Praise for R. J. Lee and
Grand Slam Murders

"A compulsively readable series debut, dripping in Southern charm, for a clever sleuth whose bridge skills break the case."

—*Kirkus Reviews*

"R. J. Lee brings an authentic new Southern voice to the mystery scene. He saturates his *Bridge to Death Mystery* with colorful characters in a small town rooted in a more genteel time in the Deep South. Lee's complex and satisfying plot is woven with wit and grace. I look forward to spending more time with the characters from Rosalie."

—Peggy Webb, *USA Today* bestselling author of
The Southern Cousins Mystery series

Grand Slam Murders

R. J. LEE

KENSINGTON BOOKS
www.kensingtonbooks.com

To the extent that the image or images on the cover of this book depict a person or persons, such person or persons are merely models, and are not intended to portray any character or characters featured in the book.

This book is a work of fiction. Names, characters, places, and incidents either are products of the author's imagination or are used fictitiously. Any resemblance to actual persons, living or dead, events, or locales is entirely coincidental.

KENSINGTON BOOKS are published by

Kensington Publishing Corp.
119 West 40th Street
New York, NY 10018

All Kensington titles, imprints, and distributed lines are available at special quantity discounts for bulk purchases for sales promotion, premiums, fund-raising, educational, or institutional use.

Special book excerpts or customized printings can also be created to fit specific needs. For details, write or phone the office of the Kensington Sales Manager: Kensington Publishing Corp., 119 West 40th Street, New York, NY 10018. Attn. Sales Department. Phone: 1-800-221-2647.

ISBN-13: 978-1-4967-1915-7 (ebook)
ISBN-10: 1-4967-1915-8 (ebook)
Kensington Electronic Edition: February 2019

ISBN-13: 978-1-4967-1914-0
ISBN-10: 1-4967-1914-X
First Kensington Trade Paperback Edition: February 2019

10 9 8 7 6 5 4 3 2 1

Printed in the United States of America

For my Angel Boy

ACKNOWLEDGMENTS

For my very first murder mystery novel, I must first thank my agents, Christina Hogrebe and Meg Ruley, of the Jane Rotrosen Agency, for believing in my decision to try my hand at a different genre. My trusty editor at Kensington Books, John Scognamiglio, also got on board with my proposal, and his delight when he read the finished product let me know that I could get out there and produce a genuine whodunit with memorable characters and an intriguing plot.

My research for *Grand Slam Murders:* A Bridge to Death Mystery was the most exhaustive I have ever done, and I was greatly aided by a number of friends, professionals, and family members. Among family, I must thank Stella Carby for her knowledge of flowers and gardens, and Bruce Kuehnle, Jr., for his guidance in matters of legal procedures, both of them my cousins from Natchez, Mississippi. Also aiding me in legal procedures was my friend Kevin Frye, of Oxford, Mississippi. For guidance in police procedure, Captain Jane Mahan and the University of Mississippi Police Department were of immense help.

Finally, for newspaper protocol, I must thank Ben Hillyer of the Natchez, Mississippi *Democrat* for his advice and counsel. All of these people made the task of creating a mystery novel a pleasurable experience, which I trust I will continue throughout the forthcoming series.

CHAPTER 1

Liddie Langston Rose caught her reflection in the French gold leaf mirror hanging in her long central hallway that also displayed all of her ancestral portraits. Had she applied her makeup just so, or did she need to return to her vanity for adjustments? After turning this way and that several times over, she decided that it would do. Then she put her hands on either side of her waist, letting them linger for a few moments to assess its size. She was pleased with the result. That also would do.

She began practicing various faces. With the fragrance of Ma Griffe she had recently sprayed on her neck radiating from her, she dramatically lifted her right eyebrow and cocked her head to one side smartly. No, that gave her a downright arrogant look. Too extreme. Next, she widened her eyes suddenly as if someone had just surprised her with a bit of juicy gossip at one of the myriad cocktail parties she customarily attended or hosted. That didn't work, either. She looked too much like a zombie from one of those old-school horror movies, or even Elsa Lanchester as the *Bride of Frankenstein,* minus the crimped, electrified hair.

What to practice next? An engaging smile? But she always

had that at her fingertips. She remained one of her hometown's great beauties, even though she had officially entered her "still handsome" phase past menopause more than a few years back. Perhaps, then, just a subtle lifting of her aristocratic chin and nothing more. There, that was just the noble façade she wanted affixed to her fine-boned face on this warm late morning in May. For not the first time, she reviewed in her head what she had done with her gray hair a little more than three months ago—abandoning the dramatic, swept-back-off-the-forehead style for bangs that hid her hairline and more. There was a bit of chiding at first, but she knew what she was doing.

"Trying to hide the frown lines?" Hanna Lewis had asked during one of their bridge games back then.

"Not at all, dear. There comes a time in a woman's life when a new look is absolutely necessary. There's no time to lose. If not now, then when?" she had answered, letting the remark fall rhetorically to the table. She let her three bridge buddies all sit with that for a while as they held their cards, and there were no further remarks during the auction—which incidentally Liddie had won.

Besides, they were hardly the ones to talk about changing their habitual coiffures or the cosmetics they applied to their faces. None of them had had the courage to update themselves all that much since their matriculation at Ole Miss over forty-five years ago. It was quite obvious that they viewed that period as the best years of their lives—volatile as it was.

Two of them, Bethany Morrissey and Sicily Groves, had even been kicked out of school for violating sorority curfew and other antics under the influence of gin. Ha! What else was new? It had been their partying poison of choice since their wild high school days in the quirky, wide-open, Mississippi River port town of Rosalie, tucked away in the southwestern part of the Magnolia State, and the high-spirited, socially prominent Gin Girls had made their mark early and often.

What had seemed like eons ago, the usually staid *Rosalie Citizen* had even done a puff piece on them in their prime, and the iconic photo that had resulted was one for everybody's scrapbook. They had lined up according to height by the side of the Rosalie Country Club swimming pool in their pastel one-piece suits with a provocative display of leg thrust toward the camera. Why, Atlantic City's bathing beauties had nothing on them, even though Bert Parks had never placed a crown on any of their heads.

Petite blond Bethany stood at the extreme left with the most contrived smile she could muster; next to her stood Sicily with her flaming red hair, that perpetual pout on her lips, and a couple of extra inches to boot; then came the lanky Hanna Lewis with her cascading brunette curls and tight-lipped grin; and finally at the right of the picture was the ringleader of the Gin Girls—Liddie, herself. When she wore heels, she topped out at just under six feet. Many a Rosalie man and woman had been intimidated by her good looks and presence over the years, and her super-exclusive Rosalie Bridge Club was the envy of many a social-climbing matron. Had she made enemies as a result of her myriad haughty rejections for cruel, specious reasons? Too numerous to count, but she never let it bother her.

Liddie finished with her latest mirror session and checked her watch. Then she fidgeted with one of her family heirloom earrings and sighed in disgust. As usual, the others were late. No matter how often she told the three of them to show up on time, it did no good whatsoever.

"Why don't you all come in one car instead of straggling in the way you do?" she had suggested now and then to no avail. "Sicily, you have that great big old thing that you refuse to trade in that practically gets no mileage. You could all pile into that easily just the way we used to in my car in high school."

But she might as well have been a teacher talking to students who insisted the dog had eaten their homework and would not back away from their story. "I always have errands to run after our bridge game," Sicily would explain. "And I don't want to have to drag the girls around with me for something like that. They'd never forgive me, would you, girls?"

So Sicily, Bethany, and Hanna would all end up coming at different times in their own cars, and Liddie found it supremely annoying. It was one of the few instances in her life in which she did not get her way. Well, enough of this waiting on pins and needles while searching for just the right expression for the bridge game she had been anticipating as never before. Time to enlist the aid of her cook and maid of nearly twenty years, Merleece Maxique.

"Merleece!" she called out with a certain urgency in her voice, turning away from the front door of her two-story, brick town house, flush with the sidewalk—Don Jose's Retreat; named for one of the venerable first inhabitants of the old Spanish Provincial section of Rosalie. There was no more historic area of the city in which to reside and call home, and Liddie never tired of reminding people of the fact that the sun could not rise or set on Rosalie without her blessing.

"Yes, ma'am?" came the reply from the kitchen.

A second later, Merleece emerged from the swinging door in her starched gray uniform and tidy white apron with an expectant yet submissive demeanor and headed down the polished, hardwood floor toward her employer. It was true that she was nearly ten years younger than the sixty-seven-year-old Liddie and her friends, but that did not quite account for the snap to her step that Liddie especially lacked these days. This, despite the "heavy lifting" of domestic work she had done around the clock for decades. Even more to her credit, however, Merleece always maintained a winning smile that complemented her rich brown skin, close-cropped hair, and strikingly high cheekbones.

"Please drop what you're doing in there," Liddie continued, poking a long, bejeweled finger in her general direction. "I'm sure they'll all be here any minute. Time for you to take a seat in the foyer and greet them as they come in."

Merleece nodded with a perfunctory smile. Her Miz Liddie had her inflexible, iconic routines that people around her disobeyed at their own peril. "Yes, ma'am. The chicken salad and the aspic—they both in the icebox ready to go. Now, you want me to go ahead and fix they Bloody Marys?"

Here, Liddie was harshly insistent and even rolled her eyes as she fidgeted with her diamond bracelet. "Yes, but they've all been complaining lately you don't make them as strong as you used to. What's gotten into you? We don't call ourselves the Gin Girls for nothing, you know. One little jigger is never enough. You put in at least two today, please."

"None of 'em ever say anything like that to me," Merleece told her, sounding almost hurt by the accusation. "I been fixin' they drinks for years without a single complaint I ever hear."

"That may be, but don't spare the shots," Liddie said, dismissing her with a wave of her hand. "The Gin Girls have their reputation to uphold. Now don't argue with me. We all need our courage for the duplicate competition in Jackson next week. When we've finished our drinks and our chatting, I'll ring the bell for the food. Then you be sure and have the coffee ready for later on. Use the Old Paris demitasse set today. We haven't used it in a while and I don't want it to think it's been forsaken. It goes all the way back to my great-grandmother, Agnes Varina Monteigne, who received it as a wedding gift."

"Now, Miz Liddie, you know I know Miz Agnes' story from beginnin' to end, and I got that face down pat, since I dust her portrait three times a week. Why you carryin' on like I don't know how to fix up yo' bridge luncheons? They all go off without a hitch as I recall," Merleece said, the annoyance clearly registering in her voice.

"Never mind the third degree. Just do as I say, and everything will proceed the way it's supposed to," Liddie told her, refusing to look her in the eye before she walked away in a huff.

Liddie brought her embroidered linen napkin up from her lap after everyone had finished up their light fare of chicken salad and tomato aspic with a dollop of mayo and a dusting of paprika at the dining room table. She took a deep breath and exhaled air still laden with molecules of gin. For just a second there, she had almost nodded off. But that came with the territory after having that second strong Bloody Mary that the others were enjoying as well. No Gin Girl worth her buzz ever stopped at one adult beverage anyway.

Upon further consideration, therefore, Liddie decided that the gossip and small talk had been in far too abundant supply for any nodding and drooping to be noticed by her constant companions. They were, as usual, full of themselves to the brim and often oblivious. So what if she had dipped her head once or twice? Though in shape, none of the others were exactly participating in triathlons these days, either.

"How are we doing, ladies?" Liddie said, surveying the table and making an effort to stay alert.

"Just fine," Bethany said. "The food's delicious as usual."

"I meant the drinks. Are they strong enough for y'all? I told Merleece to be generous with the jigger."

Sicily touched her right temple with her fingers and widened her eyes. "Another one of these and I'll be cross-eyed."

"I'm feeling no pain," Hanna added. "So I'd say we're right where we need to be."

Liddie nodded approvingly. "Excellent. I'm sure we've never played bridge sober in our lives."

"You said it," Hanna said. "And that goes all the way back to when we were sweet young things."

Indeed, if the *Citizen* had chosen to do an update on the four Gin Girls these many decades later, the reporter would have to acknowledge that they had all aged well enough. But there were some questionable decisions made.

Yes, it was true that Sicily Groves had made the mistake of trying to duplicate the fiery-red hair of her youth with that outlandish shade of henna she was using on herself at home. But Sicily had been known to go on the cheap from time to time. With her thick dark eyebrows, it was a jarring mismatch not unlike that of the late Joan Crawford in the few Technicolor movies she had made. Sicily had largely kept her figure and her most riveting facial affectation—that girlish pout. It was one for the ages that had snared for her the wealthiest man in Rosalie—Theodore "Dory" Groves of the Groves Lumber Company fortune. When he had died unexpectedly of a heart attack ten years ago, she had inherited everything, although she had never wanted for anything while he was alive. Her consumption had been conspicuous—she never tired of letting people know it—and cut from the same cloth was her only daughter, the somewhat childlike but frequently extravagant Sherry Groves Herrold.

Bethany Morrissey was a somewhat different story. Still petite, even what could be described as "terminally cute by genetic design," she no longer tried to hide the fact that her blond hair had grayed. She had settled for those streaks some women have their stylists distribute around the scalp haphazardly, but the process was not altogether flattering to her. It made her look more like her hair was always growing out from a bad dye job, but obviously she didn't see it that way when she looked in the mirror. Her trim frame was evidently enough for her. Bethany, too, had married well, although she had suffered through the misfortune of being unable to carry children to term.

At one time, Byron Morrissey had been the slickest attorney in Rosalie, practically never losing a case. He had, however, lost his battle with prostate cancer seven years ago, and as the saying goes, Bethany had more money than she knew what to do with. Her favorite use of it was to travel abroad, usually to the less frequented countries of Eastern Europe (to "spread the money around," she told people) and generally with Sicily Groves as her companion.

Then there was Hanna Lewis, who had maintained her tall, lanky frame with weekly games of tennis doubles at the Rosalie Country Club. She also paid a muscular young "exercise guru" with the ludicrously crafted moniker of Hermes Caliban to come to her house weekly for workouts. And, as the other Gin Girls often speculated, for possibly a lot more than that—even though Hanna wasn't kissing and telling no matter how often she was hounded. Alone among the four of them, she had found the secret to a seamless shade of hair color that most nearly matched that of the period of her youthful indiscretions with the others in high school and college. She remained a brunette without veering into brassy. Perhaps her only annoying trait was talking exercise all the time and trying to get the others to participate with her, knowing full well that Bethany, for instance, was a chain smoker with no intention of ever giving up the habit.

Liddie, herself, saw no virtue in sweat. She believed it was entirely unworthy of a Southern lady of genteel upbringing. "Give it up, Hanna," she had told her more than once and most emphatically. "We're all just fine the way we are. Keep your god Hermes to yourself. Once and for all, leave us alone."

Hanna's marriage to Rosalie's preeminent gynecologist,

Dr. Kelly Lewis, had resulted in the birth of two tall, strapping, if somewhat irresponsible, money-guzzling sons—Beau and Charley; but her Kelly's tragic death in a head-on collision with a drunk semi driver going the wrong way out on the interstate had made her the earliest of the wealthy widows comprising The Rosalie Bridge Club.

As for Liddie, she had found both love and an even healthier bank account when right after graduating from Ole Miss she had fallen in love with Murray Rose—he of inherited wealth dating all the way back to slavery times. The Rose Family had long ago lost Belle Rose, the sprawling crown jewel of a cotton plantation south of Rosalie, but a particularly thrifty ancestor had squirreled away enough of the original cotton fortune to keep several generations that followed quite comfortable. Liddie had inherited it all when Murray had succumbed to complications from diabetes, and she had never quite gotten over the fact that his death was perfectly avoidable. Murray had refused to take his blood pressure and diabetes prescriptions regularly, believing all doctors to be charlatans out to pad their coffers and even "kill people outright"; and he had indulged every destructive dietary habit in the annals of modern medicine. Never one to pull away from the table, his weight had ballooned to morbidly obese proportions, and it was a stroke that had actually taken him out. Liddie had remained furious with him for leaving that way and had been practically inconsolable during the visitation and funeral and even long after that.

"Damn him and his gluttonous ways!" she had cried out over and over through her tears and constant nose-blowing. Liddie's slavishly devoted daughter, Stella Markham, had tried to help but had been unable to cope with her tantrums that had continued for several months. Closure did not seem to be in Liddie's vocabulary. She also held grudges and remembered slights, real and imaginary. Crossing her had always resulted in unpleasant consequences for the offender. By some she was loved, even idolized; by others she was either envied or despised.

In the present moment Liddie rang the little silver bell for Merleece to clear the luncheon dishes. When Merleece appeared quickly, Liddie said in tones that were slightly boozy, "We'll want the coffee in about fifteen minutes for our toast. Please time things accordingly. Do not burn our tongues off."

"Yes, ma'am," Merleece said, and began removing things efficiently, although silently annoyed that her Miz Liddie would accuse her of raising blisters in their mouths. She had never come close to doing such a thing with the coffee ritual. Why the sudden chiding?

After the table had been completely cleared, Liddie at last began addressing the Grand Slam contract they would be soon be playing in preparation for the Mississippi Bridge Player's Duplicate Championship in Jackson the following week.

"I pulled this contract in spades out of Goren, of course," she told them, the remains of her inebriation still in evidence. "We couldn't do better for duplicate practice than to use this classic from one of his books. There is only one way to defeat this contract, and I want to find out if we're up to it, otherwise our championship dreams will be shattered once again. Now, Sicily, I thought you and I would be partners for this one. I always count on your telepathy when we're declarers."

Nearly as opinionated and cantankerous at times as Liddie was, Hanna balked—sounding somewhat boozy, herself—and made an ugly, throat-slashing gesture with her finger that brought everyone up short. She and Liddie had been known to get into it over practically everything.

"Wait just a second. You get to choose Sicily again? I was partners with Bethany last time. She lost our Little Slam contract when she lied about her kings. Besides, I'm tired of being the defenders."

Bethany straightened up in her chair, lit a cigarette, inhaled, and streamed smoke through her nostrils like an old-fashioned femme fatale in the movies. The others had complained about her habit many times over the years, but to no avail. Bethany was convinced she was immortal, that she would live forever and remain "cute" in the process. Neither smokes nor spirits could do her in, she had adamantly insisted.

"I most certainly did not lie," Bethany said. "You misinterpreted my response. If I recall correctly, you had three Bloody Marys that afternoon. You were swimming in gin." The last statement was no less appropriate on this particular afternoon.

"I beg your pardon. I only had two, and I never misinterpret Blackwood. Apparently, you don't understand it. You claimed you had the missing king, but you didn't. You definitely misled me."

The battle of the gin brains continued unabated. "I understand Blackwood, Stayman, Gerber, and all the conventions, and well you know it. You also know I bid short clubs and diamonds. How long have we all been playing this game together? Since we all moved into the sorority house at Ole Miss, I believe." She paused for an exaggerated smirk. "Instead of going to class, of course."

"We've been playing together too long, I think sometimes," Hanna said, averting her eyes while gazing at the chandelier overhead as if it were going to speak to her and take her side in the fuss. "But the onus is on me and Bethany to find this one way to defeat the Grand Slam."

Liddie put a finger to her lips, winked somewhat preciously, and made a shushing sound. "Girls, girls, please." The gesture got their attention, and they went silent while looking into their laps like shamed puppies. Liddie always had that effect when she focused. "I have the hands all neatly arranged in stacks over at the bridge table. We are only going to be finding out if we can duplicate the Grand Slam results that Goren created for us. If we don't, it won't be anyone's fault. We just won't have passed his test. At least, that's the way I insist we approach it. Now, no more of this bickering. It is what it is."

Liddie had laid down the law, and the partnerships were now written in stone. Liddie and Sicily would be declarers as North and South, and Bethany and Hanna, despite her strident protestations, would be defenders as East and West.

"But before we move to the bridge table," Liddie continued, "I think we need to clear the air with our usual coffee toast. We must have none of these bad feelings that were bandied about to be at our best. Merleece should have the coffee at just the right temperature soon, and we'll hoist our cups to bringing home that championship next week in Jackson. We're going to win it this time, or we're not the one and only Gin Girls of Rosalie."

All the while the Gin Girls were indulging their late-spring luncheon, gabfest, and gin guzzling in the formal dining room, Merleece had been trying her best to deal with Liddie's young hipster gardener, Arden Wilson. Just after she had cleared the table and stacked the dishes in the sink, he had wandered into her kitchen through the back door in his dirty overalls and customary red bandana tied around his neck to pass the time of day and bug her for the umpteenth time over the past several months. What had she done to deserve him, she often asked herself?

"Refill my thermos, will ya? It's hot out there. You'd think it was July, not the third week of May," he told her, thrusting it toward her. There was a hint of anger as well as entitlement implied in his action, and the frown on his narrow, sunburned face only accentuated the bullying impression.

"You got somethin' against *please*?" she said for not the first time, her hands on her hips. But it never did any good to remind him to be polite. Theirs was an uneasy truce, and the strained banter between them never seemed to get any easier.

"Just the ice water, Merleece. Nix the stuck-up manners. We're not part a' that fancy ladies' card game, ya know? We're just the servants in case you've forgotten. You act like you own the place sometimes. But you just work here." He reached back and began fiddling absentmindedly with his slicked-back man-bun, followed by a quick stroking of his dark, scruffy beard.

"I don't work for you," she said, pointing toward the refrigerator. "I got this coffee service to tend to right now. And furthermore to that, if I ever let Miz Liddie know how bad you aggravate me all the time up in here, she'd let you go in a second. You been here just barely nine months full time since that sweet daddy a' yours pass, but I been here near 'bout twenty years. I know you know I got seniority, so you better deal with it."

Arden stuck out his tongue and said, "Big deal." Then he moved to the refrigerator, taking out the pitcher of ice water and filling his thermos while making an unpleasant face. "Hey, I know my stuff. Daddy taught me well from when I was knee-high. Who has the best-looking garden in Old Spanish Rosalie? Whose garden is always on tour when the boats dock down on Water Street and the passengers ride up the hill in the buses? Who would she get to look after all her flower beds without me, then? You just take a minute and answer me that."

"I guess anybody would do who could draw a breath and got a pulse," she said, continuing to wait for the water in the saucepan on the stove to reach the right temperature. She bent near, almost hypnotically. It must not actually boil but must be hot enough to dissolve the coffee crystals. Then it must cool off quickly enough for the actual ritual. "It just take some water and chemicals and one a' them nozzles to do what you do. Seem like you want me to stand up and applaud you every time you bend over. For the record, I been witness to a whole lot better cabooses than you got goin' for ya. You near 'bout flat as a pancake back there, just in case you got any fancy ideas 'bout yo'self."

Arden mumbled something unintelligible under his breath and shot her an angry glance.

"You got somethin' important to say to me, say it," Merleece said, drawing herself up defiantly. She had better things to do than suffer this arrogant white boy who had become the bane of her existence. There were times when she dearly wanted to hit him over the head with a skillet.

"I'm saying that you don't even know what you're talking about. You have to know lots about which chemicals to use to keep the pests away."

In truth, Arden was pretty good at what he did even if he had a thoroughly obnoxious personality that showed no signs of abating anytime soon. Liddie's gardens were perhaps the showplace of Rosalie. They offered a little bit of everything for the tourists to admire when the house was open: pink Mobile azaleas, debutante and purple dawn camellias, white bridal wreath spirea, white gardenias—both dwarf and full-size—pink and blue hydrangeas, purple and pink crêpe myrtles, orange lilies and red roses, meticulously trimmed boxwood hedges with their signature bosky odor lining the geometric brick walkways, purple bougainvillea, Japanese magnolias, tallow trees, and butterfly bushes. For added semi-tropical effect there were several tall windmill palms planted at the corners with their fronds swaying in the breeze above the lush display.

Arden had planted the butterfly bushes himself at his own expense without getting Liddie's approval. Attracting butterflies and collecting them by trapping and killing them in jars was his entomological passion. Merleece found that particular hobby of his a tad bit on the creepy side and never tired of reminding him of that and his other questionable habits he may have indulged.

"Lemme tell you this straight on now. You think Miz Liddie don't know what you do out there in the shed when you got spare time? We not talkin' 'bout butterflies, neither." She stared him down intently out of the corner of her eyes. "Yeah, you know all right what I'm talkin' 'bout."

Arden took a generous swig from his thermos and produced a rude, prolonged belch that made Merleece cringe. "No, I'm afraid I don't have the foggiest. Unless you made up somethin' and told her. She's about a thousand years old. What would she know about anything I do or don't do in my spare time? You're in way over your head, Merleece."

"I wouldn't take bets on that. I think you smokin' somethin' out there, like you don't have nobody to answer to."

"Did you lie about me? I wouldn't put it past you."

Merleece thrust her chin forward and then sniffed the air as if trying to ferret out an unpleasant odor. "She happen to axe me not too long ago. She say, 'Merleece, I smell somethin' funny out in the yard all the time. You know what it is?' "

"So? The chemicals I use to make her gardens look pretty have an odor. Let's alert the media and get them right on it."

Merleece sneered. "God knows why, but I took pity on you, boy. Told her you had a new spray you tryin' out for those little green bugs that suck all the sap out—whatchoo call 'em? A-fusses?"

Arden's laugh was loud and wicked as he leaned back and showed off every tooth with its every filling in his mouth as well as his pink dangling uvula. "You mean aphids? Did you even graduate from high school?"

"Yes, I did, Mr. Smartass." Merleece again eyed him contemptuously. "And laugh at me all you want. You think you so superior, don'tchoo? But, you know what? Miz Liddie grin at me like she knew I was lyin' to her when I told her 'bout the smell. She a whole lot smarter than you think. And don't think she wouldn't turn you in to the law if she wanted. You best be on the lookout, or you gone be out of a job before you can blink."

Arden snickered. "Ooh, I'm so scared." He thrust out his hand and briefly faked some trembling. "Turn me in to the law. I bet you'd like that, wouldn't you?"

Merleece quickly pointed at him. "I think I would, now that you mention it. Lord, gimme back the peace and quiet that I have around here when Mr. Brent Wilson was alive. He a true gentleman, and he knew how to treat people. I don't know what planet you come from. Maybe they's nothin' but butterflies live there."

Arden's countenance clouded over, and there was an unmistakably dark glint in his eye. "You ever thought that maybe you aren't telling me anything I don't know about Miz Liddie and what she might or might not do with whatever you've told her about me? Maybe I'm way ahead a' you in that department."

"What's that s'pose to mean? You up to no good?"

"That's for me to know and you to find out."

"I'm warnin' you again. You gone find yo'self on the outside lookin' in before you know it," Merleece said, shaking her head.

They were interrupted by the sound of Liddie's bell ringing, and Merleece continued. "I got work to do now. You in my way, so move those dirty overalls a' yours outta my kitchen."

"Ha! It's Miz Liddie's kitchen, not yours. I can stay right here if I want to," he told her, refusing to move an inch while slamming his thermos down on the marble counter with a noticeable metallic thud. "I wanna cool off some more."

"Just stay out my way, then, good for nothin,'" she said. "You gone make me mess up."

Arden continued his sneering ways. "How you gonna mess up pouring hot water into that instant coffee? That's not a skill like my gardening is. Hey, you ever heard of apples and oranges?"

"Now you the one that don't know what you talkin' 'bout," she said, carefully taking hold of the saucepan with its temperature-perfect water. "Two a' the ladies take they coffee one way and the other two another way. Miz Liddie, she and Miz Hanna like it black with sugar. Then Miz Bethany and Miz Sicily, they drink it with cream and sugar. And I can tell you they'd be hell to pay if I don't get all that right, you know what I'm sayin' to you?"

Arden made a disdainful face, wrinkling his nose. "I still can't get over the instant coffee. Not with what's available these days to sip and sample. No true Southerner drinks that swill."

"Maybe. But Miz Liddie like it that way, and I don't axe her no questions. I do as I'm told."

Merleece busied herself fixing up the demitasse cups as she had just described, managing to hum some random little tune all the while, hoping against hope that the music might make him go away. Then she placed the cups on a silver serving tray, along with fresh linen napkins, four delicate stirring spoons, a white ceramic cream pitcher, and a matching bowl containing more of the sugar she had sprinkled and stirred in generously.

"All these little things that got to be perfect is what Miz Liddie pay me for," she told Arden, turning her back to him as she headed toward the swinging door. "Meanwhile, ain'tchoo got some chemicals you can spray around outside? Why don'tchoo do us all a favor and spray yo'self in the face real good?"

"You know," Arden called after her, "I think you got a homicidal streak buried in you somewhere."

"If I do," Merleece told him with a wry grin, "I'd use it on you first."

Merleece had just placed a demitasse in front of the last Gin Girl and stood by respectfully as her Miz Liddie began the coffee ritual.

"We are finally going to win the championship in Jackson next week. Enough of coming in second to Vernon and Carley Warren. Sometimes I think I should go all out to prove they cheat. Anyway, they've hogged the trophy long enough. They practically think it's their birthright by now. Well, we're going to take care of that. This is going to be our year, isn't it, girls? So let's hoist our cups fully confident that we will not be denied this time. Will all of you now second the motion?"

The three others did so and awaited Liddie's final words.

"I sense real confidence in our voices this time," she continued. Then Liddie blew across the top of her coffee in cautionary fashion and took the minutest of sips to test the temperature. "Aah, perfect, Merleece."

"Thank you, Miz Liddie."

"A big, healthy sip to our success, my Gin Girls. Down the hatch."

And with that, the toast was over and done with in perfect unison.

Merleece was anything but pleased to find Arden still leaning against the kitchen counter with that immature smirk of his when she returned seconds after the toast. Truly, what had she done to deserve this ever-present pest?

"My daddy always said that it must be nice to have the kind of money those stuck-up ladies in there have. Nothin' to do all day but play bridge, drink gin, and propose silly toasts to themselves," Arden said. "No everyday reality to disturb their pampered little universe. Not a care in the world."

Merleece could barely contain herself now. "You the biggest liar in Rosalie. Mr. Brent Wilson, he never talk like that about Miz Liddie and her friends. That is you talkin' and nobody else. I want you to leave my kitchen right now. You been in here long enough, and my blood pressure up way too high as it is. Next time I go to the doctor, you gone be all I talk to him 'bout. I just hope he have a pill I can take to make you go away."

Arden was fully prepared to take the argument to another level, but Liddie's bell-ringing interrupted them once again. But it wasn't the usual polite, patrician ringing, delicate as the whooshing of fairy wings, calling servants to their expected chores. There was something loud and shrill and insistent about it that was not business as usual, and half a second later it was accompanied by gargled, throaty sounds and the clatter of breaking crockery.

Merleece and Arden rushed into the dining room to a round table of horrors. No matter where they looked—in bridge terms, North, South, East, or West—there was a gruesome sight to behold. Their Miz Sicily seemed to be in the midst of convulsions, the shards of her demitasse scattered around her; only the whites of Miz Bethany's eyes were showing, as she was otherwise motionless, her cheeks a bright red; Miz Hanna was making frightening, guttural sounds while clutching at her throat; and Miz Liddie, herself, continued to ring the bell as if possessed by a demon. But she somehow had gathered enough of her wits about her to point dramatically in the direction of both Merleece and Arden.

"*You . . . !*" she cried out.

Then she, too, clutched at her throat, trying valiantly to draw a breath.

"Don't just stand there like you don't have good sense. Call 9-1-1 right now!" Merleece shouted to Arden. "Call an ambulance!"

Arden fumbled around in the pocket of his overalls and finally managed to retrieve his cell phone, summoning help in a frenzied voice. Meanwhile, Merleece ran to her Miz Liddie first, prying the bell from her hands to stop the repetitious, now almost ghoulish ringing. Instead of calling the faithful to church, it seemed the bell was announcing impending death to all within earshot.

"Hold on, Miz Liddie, hold on," Merleece told her, stroking her hand gently. "We callin' for help right now. You just hold on tight. They gone get here soon and tend to you."

Then with all the strength she could muster considering the significant trauma she was enduring, Liddie dramatically withdrew from Merleece's touch and slumped in her chair. It was clearly an act of rejection as the light drained from her eyes, almost as if she were trying to escape the grasp of a monster of some sort. Indeed, something monstrous and life-threatening was happening to all of the Gin Girls simultaneously, and the only thing in question now was how soon the paramedics would arrive upon the scene to verify that the ladies had played their last hand.

CHAPTER 2

Wendy Winchester sat at her computer in her tiny gray cubicle of the *Rosalie Citizen* newsroom trying to fight off the boredom of her job. Stoically, she suppressed a yawn and prepared to type from the copy that had been mailed to her—her request for a Word document or e-mail having been completely ignored. Not only that, but the announcement had been executed in cursive—and not very neatly. Penmanship had gone to rack and ruin. Okay, so Rosalie made its living off being a living museum of eighteenth- and nineteenth-century architecture, but did its citizens have to act like they were still living in those times? It was way past the dawn of the millennium. Nonetheless, Wendy's efficient fingers went to work at the keyboard:

> William Burns Neilson and Cynthia Varnell Neilson of Rosalie announce the engagement of their daughter, Anne Burns Neilson, to Joseph Andrew Darrow, son of Burke Taylor Darrow and Cassandra Lee Darrow of Lake St. John, Louisiana. The groom attended Louisiana State University, where he majored in accounting, and

> the bride attended the University of Mississippi, majoring in theater arts. The wedding will take place on August 12th at the First Presbyterian Church of Rosalie with the Reverend Vernon Foster officiating. . . .

Wendy suddenly decided to stop. She stuck her tongue out at the copy. Then she withdrew her fingers from the keyboard as if the letters had become white-hot, leaned back in her chair, and lazily pushed her striking strawberry-blond hair out of her pale-blue eyes. Good Lord, but these engagement announcements were tedious beyond belief. But then so were the descriptions of the actual noblesse oblige weddings and the baby showers and the sip 'n sees and all the rest that went along with being the society columnist for the venerable Rosalie newspaper.

She certainly looked and acted the part, however. Tall, slim, and soft-spoken with a disarming smile, Wendy had the impeccable manners and fashion instincts of her late mother, Valerie, who had trained her well in the social graces. Not that her mother had lacked dreams and goals beyond circulating with ease at parties with the gift of gab, along with a cocktail in her hand. Boasting a Bachelor of Fine Arts degree from Millsaps, Valerie Lyons Winchester, had put together several exhibitions of her primitive acrylic paintings of the lush greenery surrounding Rosalie and the magnificent loess bluffs upon which the impeccably preserved town rested proudly. She had done a particularly popular study called *Moon on the River,* which had sold out quickly; this was followed by another study titled *Sun on the River.* Having one of her paintings hanging on the walls of Rosalie's elite became a fad that appeared to have no end in sight.

"Find something truly satisfying to do with your life, and you'll be happy," Valerie had told her daughter during those early years when Rosalieans were snapping up her work, convinced they would eventually be the owners of valuable collectors' items. It was advice that had stuck with Wendy throughout her college years and beyond.

And yet, how many years had she been toiling at her thankless, content-challenged job at the newspaper?

Oh, yes. Going on three long ones now; and three too many, as far as she was concerned.

That initial job interview with Dalton Hemmings had gone well enough, although she had approached it with serious reservations. After all, the man had held sway at his editorial post for nearly thirty-five years, and practically no one ever challenged his tactics and journalistic philosophy. As coarse as the salt-and-pepper hair crowning his bleary-eyed countenance, he sported a voice that always sounded like it was full of phlegm; he was old-school journalism with all the favored, time-honored, male attitudes that accompanied it. Not to mention that he apparently disdained doing his laundry. His shirts were always wrinkled, and there were sometimes coffee and food stains decorating them by the end of the day as well. The man's picture was beneath the word *sloppy* in the dictionary.

"Now, Miz Winchester, you might as well know that I think the traditional way of doing things is best in this newspaper bid'ness," he had told her at the outset. He had a way of smiling at people that gave off the faintest aura of politeness, but behind it all was a first-class curmudgeon. "I have more than considerable experience in these things, you know."

Wendy was leaning forward earnestly in her chair and nodding in an attempt to convey the respect she clearly did not have for him. She knew quite well that the art of listening was her best tactic at the moment.

"Your journalism degree from Missouri is most impressive," he continued, "but as you've asked about openings on the news desk, I must inform you that we have none. However, you happen to be in the right place at the right time. Alice Mae Forman, our society columnist, is stepping down to have a family, and we do need a replacement there. I said to Alice just last week, 'You're gonna be so much happier as a wife and mother, I'm pretty sure. No more having to rush to meet deadlines and hold down a job.' "

For just an instant there, Wendy had dared to speak her mind. "Of course, you're right. There are no deadlines in running a household and raising children. There's practically nothing to it."

Hemmings's head had jerked back noticeably, and the creases across his forehead quickly conveyed his irritation. "Beg pardon?"

The man's tone was not lost on her, either, and she had retreated with a smile. "You were saying about the society columnist position, sir?"

From that point forward in the interview, she had played the game for fear of not being able to get a toehold at all in her chosen profession. Better to wait it out and then take her chances, she had figured. And Dalton Hemmings had given her the job when it was all over, although he had made it clear that her father, Captain Baxter "Bax" Winchester of the Rosalie Police Department, had put his hand in.

"I guess it won't surprise you to hear that your daddy dropped by to see me just the other day," he had told her as they stood up and shook hands there at the end. "He and I go back a good ways when he was just a rookie and I was just a beat reporter, so I thought I owed you the courtesy of at least an interview."

Wendy considered her words carefully. "Rosalie does have its trusty network of good friends, doesn't it? I suppose my father being the chief of police still counts for quite a bit."

"Yes," Hemmings had said. "Everybody knows everything about everybody else in this crazy little town. You can't keep anything hidden for very long. It all comes out sooner or later."

Wendy couldn't help herself. "Well, maybe someday I can pull some of those skeletons out of all those closets. There's a talent to that kind of rattling of cages, you know."

"The downside to that is that it can also be dangerous—even fatal."

The words just seemed to come out of Wendy's mouth without her even giving them a fleeting thought. "You speak from experience?"

Hemmings had given her a puzzled look but had said nothing further. And here she was, three years later, still describing bridesmaids' gowns and flower arrangements and the cutesy-poo "nibbles with cocktails" menus at baby showers. It was, to be sure, maddeningly repetitive and stultifying.

Throughout it all, she had actually developed a readership that swore by her, even though she felt her work was a waste of her abilities. Sometimes, she even received a visit from one of her fans—mostly gushing brides-to-be or their mothers—who never failed to tell her how "sweet" she looked in person or that her write-up of their social event was "too perfect for words" and so appreciated by the family.

"You described everything precisely, and my aunt Sybil was so thrilled you mentioned her ladling at the punch bowl. No one ever thinks about the art of ladling these days, you know," Priscilla Newellton of the Dulcimer Street Newelltons had told her, having been escorted without permission to her cubicle by one of the interns.

At other times she got credit for what the *Citizen*'s veteran photographer, the cue-ball Oscar Norris, produced.

"You got a terrific shot of my husband and me dancing. Is

there any way you could e-mail us a digital copy?" Elissa McMahon of the Adams Street McMahons had said, ambushing her at the front door as she was heading out to lunch.

The sincerity of her following aside, every patronizing smile and pat on the shoulder she received on nearly a daily basis from Dalton Hemmings continued to feel like an insult. It was getting more and more difficult for Wendy to bide her time for the opening that might never come; and even if it did, could she ever get the consideration for it that she firmly believed she deserved? Or would some man—any man on the staff—line up in front of her and snatch the goodies?

Hemmings aside, the rest of the cast of characters at the *Citizen* weren't particularly palatable to Wendy, either. The assistant editor, Logan Brady, an older man who was largely responsible for the layout of the paper, spent most of his spare time doing crossword puzzles and occasionally would ask for help around the office with words that fit, but was otherwise noncommunicative. The "classified girls," as they called themselves, were a gossipy clique who giggled and whispered a lot in the break room and were standoffish in the extreme. The muscular young sports editor and ladies' man, Terrance Baylor, had stopped speaking to her since she had made it perfectly clear more than once that she was not interested in going out with him. It wasn't just that she found his pickup lines smarmy beyond belief; it was more that she had plenty of opportunities to observe him in action with the classified girls and knew what she would be in for if she ever said yes to him.

Wendy was about to return to the thrilling finale of the Neilson-Darrow nuptials when Jack Manning, the *Citizen*'s police beat reporter, sprang up from his cubicle across the way.

"Unbelievable!" he cried out. He repeated the word twice more, quite audibly, and then headed toward Dalton Hemmings's office as if he had been doused with gasoline and set on fire. Then, after knocking on the glass pane with noticeable urgency, he disappeared inside, shutting the door behind him.

Wendy's brain went into overdrive as she kept her eyes trained on the editorial office. What on earth could get "Li'l Jack Horner" Manning, as she had nicknamed him contemptuously in her head, that excited and truly off his duff for once? A thin and pale, monosyllabic specimen of a man who seemed perfectly content to monitor the police scanner all day and then churn out the pedestrian burglary and criminal mischief reports with passionless efficiency, he also seemed to have been born without smiling muscles. Wendy could not recall a single instance when he had bared his teeth or cracked a joke or even given a reasonable imitation of a flesh-and-blood person rather than a cardboard cutout. She could only conclude that something far beyond sensational had finally pushed his sluggish hot buttons.

Had aliens landed?

Several minutes crawled by. Wendy continued to ignore the Neilson-Darrow announcement, frozen in place by her curiosity. The computer screen was her enemy, the cursor blinking impatiently where she had left it, as if demanding to know why she had taken such an inordinate amount of time off. If it actually could have spoken, it would have screamed at her.

Finally, Manning emerged, his face looking flushed and distracted as he sprinted to his cubicle. It was all Wendy could do to keep from dashing over to get the lowdown from him, excruciating a process as that would be for her. But she needn't have even tried, for Manning was soon headed out the front door after gathering a few items from his cubicle and collecting Oscar Norris along the way for the photos.

No matter. All she had to do was knock on Dalton Hemmings's door to find out what was going on. However, the crusty editor beat her to the punch, emerging from his office and addressing the entire newsroom.

"Ladies and gentlemen," he began, clearing his throat noisily. "May I have your attention, please?"

Heads popped up over the gray cubicle dividers around the room, then turned to face him as he continued.

"We have Rosalie's story of the century on our hands, it appears. It's nothing short of improbable. Manning just learned that all four members of The Rosalie Bridge Club were DOA at the hospital a few minutes ago. As most all of you know, those ladies were also known as the Gin Girls and were among the most prominent citizens of our town. This newspaper has followed their family activities, accomplishments, and charity work very closely over the years. This is a tragedy of epic proportions."

Amidst all the gasps and buzzing that broke out, Wendy was the first to raise her hand and then ask the obvious. "What in the world happened, Mr. Hemmings? Were they in a bad car wreck or something?"

Hemmings shook his head, his tired eyes taking on a hint of life. "Or something. From what little I gleaned from Captain Winchester, it appears they all fell fatally ill in Miz Liddie Rose's house shortly after eating lunch. Who'd ever have imagined such a crazy thing? All four of them at the same time." He snapped his fingers as if summoning a servant. "Gone, just like that." But there was not even a hint of sorrow and regret in his tone.

Several comments burst forth, blending together at once from various people around the newsroom with incredulous expressions on their faces and genuine emotion in their voices:

"Sounds like food poisoning . . ."

"Or maybe just plain poisoning . . ."

"Imagine those poor families . . ."

"I simply can't believe it . . ."

"What are the odds?"

While Hemmings continued to ramble on about how important to the community it would be that the entire staff devote themselves to covering every possible angle of the shocking development, Wendy began drifting off into surreal conjecture of her own. Everything surrounding her suddenly became very muted background noise. Perhaps she was in shock.

The soles of her feet were tingling the way they did when they'd gone to sleep and were starting to wake up on pins and needles. It was not a pleasurable sensation. She felt weak and dizzy, as if she might spin out of her body entirely into an alternate universe. Was this some sort of unthinkable accident? Or worse, had someone deliberately poisoned the Gin Girls?

Alone among the employees of the paper, Wendy had a personal stake in this tragedy. Just a few months earlier, she had been provisionally accepted into The Rosalie Bridge Club, the first new member since Liddie Rose's daughter, Stella Rose Markham, some fifteen years earlier. Of course, Stella was a family legacy as well as an alternate, sometimes taking her mother's place on the extremely rare occasions when Liddie was out of town visiting relatives or on some other social errand.

Qualified women with and without social pedigrees right and left had been turned down year after year for membership in the club. Or more accurately, Liddie Rose had turned them down as the supreme potentate, even when some of the others had lobbied vigorously for one of their friends or relatives. Had that behavior been the catalyst for this unspeakable horror? Or was this simply a case of virulent and opportunistic botulism?

In that case the finger would be pointed at Merleece Maxique for culinary carelessness of some sort. In the months since her provisional acceptance into the club, Wendy had gotten to know Merleece very well. Wendy had been allowed to sit in on a number of hands so that she could observe the four veteran players at their best and learn from the experience. Merleece had always been there serving the food and adult beverages made with gin, of course.

Now and then, Wendy had gotten permission to slip away into the kitchen to take a break and chat. She had found Merleece to be warm and friendly, as well as tireless and efficient in the performance of her considerable duties. She never failed to snap to attention at a moment's notice whenever her Miz Liddie barked orders or rang the bell from the dining room or the bridge table. As a result, Wendy was finding it difficult to believe that Merleece could have served food or drink to the group that was anything but pristine. Her aspics, chicken salads, and sherry custards that usually accompanied the bridge club luncheons were all delicious, state-of-the-art creations—the best Wendy had ever put in her mouth.

So, then, if Merleece's food and drink weren't the likely culprits, what was? Was this truly a case of outright and blatant poisoning? Wendy shuddered at the thought. What type of sociopath could have done such a thing to these mighty—if admittedly foolish and flighty—society matrons of Rosalie?

It was beginning to appear to Wendy that she was never going to learn the game of bridge the way she had fervently hoped to. Even now, she had not quite mastered the requirements for an opening no-trump bid. Fifteen points? Not enough. Twenty? A little too strong for one no-trump. It seemed she was always zigging and zagging at the wrong time on this one. More than once, she had been severely reprimanded by Miz Liddie when she had entered the auction without a real stopper in one of the four suits, God forbid.

"You can't always count on your partner to have the stopper if she hasn't mentioned your weak suit," Miz Liddie would point out in that superior way of hers. Then the rest of her scolding would go something like this: "If neither of you has it, the defenders can rip right through you and run off every card they have in that suit. They'll run away and hide, you're toast, and you'll never recover. You'll be beating yourself up the rest of the afternoon for such stupidity and make even more foolish mistakes. Bad leads, miscounting trumps, reneging. It will all end up a train wreck, and your only solace will be to drown your sorrows in adult beverages. At least we have plenty of those and plenty of practice at that."

A gruff voice broke through Wendy's fevered speculation and bridge game replays. "I say again, Miz Winchester?"

Wendy came to and realized that her editor was standing above her with a frown, trying to get her attention. "Oh . . . yes, Mr. Hemmings?"

"I'd like to see you in my office."

Wendy did not like his tone. It was far from welcoming. She envisioned being chewed out for something or other but could think of nothing she had done to deserve such a thing.

Once the two of them were seated across his desk, Hemmings said, "Your father tells me you're dating that police detective, Ross Rierson. Are you two still somewhat of an item?"

Completely surprised by his line of questioning, Wendy stalled for time by scanning all the plaques and awards hanging on the wall—mostly local, but also a few statewide honors. "Well . . . umm . . . you see, the truth is, we're not exactly a couple yet. Ross thinks we are, but . . . we really aren't. It's pretty one-sided at this point, although things could change."

Hemmings looked supremely displeased by her rambling. "I didn't ask you to go into all that silly, schoolgirl rhetoric, even if you are our semi-gossip columnist. I just wanted to confirm that you and he were friends. Is that the case?"

"Yes, we are definitely friends."

"Good. I think between your friendship with him and

mine with your father, we can get some additional inside information on the story. It should give us that decided edge we need to make it more interesting and compelling for our readers."

"Don't you trust Jack Manning to do the job?"

Hemmings seemed more annoyed than ever. "Of course I trust him. Why would you even ask that? Do you have something against him?"

Wendy did not dare say what she really thought about her milquetoast coworker who looked like he had never spent even one day in the sun. "No reason. So you want me to pry things out of Ross, is that it?"

Hemmings leaned forward, staring at her with every one of the broken capillaries in his eyes and on his bulbous nose in evidence. No little child having a nightmare could have conjured up anything scarier at close range. "Listen, I know how this works. They're not supposed to share anything about ongoing investigations at the station. They just give us bits and pieces to run with because they know they have to give us something. But sometimes, husbands and fathers and boyfriends let a few things slip after a hard day's work. I want you to see what you can do when you're with Rierson. In fact, you could do us a favor and start seeing him more often as things progress. Just think of it as a special assignment. You can even go undercover if you want." Hemmings gave her a wicked wink.

Wendy recoiled visibly, and it was easy to see her adrenaline was flowing because of her sarcastic tone. "So I get to do the research—in a manner of speaking—but I don't get to write the story, is that it? I'll just be one of those anonymous sources. Of course that's why I went to journalism school."

Hemmings pulled back dramatically and briefly studied her in silence. "Your job is to write the social column and anything related to it. Manning's job is the police beat and anything related to that. There's not a great deal of overlap. You've made noises from time to time that you'd like to do more for the paper. I'm not deaf. I like to think I'm a fair man. This would be a way for you to contribute to our effort. We've got to stay on top of this. The people of Rosalie will demand it, of course. It'll be the talk of the town for the foreseeable future. Even after we get to the bottom of it, I'm sure. We'll sell more papers because of it, no doubt."

"If you don't mind my saying, you don't seem all that broken up over the deaths of these ladies. I know I'm still in shock," Wendy continued, trying a different tactic. She did not like being marginalized one bit.

Hemmings surprised her with a chuckle that ended in a peculiar snort. "I'm an old hand at dealing with and reporting tragedy. But you want my angle on the Gin Girls? Okay, I'll give it to you." For this, he paused dramatically, squaring his shoulders and puffing himself up, as if he were a leaking tire being quickly pumped with air.

"I know all about their wealth and social status, of course. But they were somewhat trying, to put it mildly. Miz Liddie would call up here all the time and demand that we cover this and that event she was attending or hosting or whatever else it was. Didn't matter how newsworthy it actually was. Most of the time it wasn't even close to being a real item."

"You don't have to tell me. I was the one who had to write up all those little bits of nothing once you hired me," Wendy said.

"Yes, well, we always covered it because of who she and her family were—the Langstons and the Roses—two of Rosalie's pioneer families. Same for the others, though none of them were ever quite as snippy with me as she was. They'd back off if I told 'em a little white lie and said we didn't have room on any page. Miz Liddie just took it for granted that the *Citizen* would comply with her social agenda, and I have to say that we never turned her down. Guess that's all on me. I didn't want a vendetta from the likes of her, I'll tell you that."

"I could be mistaken, but it almost sounds like you're glad to be rid of her. All of them, really."

Hemmings went silent again, and Wendy began to wonder if she might have gone too far. She looked down into her lap and counted her fingers to handle the tension. Yes, they were there—all ten of them—neatly filed with clear polish. She was greatly relieved, therefore, when he finally spoke up without a hint of anger, leaning instead toward the magnanimous.

"I'll let you have that one because of your father, Miz Winchester. But I think you need a bit of an attitude adjustment if you want to really make a contribution to this paper."

Just where it came from, Wendy did not know. But suddenly, even in the midst of her restrained confrontation with her boss, a brilliant idea popped into her head. Being intimidated was the last thing on her mind, and she found the courage to forge ahead. "I think you're absolutely right, Mr. Hemmings. I've already adjusted my thinking right here on the spot as we speak. Could I run something past you?"

He nodded without conviction.

"Well, according to you, since I'm going to be pumping Ross and maybe even Daddy for tidbits about the case, why don't you authorize me to go a step further and write a feature story for the paper from an entirely different angle? I assume Manning will be getting the spoon-fed releases from the police department and expanding upon them, and I'm sure you'll be writing some kind of editorial about Rosalie's stunning loss, won't you?"

"Yes," Hemmings said, again without enthusiasm. "I'll have to put something together for tomorrow's edition as soon as you leave. I pretty much say the same thing about all our movers and shakers when they leave us. It's not quite a form letter editorial, but it's close, and it always works."

"I was sure you'd be having something to say, and as you've said, I'm the society columnist. These ladies were at the top of the social pecking order. I could go behind the scenes and interview family members and write about what the Gin Girls meant to Rosalie. You know—who were they really? I mean, that's supposed to be my beat, right?"

Hemmings nodded hesitantly again.

"You know as well as I do that I know my way around the social swirl of Rosalie," Wendy continued, feeling she was on her way to gaining the upper hand. "Manning doesn't have a clue about all that. I have all the contacts, and I know how to tap into them for anything that's pertinent. After all, there's no scanner to monitor for social events, large and small."

"That's true enough," Hemmings said, his interest clearly breaking through his listlessness.

"It could even be a series. We'd have to give each of the four ladies equal time. That would really start a feud if we didn't."

Suddenly, Hemmings seemed a different man altogether, grinning and rolling his eyes at the same time. "Believe me, we don't want to get into that. We'd never hear the end of it."

Wendy kept the relaxed mood going with laughter of her own. "You should have seen some of the arguments the ladies got into when one of them trumped the other's ace during one of their bridge games. As their newest member, I was allowed to observe and occasionally even play a hand. I'm afraid I can't repeat the language they would use, or I'd blush. But they could pretty much hold their own with the dockworkers on Water Street."

"I'm sure it was no worse than some of the shots Miz Liddie took at me from time to time," he said. His smile had completely disappeared as he looked away lost in thought. "I don't think this idea of yours is half-bad, though. I'm seriously considering giving you the green light. But you've got to remember to tread lightly. These are four of Rosalie's oldest and wealthiest families, and we want to feature them in the best possible light, especially in the midst of these untimely deaths."

Wendy was beaming, her soft pink skin growing even pinker. Had Hemmings just okayed her path to greater responsibility and a possible promotion at the *Citizen* without realizing it? Did she have him where she wanted him at last? She was almost giddy with excitement.

"But here's the caveat of all caveats," Hemmings continued. "Keep in mind that some of the family members might not be willing to cooperate with you. They may shut you out, and it'll be up to you to get around them tactfully. People handle grief in different ways, and we don't want to intrude. It's one thing to describe place settings for banquets and dresses for weddings as you've been doing, and quite another to pump people about their feelings in a time of tragedy."

Wendy nodded perfunctorily and listened to him drone on using such clichés as "treading lightly" and "using kid gloves" during her interviews, but then another thought came to her. For once, the curmudgeonly Dalton Hemmings almost sounded human with these TLC warnings and directives. Wasn't that a kick in the head? Perhaps he'd even had a mother. And even a girlfriend once. There were rumors that he'd been stood up at the altar by the love of his life and that he had never quite recovered. As it happened, no one had ever seen him with a woman in all the years he'd been running the paper like a dictator. Confirmed bachelor he seemed to have remained.

When he had finally wound up his sermon, Wendy said,

"When do you think it would be proper for me to start on the article? I was thinking I should wait until after the funerals are over and done with."

"That's an excellent instinct," Hemmings said. "These families need some closure first."

But even as he said the words, Wendy was disagreeing with him in her head. It seemed to her that there were two propositions to consider, both of which were equally ghastly. The first was the inescapable reality that the four women had died together under untimely and unfortunate circumstances, and that was difficult enough to accept and comprehend no matter what. The second, however, would be the sort of scenario that would haunt the citizens of Rosalie the rest of their lives, and no real closure would be possible: namely, that the ladies had been murdered, rudely jerked out of life by design. In fact, foul play seemed more than likely, and that meant a murderer was afoot in Rosalie. Would the Gin Girls be the only victims, or would there be more deaths to follow?

"Meanwhile," Hemmings continued, "get back to whatever you were doing. We have a paper to get out as usual."

Wendy left his office feeling energized as never before as an employee of the *Citizen*. With this new assignment looming ahead, no engagement announcement, no bridal shower, no sip 'n see, no wedding, large or small, could possibly drag her down and keep her there. The glass ceiling that had frowned down upon her the last several years seemed ripe for crashing and breaking into little pieces.

She was barely seated at her desk, however, when the call came through from her father on the landline.

"I assume Dalton's given all y'all the news down there at the paper," Captain Bax Winchester said in that deep, booming voice of his, while skipping the customary hello. Wendy could picture him in his XL navy blue uniform, his sturdy legs propped up at his desk with the receiver wedged between his ear and his shoulder. The expression on his broad, square face would be solemn and yet strangely reassuring. He was a man who had always seemed firmly in control of whatever challenge police work handed him, and that had earned him captain status in record time.

"Yes, we have, Daddy. I just came from Mr. Hemmings's office. We were discussing how to approach a feature on each of the Gin Girls," she told him. "You know, who they and their families were, what they meant to Rosalie, that sort of thing. It may help to get people through all the gut-wrenching emotions they'll probably be feeling for a very long time to come."

There was silence for more than a few seconds at the other end. "How you doin', daughter a' mine? This may be the worst tragedy to ever hit Rosalie. Certainly in my lifetime."

Wendy managed a smile. She knew exactly what that daughter phrase meant. He always used it when he was genuinely worried about her—or unusually proud of her. "I'm okay. More than a little shocked by it all, though. I don't think it's really sunk in completely yet."

"Yeah, I thought you might feel that way. You were getting to know those ladies pretty well, weren't you?"

Wendy hesitated at first, but then decided to tell him the truth. "They were still kinda holding me at arm's length, Daddy. There was a generational reserve in play, I think. I hadn't been officially approved as a member, you know. I had a few more months of kibitzing and even sitting in as dummy to observe and learn from it all. None of them really opened up to me all that much—at least not as far as their personal lives were concerned. Now the game of bridge was another matter. They were all happy to put in their two cents on that. No shortage of opinions there. Especially when they'd all gotten a couple of their stiff gin cocktails in them."

"Hmmm," he said. "I guess I'm not all that surprised. Liddie Rose, for one, was a formidable woman."

"That she was. I wouldn't have wanted to get on her bad side just from what I observed at the bridge club."

"I'd certainly agree with you there. Anyway, I have a message to deliver from Ross. He said you may have to be flexible about your dinner date later on at the Bluff City Bistro. I've made him lead detective on this Gin Girls case. He's gonna be interrogating the two witnesses in a little while here at the station, and then he'll go on over to Don Jose's Retreat to see how the processing's going. He said he'd text you when he got an inkling about when you two could go out for dinner. I'm sure you'll be able to work something out."

Wendy thought for a moment about Hemmings suggesting that she do "undercover" work to pry bits and pieces from her boyfriend. She mentally banished the image of his sleazy smile and focused instead on the fortuitous news she had just received from her father. Being lead detective, Ross would indeed be privy to things that might assist her in writing her articles. He might not even know he'd let something slip, although she fully intended to try and respect his professional boundaries. Of course, she always had her father as a backup source.

Then a further momentous idea surfaced for the first time. What if her interviews and the scraps she could collect from Ross and her father actually enabled her to help solve the case? It hardly mattered if it turned out to be an incredible accident or a homicide. If she could get to the bottom of it on her own, Hemmings would have no choice other than to give her the juicy promotion she felt she deserved. A pox on his antiquated belief that women should only write about "women's stuff." What did that mean these days, anyway, since women were doing practically everything that men did?

"Thanks for the heads-up, Daddy," she said, coming to.

"Sure. It's a sad day for Rosalie, isn't it?"

"Yes, I imagine we might even make the evening news around the country. All those cable stations just love this kind of sensationalism. You know, anything to outdo each other for ratings."

"Hard to keep things private anymore," Bax said. "Everything eventually comes to light, and sometimes it surprises the hell outta everybody when the truth is finally revealed."

"So maybe what this case needs is a fresh pair of eyes and a brain to go right along with it."

Bax enjoyed a hearty laugh. "Is my daughter volunteering?"

"Maybe I am," she told him. Her voice was quiet, but her adrenaline was flowing. "Maybe I just am."

An hour and a half later after putting the day's engagements and other social trivia to bed, Wendy headed toward the parking lot and slid into the black Impala her father had so generously given her on her twenty-first birthday a few years back. Then she made her way to Don Jose's Retreat on historic Minor Street. It was a mere three blocks from the *Citizen* building, so she arrived at the crêpe myrtle-lined avenue of privilege in no time, parking her car a half block north and then walking the rest of the way.

There was still a small crowd of onlookers gathered in front of the venerable brick town house now fully encircled by crime scene tape. Heads down and otherwise oblivious, most of them were texting with their cell phones or staring straight ahead at the front door, as if expecting it to open at any moment and a full explanation of everything given to everyone's satisfaction. Such was the nature of the rubbernecker and the gawker. A tall, stoic-looking police officer with a buzz cut—Wendy recognized him instantly as Sgt. Ronald Pike, who sometimes partnered with her boyfriend, Ross—was stationed on the sidewalk to prevent any of them from lifting the crime scene tape and interfering with the processing still going on inside and around the perimeter of the house.

How out of character it was for this neighborhood—one of the more remarkably preserved of those built by the Spanish colonials in the 1790s—to have the aura of crime hanging over it while creating one of those tabloid headlines at the supermarket checkout counters. Ugh. She fervently hoped these crimes would not end up there for the country to consume like buttered popcorn at a movie theater. Nothing close to this had ever happened along very proper Minor Street, or any other street in Rosalie for that matter, as far back as Wendy could remember, even though her life span amounted to a little more than twenty-five years. There had been car wrecks and robberies and even a few street shootings in run-down neighborhoods, to be sure, but nothing had reached out and rippled across the community the way these quadruple murders were doing right at the moment. There was about it nothing short of a flash-fire effect.

Wendy's intention in swinging by was simply to "see for herself," even though she knew Ross and some of the other CID officers were busy on the case already. Some part of her brain was still trying to convince her that this terrible tragedy was just an elaborate joke staged by the insufferable Dalton Hemmings, possibly to test her for whatever insane reasons he had concocted. He had been known to pull practical jokes on his employees before, even if this particular one—if that was indeed the case—was in the poorest possible taste.

But the yellow crime scene tape strung out everywhere instantly told her otherwise. Reality was cemented in place securely for her like a crown over an exposed, broken tooth. Those four women she had barely gotten to know in any significant way and who had just begun to teach her the finer points of the game of bridge really were gone forever. She would be interacting with them no longer, and her dreams of becoming a championship bridge player would just have to be put on hold for the time being.

Then, as a reflex action, she found herself gasping softly. What in the world was wrong with her? Where were her values of decency and empathy? How could she possibly be concerned about a trivial card game when four women had just lost their lives in a horrifying manner? Learning the art of finessing or doubling or preemptive bids or the various conventions had to take a back seat for now—and perhaps for a very long time after. The game of bridge was certainly not a matter of life and death, the fate of the Gin Girls notwithstanding.

Wendy's cell phone vibrated in her pocket. She retrieved it and saw that it was Ross checking in with her.

did Bax give u my message?
yes, she texted back.
just started interrogations, may take a while
daddy said 2 witnesses
can't spell her name right
Merleece?
that's it
who else?
the gardener, they were both there, text u when I'm done
let me know asap
u got it

After they'd both signed off and Wendy headed back toward her car, her thoughts turned to Merleece and how she would be able to hold up under Ross's unique but deceptive style of interrogation. A memorable conversation she had once had with Merleece in Liddie Rose's kitchen quite a while back flashed into her head and stubbornly remained there, front and center. How the subject of law enforcement had even come up that particular day, she could not quite recall, but it had piqued her interest back then and certainly was doing so now.

"Lemme tell you right now, I don't trust the *po*-lice," she remembered Merleece saying to her.

There was much more from Merleece, and it all left a lasting impression. Something about black folks in Rosalie always having to be cautious about everything they did and said, and always looking over their shoulders to be safe from harm. Something about black folks getting the blame too much for the wrongs that white folks did, and nobody doing anything much about it. Merleece had implied that things had always been that way, and they were never going to change in her lifetime.

"But don't you worry. I can't imagine you'd ever get into any kind of trouble, Merleece. You are one of the most hard-working, upstanding citizens of Rosalie," Wendy had said to her.

Merleece had given her a strange, sideways glance, as if she might possibly be hiding a secret of some kind. Then she had said something else that Wendy clearly remembered. "You never know where trouble come from. Things sometime not what they appear to be."

Odd that that image and those words had not only stuck with Wendy but had stepped up and refused to fade in the midst of this once-in-a-lifetime tragedy. Were these random remembrances going to be par for the course in the days to come? Could they possibly lead her to a solution that no one else would see coming?

CHAPTER 3

Detective Ross Rierson of the Rosalie Criminal Investigations Division was a man who liked to get right to the point when it came to interrogating suspects and witnesses. He had crafted a hybrid approach involving aspects of "good cop" versus "bad cop." It had proved to be very successful for him, namely "kill 'em with kindness"; then—move in for the kill. He was, in fact, just the man to pull off such a one-two punch. He had one of those dazzling smiles full of teeth so white that it was impossible to look away. The baby blues and shock of dirty-blond hair that graced his forehead didn't hurt him, either. The combination was hypnotic, especially when combined with his disarming, low-key manner of speaking. And when he had his person of interest right where he wanted them, he generally was able to close the deal by leaning in further while keeping that smile on his face and saying something like, "You know you need to tell me the whole truth, don't'cha? Otherwise, this won't go well for you." The fact that it came out sweet and guileless there at the end made it all the more effective as a ploy. Only the most abrasive and abusive of his suspects made him veer from this formula.

Ross's meteoric rise within the Rosalie Police Department and then the CID was not unlike that of his supervisor, Captain Bax Winchester, a couple of decades earlier, and it was not Ross's imagination that Captain Bax had taken him under his wing from the get-go, perhaps as the son he never had. It was also quite apparent to Ross that the man heartily approved of his ardent pursuit of Wendy, even if she hadn't quite returned his interest yet.

Ross had also made it clear to Wendy, however, that she must pursue her questioning of suspects and survivors for her feature articles on her own. He would do what he had to do in the interrogation room at the station or out in the field somewhere, and she would have to devise the ways and means to engage those same people without his help.

But Wendy wasn't particularly concerned. She knew her father would leak a few things here and there if she asked. As for Ross and this "undercover" business that Hemmings had suggested—well, she was her own woman, and she would be the one to decide what approach she took with him.

Thus it was that Wendy's first in-depth interview with Merleece took place at Simply Soul on the north side of town over lunch the day after the murders. Famous for its greens, mac and cheese with bacon, fried shrimp, catfish, and cornbread, Wendy often dropped in by herself when her workload at the paper allowed her time. There was always a B. B. King or other blues tune playing in the background, and it all gave Wendy a much-needed respite from her tedious, frustrating job.

"I know this is going to seem repetitive," Wendy began, taking a sip from her sweet tea tumbler as they sat together at their cozy corner table with its catfish art scattered across the cloth. "I know you finished up with Detective Rierson down at the station yesterday. But I need to know as much as possible for these features I'm going to be writing for the paper about Miz Liddie and her friends."

Merleece seemed game and waved her off quickly. "Go right on ahead, Strawberry. Mr. Rierson, he say that the evidence pointin' to me right now, and I'm not likin' that one bit. Maybe you can help me out. You one smart girl."

Wendy smiled as she often did when she heard the nickname Merleece had invented for her. It had happened during one of the bridge games at Don Jose's Retreat that Wendy had been allowed to observe during her fledgling membership. Excusing herself to the kitchen during a break, Wendy and Merleece had chatted amiably, and Merleece had raved about her strawberry-blond hair.

"You mind if I call you Miz Strawberry?" Merleece had said there at the end.

Wendy had laughed and told her, "Drop the Miz. I'll call you Merleece, and you'll call me Strawberry."

From there, their friendship had blossomed even further every time Wendy had come for one of Miz Liddie's luncheons.

"So tell me more about working for Miz Liddie," Wendy said, poised with her pen and notepad. The greens and cornbread plates they had ordered had not yet arrived. "How long were you there again?"

"Near 'bout twenty years," Merleece said. "The maid she inherit from her mama—it was Jawnita Silers—she die of a heart attack, poor thing, and Miz Liddie need somebody new. We hit it off on my first interview, and I been there ever since."

"Could you go a bit more into detail?"

Merleece took a deep breath and brought her hands together. "Miz Liddie have her ways and list of things for me to do. But I learn 'em fast, and she always satisfied. She pay me well for my work, and whenever I want a raise, she give it to me. When Mr. Murray was alive, I would go in five days a week to clean and cook. After he die, though, we cut it back to three unless Miz Liddie have a party or one a' her bridge luncheons she want me to show up for. She always pay me extra for that, too. But I stop cookin' so much these last few years. She just want the cleanin' mostly, she say."

Wendy busied herself making notes and continued. "It was nice that you were always well compensated. Maybe you already know this, but Mr. Rierson says your fingerprints were all over everything, including the coffee cups. But that makes perfect sense considering all the work you did in that house."

"I know that's right. You think I work with gloves? Well, maybe when I wash Miz Liddie best china by hand I put on the latex." Merleece hesitated, and there was the slightest hint of emotion in her tone. "Or when I did wash the china all them years. I keep talkin' 'bout her like she still alive."

"Yes, I imagine that was a shock to walk in on it all the way you did. My sincerest condolences to you."

"I thank you for that, but I don't know if I wanna call it a shock right now. Maybe I give it a name when I get outta bed tomorrow, if I can get outta bed. This mornin', I forget for a minute 'bout what happen. I get all the way to my kitchen to start fixin' up my coffee, and then I remember everything. I near 'bout fell to the floor."

"I know it must be horrible for you," Wendy said. Then she referred to a few notes she'd scribbled after talking briefly over the phone to her father. "The Rosalie crime lab has already established that there was potassium cyanide in all the coffee cups. It was an extremely nasty way to go, I've been told. Considering how it works on the human body, none of the ladies could draw a breath there at the end. They were all oxygen-starved."

Merleece closed her eyes and shuddered, waving her hand in front of her face as if she were swatting a gnat. "Please, please. Don't make me think 'bout it. I don't think I can stand it."

Wendy gave her time to gather herself, respectful of her growing vulnerability. "Their families all want autopsies, of course. I fully expect when the results come back from Jackson, they'll confirm that this is what did in these poor ladies. Did you serve the coffee to them, Merleece?"

Merleece did not hesitate. "Yes, I fix it up, too. I always do that . . . I mean, did that . . . for Miz Liddie bridge luncheons. I fixed up everything she serve."

"How do you think that potassium cyanide got into the coffee cups?"

"I don't know, Strawberry. I know I didn't put it in there, but I got a good idea all the same," she said, leaning in with a confidential squint. "That crazy gardener you need to question. He got all kinda chemicals and drugs out in the shed. You watch him squirm all over the place when you talk to him. I say you don't squirm unless you guilty."

Wendy maintained her poise. "I'll get to that later. Meanwhile, tell me everything you can remember about fixing up the coffee service."

"It was the same as it always is," Merleece began. "I have to heat up the water just right. Cain't be boilin', but have to be hot enough to dissolve the crystals and all like that. Then I have to let it cool just so. Miz Liddie, she like . . . she liked . . . the instant coffee."

"Really? I wouldn't have thought that in a million years," Wendy said.

"Cain't stand any a' that instant coffee, myself. I brew my coffee at home from scratch."

Wendy focused. "And you didn't notice anything unusual about the coffee? Maybe something about the crystals?"

Merleece's expression indicated she might just be in the middle of an aha! moment. "To tell you the truth, Arden was botherin' me at the time. I didn't pay attention like I usually do."

"Arden?"

"Yes, Mr. Arden Wilson. The gardener you need to question 'bout everything under the sun. I know Mr. Rierson question him right after he get through with me down at the station."

"Right."

Merleece leaned in even farther and lowered her tone to a whisper. "Arden, he downright crazy. He got all them butterfly jars out in the shed. Killin' jars, he tell me they call 'em. Now you tell me. What kinda person go round makin' a hobby a' killin' pretty butterflies?"

Wendy was frowning now. She had always thought butterflies were among the most beautiful creatures in nature and had been fascinated with them since her Girl Scouts days. She had even earned a badge once by identifying ten different species. Monarchs had been her favorites. Black swallowtails next. But the thought of killing them had never crossed her mind. Such fanciful creations needed to be free to fly about and thrill the hearts of people everywhere during their brief time on the earth.

"I assure you everyone will try to find out—the police and myself included. But, for the record, Daddy says they already know about those killing jars."

"You be sure you don't forget 'bout that," Merleece said. " 'Cause I know I hear Arden say he got some kinda cyanide out there. Plus, I think he out there smokin' somethin' if you want my opinion. Seem like you can put two and two together from that. No good come from doin' drugs, you know what I'm sayin'?"

"You don't like Mr. Wilson very much, do you?"

Here, Merleece drew back dramatically as if she had just spotted a snake concealed in the grass that was about to sneak up on her and strike. "I do not. He mind himself at first, but then he was all the time comin' into my kitchen and botherin' me. Wouldn't leave me alone as God is my witness. Want me to do this and do that for him, and don't even say *please*. My job was to take care a' Miz Liddie and her friends, not put up with that sorry fool and his crazy ways."

"I take it you would have been very happy to see him go and never cross your path again?"

"You got that right, Strawberry. He got on my last nerve and any I got comin' my way in the future."

Wendy decided to go for it. "What I'm going to say to you is not something I believe, but the police may make a case that he got on your nerves enough for you to frame him for murder. They'll say you could have swiped his potassium cyanide from the shed and put it in the coffee cups yourself. You've already admitted you pretty much knew about everything that was going on out in that shed."

The everyday mask came off, as if ripped by an invisible hand, and Merleece was nothing short of indignant. "So they think I'd harm Miz Liddie and her friends? They crazy if they think so, no matter how much I cain't abide that Arden Wilson. I am a churchgoin' woman. I don't miss a Sunday. You just axe anyone who go to my church. Thou shalt not kill is a commandment, and they better take me at my word that I take it seriously."

"I have no reason to doubt that, Merleece," Wendy said in soothing tones. "Let's move on. I'll tell you now that the crime lab has confirmed that the potassium cyanide was not in the coffee crystals. It was actually in the sugar bowl on the tray you used. So let's talk about the sugar. Did you put sugar into all the coffee cups, or was that something the ladies did for themselves?"

Merleece slowed down her explanation, pausing frequently. "Yes, Strawberry. I fix up everything. All four of the ladies . . . they take sugar in they coffee . . . and two take cream. If I didd'n get it right, they was a price to pay."

"Did you ever get it wrong?"

"Just once, and that was enough. You never heard such carryin'-on, and all over a cup a' coffee."

"Did you notice anything unusual about the sugar?"

"No, it look white like sugar suppose to look. I never give it any thought. Cain't say more'n that. But like I also say, Arden, he was aggravatin' me the whole time like he usually would do, so I wudd'n payin' that much attention."

"Do you think he was trying to distract you deliberately?"

Merleece smirked. "Could be. But he always doin' that anyway."

"So, nothing out of the ordinary there." Wendy's tone continued to be calm and even, causing Merleece's facial muscles to relax somewhat. "Talk more about what the ladies expected you to do."

"You already know most of it. Miz Liddie have these bridge luncheon rituals, see. I had to fix gin drinks first, then tomato aspic and chicken salad for they lunch—and sometimes they had custard for dessert, but not this time. Don't know why, but that was Miz Liddie decision. Then coffee afterward so they could make a toast before they bridge game. I heard her say they gone win the championship in Jackson next week. They never had done it even one time, but this was they year, she tell me."

Wendy scribbled something quickly and then looked up. "So, we can say—nothing out of the ordinary there, either."

"'Cept they never got to play this time." Finally, Merleece's voice began to tremble quite a bit. "Miz Liddie, she say she have this great Grand Slam hand all dealt out at the bridge table in the living room. The hands, she have 'em all stacked up facedown—North, South, East, and West. Miz Liddie, she always sit North. She explain to me once that whoever sit North mean they on top of the world. Now, that seem like a lotta nonsense to me. Anyhow, I know just a little bit about bridge from just hangin' around all these years. She been talkin' to me about this particular hand all mornin' before the rest of the ladies show up. She say they just gotta win that duplicate title this time up in Jackson. You cain't work for someone that start up The Rosalie Bridge Club and not understand they lingo. The cards prob'ly still there the way she left 'em."

"No, as a matter of fact, they're not there anymore. My father said they were bagged and they're down at the station," Wendy told her. "Daddy says they consider them part of the evidence, and you were very helpful to them in explaining the bridge game that was supposed to take place when the police officers first arrived to start processing the house and grounds."

Merleece cocked her head and frowned. "I was happy to help, but I still don't see how the cards be evidence when the ladies never play with 'em."

"The truth is, you just never know what might be useful in an investigation. You can't overlook anything."

There was clearly a pleading element in Merleece's voice now. "I'm tellin' you, Strawberry, that I had nothin' to do with the deaths of the ladies. I don't know how that poison get in the sugar, but I'll say it again. I wouldn't put it past Arden Wilson to do such a wicked, sinful thing. In fact, he tell me somethin' earlier today . . . lemme see . . . how did he put it? That he just might have Miz Liddie figure out, and he was stayin' ahead of her—somethin' like that. He wouldd'n tell me exactly what he was talkin' 'bout, though. No tellin' what kinda deviltry inside that man. Maybe his brains pull too tight by that man-bun thing he wear all the time. Silliest thing I ever see on a grown man. To me, it just not right."

"And why do you think he would be plotting against Miz Liddie? Aside from the fact that you don't like him and the way he treats butterflies."

"'Cause I think that Miz Liddie ready to fire him. Maybe for smokin' dope out there in the shed, and I think she intend to turn him in to the law."

"Tell me honestly. Did you put the idea of Mr. Wilson smoking dope out in the shed in Miz Liddie's head?"

Merleece raised her voice a notch, putting her hands on the table. "He told me hisself he was doin' it out there."

"But you didn't answer my question, Merleece. Did you mention it to Miz Liddie?"

"No, Strawberry, I did not. I only answer Miz Liddie when she mention somethin' about the smell out in the yard. I tell her that it have somethin' to do with all those chemicals he use for the gardens."

"Did she believe you?"

"Cain't say. But I think she suspeck all the same."

Wendy took another sip of her tea to gather her thoughts. "Let's assume for a second that you're right about Mr. Wilson killing Miz Liddie. Why kill the other ladies if his beef was only with her? Doesn't that seem odd to you?"

"I would'n know what he have against the others." Then Merleece gave out a barely audible gasp. "But maybe they just at the wrong place at the wrong time, you know what I'm sayin'? That can happen, cain't it?"

"Yes, it can. Daddy's had cases over the years in which there was collateral damage," Wendy said.

"*What* kinda damage?"

"Never mind. Let's just move on to something else. Think carefully now. Do you have any idea who else besides Mr. Wilson might've had any reason at all to kill Miz Liddie and her friends?"

Merleece's light brown eyes moved from side to side as she frowned and considered. "Like I told Mr. Rierson, they was two people. Just this past week they come by for a visit. Not on the same day, though. They come on different days for different reasons, and they raise hell and aggravate Miz Liddie so bad she have to go and lay down on the bed for a while."

"Tell me about that, please."

"The first was Miz Selena Chalk."

Wendy perked up, and the surprise on her face was quite noticeable. "The owner of the Bluff City Bistro? Mr. Rierson eats there all the time. We were supposed to have dinner there last night, but he had to work too late, so we called it off."

Merleece's face lit up as well. "You and he goin' out together, Strawberry?"

Wendy sounded a bit mischievous. "Kind of. I'm not quite sure how serious it is yet."

"Really, now? That Mr. Rierson, he quite a looker, you know."

"That's another subject for another day," Wendy said, lifting her tumbler, rattling the ice cubes, and taking another big swallow. "Back to business, please."

Merleece said nothing, drawing back with a skeptical glance. Then their lunches came, and they paused long enough to take a bite or two of their mustard greens.

"What do they put in these greens, Merleece? I'm always in heaven when I taste them."

"Salt pork. And they cook 'em down for a long time."

They both continued eating for a while; then Wendy finally picked up where they'd left off. "Let's get back to the Bluff City Bistro and Miz Chalk, why don't we?"

Merleece's tone went from chatty to somber. "That was why Miz Selena come by to see Miz Liddie."

Wendy noted the change with great interest. "*What* was why she came to see Miz Liddie?"

"Her restaurant. It was 'cause of the letter Miz Liddie and her friends write to the paper a coupla months ago, talkin' 'bout it so mean. They trash it pretty good, the way I remember it. I never been in it to eat, so I don't know if what they say was the truth, but it seem to me like you don't want people sayin' all those bad things the ladies say 'bout it."

"Yes, I recall that only too well. They all signed it and pretty much called out the menu and the service especially. I disagreed with just about everything they said, and if I'd been Dalton Hemmings, I wouldn't have published it as a simple courtesy. Don't know why he did. The ladies didn't have anything positive to say, and he had to know that some people in Rosalie would pay attention to what they said because of who they were."

Wendy knew that Ross had seriously considered writing a letter refuting the Gin Girls' attack, since his experience with Bluff City Bistro had been nothing but gastronomically pleasant, and he had never had an issue with the service. His favorite meal was the Bluff Burger stuffed with blue cheese, along with the steak fries, and he often dropped in on the Broad Street brick and lacework building overlooking the Mighty Mississippi for a quick lunch when his duties permitted. Furthermore, he had told Wendy he had been waited on by several different people who had gone out of their way to please him. One had even brought him an extra helping of fries without charging him, doing so with a smile and a wink.

But Miz Liddie and Company had called out the waitstaff in no uncertain terms. They had referred to being ignored constantly, having water spilled on them, and getting orders mixed up more often than not. Ross had told Wendy that he wondered if the Gin Girls had had some other bone to pick with Selena Chalk that they were keeping hidden. Did they not approve of or dislike her because of the plus-size clothes she had to wear? Had she approached them with bad breath? In the end, however, Ross had decided to stay out of the fray, continuing to patronize the restaurant whenever he could and hoping to do his part to help it prosper. He had even recommended the food to all his buddies at the station.

The last time he and Wendy had eaten there about a week ago, she had commented on the obvious trend. "Every time we come here, there seem to be fewer and fewer customers. I know it's not my imagination, either."

"Offhand I'd say that Miz Liddie's critical letter in the *Citizen* has taken its toll," he had reminded her.

"Words have consequences," Wendy had replied. "Sometimes very serious consequences. They can cut deeper than a knife."

And now that rambling, vitriolic letter was popping up again in a police investigation regarding the deaths of Miz Liddie and her friends. Some things indeed had long legs, and Wendy focused as Merleece began describing Selena Chalk's troublesome visit.

"Well, what happened was Miz Selena come to the front and she demand to see Miz Liddie. But Miz Liddie say to tell her to go away. Miz Selena, she wouldn't take no for an answer. She got her big, fat foot in the door so I couldn't close it shut. So, finally, Miz Liddie, she come out in the hallway and they do everything but slap each other in the face and pull each other hair out. I was there standin' right behind the two of 'em the whole time."

"What did they say to each other?"

Merleece took on the appearance of a medium, closing her eyes as if trying to project the exact images. "They raise they voices, and Miz Selena tell Miz Liddie that the letter she wrote would be the cause of her goin' outta bid'ness soon if somethin' don't turn around. Her trade had drop off somethin' awful, she tell Miz Liddie. Then Miz Liddie say somethin' like, 'Why on earth should I care? You run uh awful restaurant, and it *should* go outta bid'ness.' "

"That's pretty harsh, and I think it couldn't be further from the truth. Was that it, or was there something more?"

Merleece seemed hesitant at first, but then blurted it out.

"Miz Selena tell Miz Liddie that she want her to take back what she wrote in the paper and send a new letter to the editor. Then I remember Miz Selena exact words: 'I could just kill you and those drunken cronies you hang around with for what you did to me, and don't think I won't find a way.' Far as I know, nobody ever call Miz Liddie and her friends—drunken cronies. Maybe some people think it, though."

"Strong words. Do you think she was serious, or that maybe she just lost her temper in the heat of the moment?"

"From the look on her face and the way she screamin' at the top a' her lungs, I'd say she was dead serious."

"Interesting choice of words. How did it end?"

Merleece brought her hands together with a light smack. "Miz Liddie and myself manage to push her out to the sidewalk and slam the door on her. Then I lock it. That was the end of it. Well, maybe not quite. Miz Liddie, she was some upset with me 'bout lettin' that woman get in like I did. But I just turn my head for a second, and Miz Selena just barge in. She a big, heavy woman, all the time huffin' and puffin', and I couldn't push her out 'cause you see I'm small. But together Miz Liddie and me, we able to do it there at the end."

"So things definitely got physical."

"They did, and it wudd'n a pretty sight to behold. It was a good thing there wudd'n no weapons around."

Wendy paused briefly to digest the highlights of what Merleece had told her, knowing that her notes and perhaps a session with her father or Ross would enlighten her further. "Did Miz Selena go into your kitchen at any time while she was there? You see where I'm going, don't you? If she did, that would have given her the opportunity to poison the sugar."

"No, she stay out in the hallway the whole time until we finally manage to shove her out."

Wendy finished up her notes and said, "You mentioned there was another person and another incident to report?"

"Yes, Miz Crystal Forrest. She just move to Rosalie last year, and I b'lieve she inherit all this money from her husband when he die. So she bought Old Concord Manor just down the street in the next block and put all kinda money into it, tryin' to outdo everybody on Minor Street, it seem like. It was all run-down and 'bout on its last leg when she took it over. And it also seem like they wudd'n a day that go by when Miz Liddie don't complain about her and her uppity ways. Miz Liddie, she say . . . wait, what was that word? They's one she use 'bout Miz Crystal all the time like when someone get they hands on lotsa money all of a sudden and don't know what to do with it and then throw it all over the place to impress people."

Wendy pondered it all for a few moments; then everything easily fell into place. Rosalie had more than its share of such people showing up all the time to pretend they'd been there forever. "Was it possibly nouveau riche?"

"Yes, indeed, that was it," Merleece said, nodding her head energetically. "All these fancy clothes she wear, and the way she talk like she British or somethin' and like her nose stopped up, too. So what happen was Miz Crystal call up Miz Liddie and say she want to speak to her 'bout the horse-drawn carriages that clip-clop along Minor Street and slow the traffic down so much she cain't get to her driveway when she in a hurry. She say she want to cut down the hours when they can ride by."

Wendy looked incredulous, putting the palm of her hand to the side of her face. "You're kidding? I've never heard of anyone complaining about the tourists in the carriages. Everyone knows it adds to the local color. I've never even heard of anyone honking at the carriages. If you have any sense, you know it spooks the horses."

"I never hear anyone honk at the horses, neither," Merleece said. "I don't know why Miz Liddie give that woman the time of day and take her serious, not with the way she feel about her. But for some strange reason, she did, and when Miz Crystal come by, it turn out what she really want is to talk Miz Liddie into lettin' her join The Rosalie Bridge Club. Miz Liddie, she turn her down already, so this wudd'n the first time she try to worm her way in. I was in the kitchen when I hear 'em raise they voices, and I rush out to see if Miz Liddie need me. 'No,' she say to me, holdin' her hand out like she directin' traffic. 'I can handle this.'" Merleece took a couple of breaths, but it was clear that she was enjoying relating the drama of the situation and was playing to an imaginary back row.

"What happened next?" Wendy said.

"Some angry talk back and forth, and I hear Miz Liddie tell Miz Crystal to leave or else. When she gone, Miz Liddie come into the kitchen with her face on fire. I never seen her look like that in all the time I work for her. Not even when she got mad at Miz Selena, and she plenty mad then. She tell me that Miz Crystal have the nerve to offer her ten thousand dollars to join the bridge club. I had to shake my head. Cain't be nobody that want to play cards that bad."

"Nothing surprises me anymore. Anyway, that's a whole lotta money to pay just to play a game."

"I wish I could get my hands on that much money at one time," Merleece told her.

Wendy was startled by the mercenary comment but said nothing.

"Then Miz Liddie say that Miz Crystal threaten her," Merleece continued. "She say that Miz Crystal tell her she would regret not lettin' her in the club big-time. Then she repeat *big-time*."

"Nothing more of interest? For instance, did Miz Crystal ever go into the kitchen that afternoon?"

"No, she didd'n. You think they's anything to these two ladies actin' up the way they did with Miz Liddie?"

"There might be. I'm sure the police will question them both."

There was a hint of panic in Merleece's voice. "You think the police have enough to arrest me, Strawberry?"

"I don't know."

"I cain't afford no lawyer, you know."

"One will be appointed for you if it should come to that. Let me just say right now that I know you're a person of interest. There's evidence that points to you, and that can't be disregarded. I'm sure Mr. Rierson told you not to leave town. It would be an admission of guilt if you did."

Merleece put her hand over her heart as she heaved her chest. "Yes, he tell me that, but I swear I didn't have nothin' to do with this. You just remember what I say about Arden Wilson and his crazy ways."

"I'm sure the police won't forget that," Wendy said as she took a bite of her cornbread and another swallow of tea. "One last thing. Did any of the other ladies come into your kitchen for any reason once they'd arrived?"

"No, none of 'em did. They all stay out in the dining room while I serve 'em lunch and then they coffee."

"Which means they couldn't have fooled around with the sugar."

Merleece nodded but said nothing. Perhaps it had just occurred to her that it might be better if at least one of the ladies had spent any time at all in the kitchen. As it was, the focus remained on herself and Arden Wilson.

Near the end of the meal, Merleece finally addressed what was surely her greatest fear. "I got a real bad feelin' 'bout all this, Strawberry. I don't wanna take the blame for somethin' I didd'n do. It happen to black folks all the time."

Wendy reached across the table and gently took Merleece's hand. "If I have any say in the matter, you won't."

CHAPTER 4

Over the phone, Ross had told Wendy to brace herself if she decided to interview Arden Wilson. "He's really out there all by himself," he had continued. "I don't know if you really need to see him anyway. He doesn't know very much about the Gin Girls from what I was able to get out of him. But he's as much a suspect as Merleece is."

"I need the practice if I'm going to realize my dream of being an investigative reporter," Wendy had told him. And Ross had dropped the matter graciously.

Arden had been living with his father, Mr. Brent Wilson, before his death and then had inherited his childhood home outright. It was a modest little Queen Anne cottage on Dulcimer Street, painted a pale shade of blue, but the yard was impeccably tended, full of gardenias and azaleas with a fanciful ceramic birdbath off to one side. As a result, it was often either fragrant or colorful, depending upon the time of year, and Wendy was impressed with its design and tidiness as she walked up the sidewalk onto the porch and rang the doorbell.

She was hardly impressed with Arden's appearance once he greeted her at the door and ushered her into the somewhat unkempt parlor, however. It was as messy as the yard was pristine—newspapers and magazines strewn all over the floor and what appeared to be grease stains on the sofa cushions. Wendy kept remembering Merleece's snarky comments regarding the man-bun atop his head—something about his brain being pulled too tight by all that long hair swept back. A humorous image flashed into her head of Arden's roots screaming at the top of their lungs—if indeed they could have vocal cords—at the ordeal of being stretched like that to the limit.

But it wasn't just the man's hair. Arden and his stale sweat didn't smell very good, and those definitely were dirty overalls he was wearing. Wendy wondered how long it had been since he had taken a bath. He also started out being little more than monosyllabic when questioning began on the living room sofa.

"So tell me about these killing jars you had out in the gardening shed. That's a new one on me."

Arden shrugged and leaned back against the sofa cushions. "A hobby a' mine."

Wendy dug in with her pen and notepad ready. "Could you please elaborate?"

Arden looked and sounded bored. "I collect butterflies. Unless you live under a rock, you surely know that lots of people do that. I didn't invent it, you know."

"Please explain to me how these jars work. What do you need the potassium cyanide for?"

Arden began opening up, gesturing with his hands. "Simple. You put the butterfly in the jar, and it prevents the butterfly from thrashing around and tearing up its wings. That'd ruin the specimen. That's the object, you see. Puts the butterfly right to sleep, so to speak. No harm done, and your butterfly is pristine."

Wendy nodded after taking notes. "I suspect the butterfly

"Looks like her feelings about you are mutual."

"So what?"

"That's the question, isn't it?" Wendy said. "And the answer is that it would have given you a motive to take Miz Liddie out if she thought you were smoking grass on her property. After all, you had already had the opportunity, and you had the potassium cyanide on hand. Plus, this isn't Colorado. This is Mississippi. Possession of dope would land you in prison."

Arden shrugged again, the complacency oozing from his every smart-aleck pore. "So did the police find any grass in the shed?"

"I don't know."

Arden leaned in with a triumphantly smug look on his face. "I know for a fact that they won't."

"And why is that?"

"Because I never smoked dope at any time out there in the gardening shed. Never ever happened."

"Or anywhere else?"

"No comment. The world's a big place to do things in. But I will say I liked to fool with Merleece's head. It's pretty easy to do. I made her think I was blazing up. She's pretty naïve behind all that street-smart lingo of hers. Hey, she bugged me, so I bugged her right back, and I'm willing to bet she made all that up about Miz Liddie getting ready to fire me. So, you see, there goes my motive." He drew back a bit and noisily cracked his knuckles in what was clearly a macho ritual of his. "Did Merleece mention Miz Liddie's finger-pointing?"

Wendy considered for a moment. "I . . . no, I don't recall that."

"When we rushed into the dining room to see what all the commotion was about, Miz Liddie pointed straight at Merleece and said, 'You!' The way I see it, she was fingering her murderer."

Wendy reviewed her conversation with Merleece carefully. "If that was the case, Mr. Arden, what would Merleece's motive have been to kill Miz Liddie and her friends? She told me herself she was well-paid, and she'd been there for twenty years."

Now, Arden was laughing outright. It seemed as if he would never stop, and Wendy liked him even less for that. A few seconds more, and she would have gathered up the courage to tell him to shut up as politely as she could.

"Did Merleece tell you about Hyram Maxique, her one and only son?"

"I don't recall her mentioning the name, no. Do you have something to tell me about him?"

It was apparent that Arden thought he had the upper hand now, and his erect posture and the sneer on his lips reflected it.

"When I first began working for Miz Liddie after my father died, Merleece didn't have her guard up the way she does now. One time when she'd gotten into Miz Liddie's sherry—and I happen to know that she did that more than a few times—she told me that her son, Hyram, had had to leave town after slapping his girlfriend around. She wasn't seriously injured, but the girl was ready to press charges for assault and battery anyway. Merleece called him a good-for-nothin' all the time, but I know she was still sending him money to live on, wherever he is. I think she even hinted he had a new girlfriend up in Chicago or somewhere with very expensive tastes in everything. She once said to me, 'I cain't say no to my flesh and blood.' But I can tell you he was eating up a lot of her money, and she needed even more because of it."

Wendy dismissed the revelation with a sweep of her hand. "So? Merleece told me Miz Liddie gave her raises every time she asked."

"You're missing the point. Merleece also told me there before we had the falling out that Miz Liddie was going to leave her a tidy little sum in her will for all the years she had worked for her. There's Merleece's motive for doing her in. She'd have all the money she needed for herself and her bum of a son and all those women he fooled around with."

"And what about the other ladies? What was her motive for that? Everybody agrees that Merleece made the coffee and stirred in the sugar. Why poison the other ladies, then? She could have poisoned only Miz Liddie and let the others live."

"Collateral damage if you ask me," Arden said without hesitation. "You confuse things by killing them all. You know—which one was the real victim? Seems like an excessive move, but it'll do the trick."

"Sounds like you're speaking from experience."

Arden remained placid. "Nah, just saw it on one of those popular TV crime shows once. I forget which one."

The red flags were waving in front of Wendy's eyes like semaphores. Both Merleece and Arden had offered up the same concept of the ladies being at the wrong place at the wrong time. Separately. True, Ross had told her they had been separated as witnesses as soon as all the CID officers had arrived. But had the two of them somehow still managed to coordinate their stories before then? Even though both seemed intent on accusing the other of the crimes, were they actually doing so to confuse things? Or make it more difficult for the actual truth to emerge? Was that truth something ingenious or practically impossible to conjure up?

"I'm sure Mr. Rierson advised you not to leave town," Wendy told Arden. "You are a primary suspect in this investigation at this point."

"Yes, he told me. But what about Merleece?"

"Yes, both of you are."

"I take exception to the both part."

Wendy leaned in and spoke calmly. "That's your privilege, but my father says the police could go to the D.A. and get a warrant for your arrest at any time for probable cause."

Arden sounded not the least bit perturbed and cracked his knuckles again. This time, the gesture seemed more defiant than macho. "If all the evidence they have is that I used potassium cyanide for my butterfly collection, I don't think that'll hold up in court. My fingerprints weren't anywhere near that coffee service. There might be a few on the kitchen counter since I hang around there all the time, but that should be about it. I'm not your man." He rose from the sofa and pointed insistently toward the foyer. "I hope you've written down everything, Miz Winchester, 'cause I don't have any intention of repeating it. I'm about ready to lawyer up with all this questioning. I think we're done here, unless you want me to give you the grand tour of my butterfly collection. It's just off the kitchen on the screen porch if you're interested. I have nearly one hundred and fifty specimens."

Wendy managed an insincere smile. "Thanks for the invitation, but I think I'll take a rain check."

At the door, Arden said, "All of you are really barking up the wrong tree after me. I'm totally innocent, and the way I figure it, I'll always be as free as a butterfly."

"Not the ones in your killing jars," Wendy said, getting the last word and noting the trapped expression on Arden's face.

Wendy slid into the front seat of her car after her interview; she took her cell out of her pocket and glared at it while she took a deep breath. Why had Merleece failed to mention to her Miz Liddie's finger-pointing and the accusatory, "You!"? And then there was the revelation about her son, Hyram. Had Arden Wilson been telling the truth about these things? Wendy intended to put Merleece on the spot immediately but tactfully, as befitted a fledgling investigative reporter. Both Ross and her father had warned her that digging around in the dirt was frequently a very messy business, and she needed to proceed carefully.

"I cain't remember every little thing," Merleece told her over the phone a minute or so later, sounding very annoyed. There was a pause, after which Merleece seemed to have calmed down somewhat. "But she wudd'n pointin' that finger at me, she was pointin' at Arden."

"That seems like a pretty big thing not to remember to tell me. So you confirm that she actually did say that while she was pointing?"

"Yes, she did," Merleece said.

"Did both of you enter at the same time?"

Merleece took a great deal of time answering, and this time her voice lacked confidence when she finally spoke up. "I come in first. Miz Liddie, she got a swingin' door as you know, so two people cain't use it at the same time. More than once, I got to slam it in Arden face. It give me great pleasure to do so."

"So Arden was behind you in this instance."

"Yes, but when Miz Liddie point and say, 'You!' like she did, we side by side not believin' our eyes when we saw the ladies all convulsin' and gaspin' for breath. I like to have fainted, but at least I did somethin'. I did what I could. Arden, he was just standin' there like he don't have good sense, and I had to shout at him to call 9-1-1. It was like he was bein' slow on purpose. Yes, I do believe he was slow on purpose. You think 'bout that for a while, Strawberry."

Wendy was turning over everything as fast as she could. "Has it occurred to you that she was referring to both of you at once?"

"No, I tell you again, she meant him—Arden—not me."

Wendy changed the subject abruptly. "I think we've got that covered. Now, please tell me about your son, Hyram. You do acknowledge him, don't you?"

At the other end of the call, Wendy could not see Merleece's eyes widen to the point they looked about to pop out of her head. "Yes. Whatchoo want to know about him?"

"Where is he now?"

"Cain't say. Don't know. He call me now and then. I wish I could tell you he was a credit to me, but I'd be lying if I did. Early on, he wouldn't pay attention to right and wrong. Stole this. Lied about that. Who tell you about him, Arden? I got in my cups once and let all that spill outta me. My bad."

Wendy was not about to let up, however. "Do you send him money?"

"Sometime I do. Is they a crime in that?"

"No. Arden said your son needs money to keep his current girlfriend in style. Anything at all to that?"

Merleece raised her voice noticeably. "That's a big, fat lie that crazy fool make up. He all the time exaggeratin' just to worry me to death."

"Have you seen your son around here lately?" Wendy let the question sit there, and Merleece continued her fit of anger when it finally sunk in on her.

"You accusin' my son of comin' back here to Rosalie and killin' Miz Liddie and her friends? 'Cause you don't even need to worry 'bout that. I can tell you, it never happen."

"Now, Merleece, I didn't go there at all, but you certainly did. I only asked if he might be in town."

Merleece seemed to have cooled off slightly, as if sensing she was being overly dramatic and not making a very good impression on her friend at the moment. "Already said I don't know where he is right now. Could be anywhere—Chicago, Detroit, Memphis—you name it."

"I keep worrying about Miz Liddie's will," Wendy said, changing the subject. "It could make a difference if she was actually going to leave you something."

Merleece went from calm to nonchalant. "I just don't

know for sure. She tell me she was one time when the two of us have a cocktail together one afternoon. Miz Liddie, she was mighty lonely after Mr. Murray die, and we used to drink a toast to him in front of his fancy paintin' in the dining room. He up there frownin' down at us while we salute him. Both Miz Liddie and Mr. Murray, they good to me all the time I worked for 'em. You think I'd kill her for whatever she gone leave me? You better think that over again."

"Duly noted," Wendy told her while adjusting the phone so she could make more notes.

"Miz Liddie put the finger on her killer when Arden come into that room. How she know that, I don't know. But that creepy butterfly killer the one you lookin' for. Lissen, Strawberry, I cain't afford to have you doubtin' me. You practically all I got on my side."

"I understand, Merleece. I just needed to check things out with you," Wendy said. "I still believe you're innocent."

"Seem like you the only one who do right now."

CHAPTER 5

Things began to unfold quickly over the next twenty-four hours. At first, the Rosalie grapevine referred to the investigation as the Gin Girls' deaths. Among the snarkier comments that circulated among those who did not particularly care for one or more of the ladies was, "I bet they drank themselves to death!" Predictably, the horrific incident continued to be the subject of conversation throughout Rosalie over breakfast, lunch, dinner, throughout everyone's workday, and up until retiring at night. Among the many who admired them, the sentiment was universally, "Who in their right mind could have done such a thing?" Liddie Rose, Sicily Groves, Bethany Morrissey, and Hanna Lewis had been among the Rosalie elite, and losing all four of them simultaneously had brains reeling, tears streaming, and even an element of fear creeping into the imaginings of the community. Was someone on the prowl to take out wealthy widows, and if so, why? Was this only the first act of evil? Who might be next in line?

Then when Jack Manning revealed in the *Citizen* that the autopsies from Jackson proved all four of the ladies indeed had had lethal doses of potassium cyanide administered to their systems, and when it was further leaked by person or persons unknown that they had been preparing to play out a Grand Slam contract at Miz Liddie's Don Jose's Retreat, the moniker of choice became The Grand Slam Murders. It captured the public's imagination—appealing to the dark side that exists to varying degrees in everyone.

Dalton Hemmings embraced it and told all employees to refer to it as such in their everyday conversation. It was good for circulation, he explained, trying to insert an empathetic tone as he said it but failing miserably. The new catchphrase made the incident no more understandable or any less frightening, but when regional TV crews from Jackson and Hattiesburg began showing up to question townspeople, there was no shortage of those eager for their fifteen minutes of fame with their "If you ask me . . ." and "This is what I think . . ." opinions. It quickly became a media circus and even the talk of the entire state of Mississippi.

Hemmings's directives to Wendy were to attend the joint memorial service at St. Mark's Episcopal Church—all four of the ladies had eagerly embraced the term *Whiskeypalians*—even if they were almost exclusively devoted to gin. As the paper's social columnist, she was to pay her respects for appearances, he told her further. Never mind that she fully intended to do so on her own. She knew quite well that it was the ideal circumstance to begin putting together her behind-the-scenes Gin Girls' pieces in a tactful and patient manner as they had discussed originally. This while Ross and the other CID officers would be continuing to gather evidence and interrogate the many persons of interest.

"I'm not a bit surprised by the joint service," Wendy said after she had received her marching orders in Hemmings's office. "Everyone knew they were all inseparable. They were still talking about some of their escapades in high school, college, and even during their married lives on those occasions I was there kibitzing to become a full-fledged member down the road. You might think some of those things had just happened yesterday."

Hemmings looked pleased. "Then you've got that much of a head start on this. But I do expect you walk that tightrope between the endearing and the gossipy. We don't want to be sued for anything."

"I've dodged many a bullet from fussy brides, pretentious mothers of the bride, bossy bridesmaids, tacky in-laws, and just about any other category you can think of," Wendy told him, somewhat amused with herself. She had indeed developed a very thick skin since coming to work at the *Citizen.*

"That's what I'm counting on, Miz Winchester," Hemmings continued with a conspiratorial grin. "You do have a considerable following here in Rosalie. You make all these fancy parties and dinners and such sound like the agendas of Hollywood royalty at the Cannes Film Festival or something. And yes, I'm well aware that more than a few people in Rosalie have thought they were the kings and queens of the Deep South for a century or two. I think some of it may have to do with the respect your father commands in this community. Be that as it may, your ability to draw things out of folks that nobody else can is why I'm giving you a chance to prove how much more you can do for the paper."

The conversation ended with Wendy being more buoyed than ever about the assignment as she headed back toward her cubicle. One irrefutable fact still nagged at her, though: this promising opportunity was being made possible by the horrific murders of four pillars of the community. There was just no way around the ugly, visceral nature of it all.

Did she think she was up to it? Yes. Did she think she had something to prove to herself and Dalton Hemmings? Absolutely. But at her core of decency, she devoutly wished the circumstances could have been otherwise.

★ ★ ★

Wendy was impressed with the turnout for the Gin Girls and their families at the joint memorial service. Each stained-glass church window was appointed with tall, clear glass vases containing silky white lilies, providing a tasteful counterpoint to the many mourners in black and the red carpeting that ran from the front door to the altar rail. Then, too, Reverend Gerard Blough had started out well enough with his Gin Girls' eulogy. Mention was properly made of their prominent family backgrounds, their devotion to the game of bridge, and then the civic and charitable endeavors all four women embraced, particularly their support of St. Mark's Orphanage and St. Mark's Senior Citizens' Center. It was made abundantly clear that both of those institutions would have gone under without the support of the Gin Girls over the years. Wendy understood and appreciated the necessity of giving each of the ladies their due for all their good deeds, and in the beginning, heads were nodding and understanding smiles were affixed to most of the faces in the pews. Everything was proceeding at a reverent pace, and nothing seemed out of place.

But the good rector had his flaws, one of which was to drone on and on in his sermons well beyond the attention span of the politest of Rosalie's citizens. Succinctly put, this tall, spindly, and bald man who was engulfed by his black and white robes loved the sound of his surprisingly deep voice. On this occasion, he also turned out to be fond of anecdotes that—in his opinion—uniquely illustrated the characters of the dear departed. So, each Gin Girl was revisited and reanimated with notes of levity, most regarding bridge-playing and gin-drinking. His frequent pauses also indicated that he expected the congregation to play along with their tittering as if they were all part and parcel of a lengthy and slightly off-color spiritual skit. Had the man himself had issues with one or more of the ladies?

"Here's something many of you may not know," Reverend

Blough was saying at one point. "Our world traveler, Bethany Morrissey, did manage to bring home a piece of the Berlin Wall on one of her many trips to Eastern Europe. But as she once told me at a cocktail party, her decorator approved of political freedom but not common graffiti, and therefore refused to let her display that chunk of 'protest concrete' on her living room coffee table—which is what she devoutly wanted to do. She considered it avant-garde of the highest order."

Some of the muted chuckling was genuine enough, but there was also an undercurrent of whispering that suggested that "enough was enough, and it was time to move on." After all, the ladies had not passed on due to old age and natural causes, they had been murdered and endured ghastly suffering in the process. Reverend Blough was pressing the envelope a bit but seemed determined not to let up.

"Our Miz Sicily Groves once told me," he continued soon enough, "that being a natural redhead was an enormous responsibility. She insisted that if God gave you that kind of striking hair color in the first place, you had to live up to it. You couldn't be boring or ordinary. You had to be absolutely memorable, which I think we would all agree she was in every way. I know I wouldn't disagree since I don't have any hair to speak of anymore."

There followed a prolonged, genuine laugh from the congregation, obviously relieved that the man could make fun of himself as well.

But Reverend Blough just couldn't leave well enough alone. "Of course, we would also have to agree that Miz Sicily got away from the natural redhead part there at the end."

Even the good reverend could tell that his extra attempt at humor had not gone over all that well, and he drew back slightly from the pulpit in silence until the whispering had died down. Eventually, however, he gathered himself, glanced down at this notes, and took aim at Hanna Lewis.

"Our Miz Lewis was born a bit too late, I'm afraid," he began. "Don't worry. I'm going somewhere with this. Considering her prowess on the tennis court, I believe that if Billie Jean King hadn't taken down Bobby Riggs in that Battle of the Sexes, our Miz Hanna would have found a way to do something similar herself in some other venue. She would have taken no prisoners, just as she always did out at the Rosalie Country Club courts."

Finally, he seemed to have hit the bull's-eye with a comment that was overwhelmingly positive and humorous without being snarky. All the head-nodding and pleasant smiling were general testaments to that among those in attendance.

Toward the finish of what turned out to be well over thirty minutes of increasingly labored reminiscences, Wendy began to tune out; not as an act of disrespect, but as a reminder that some of the survivors of the Gin Girls were sitting in the front row, and her assignment would be to interview them soon enough without overstepping her bounds. Would they refuse to cooperate and perhaps shut her out? Then where would she be?

As if reading her mind and assuaging her fears, however, Stella Rose Markham, Liddie's daughter, sought her out amidst the significant crowd milling around at the reception that followed, consisting of several tables of spiked punch and sandwiches in St. Mark's Parish House next door. Perhaps it was to be expected, as Stella and Wendy were the only two additions to The Rosalie Bridge Club in its storied history, and now they were simply the only two remaining members. Could the club even survive under those circumstances? More to the point, should it just be allowed to die with the Gin Girls? It had, in fact, always been an exclusive reflection of their inflated opinions of themselves.

"It's so good to see you," Stella said, holding on to Wendy's arm. The gesture seemed to be more a balancing act than one of affection. Perhaps Stella had had a few nips for courage before the service. Her unsteadiness showed up in her speech as well. "You . . . and I—we're . . . well, we're all that's left of the club. We . . . don't even have enough for a game anymore." Stella dabbed at a tear with her finger. "And I honestly don't know if I have the energy to remedy that."

Stella had been gracious to Wendy from the beginning. Though twenty years apart in age, the two were somewhat similar in the way they dressed impeccably and presented themselves and their social graces to the public. They were both soft-spoken and deferential to their elders—Stella particularly so to her mother. Not as tall as Liddie and with features far less delicate and striking, however, Stella was in no danger of being heralded as her mother's second coming.

"The truth is," Stella had told Wendy confidentially that first time they had met at one of Liddie's bridge luncheons, "that I'm pretty much Alternate Number One. You know, an extra if anyone gets sick or is off traveling. I hope you won't be too disillusioned to hear that you will officially become Alternate Number Two. Miz Bethany and one of the others sometime travel together to Europe and stay a month or longer. The Girls just can't go that long without a game. It would be like going cold turkey off the gin. We would hear the shrill screams of withdrawal all over Rosalie, worse than the tornado siren that makes everyone jump out of their skin."

Wendy had enjoyed a good laugh then, but today was the time for proper decorum as they moved to a quiet corner of the room and sat down beside each other in comfortable armchairs. "I wanted to express my shock and sorrow to you again. I can't imagine what you're going through. Losing my father that way would just devastate me, and don't think the possibility hasn't crossed my mind with him being in the police business all these years. I worry about him all the time even though he's graduated to paperwork and making assignments mostly. But there was a time when both my mother and I wondered if he would be coming home to us at the end of the day. It's a very unsettling profession for other members of the family."

"I understand, but I've never been one to wear my emotions on my sleeve," Stella told her. "I'm the type who presents a brave front in public and then goes home and cries buckets until I'm exhausted. I hope my eyes don't look too red today. I spent a lot of time on my makeup, and I've got a prescription or two flowing through my veins today to make me cope a little better with everything. Believe me, I don't think I could make it through this ordeal without them. So if I seem a bit wobbly, that's the reason."

Wendy gave her shoulder a sympathetic pat or two, easily spotting the hurt in her eyes. "I understand what a loss this is for you. But you look like a true Rosaliean. I know Miz Liddie would be very proud of you."

"Mother and I were completely devoted to each other," Stella added, sniffling just a bit. "We saw the world the same way. After my divorce from Peter, I sort of threw myself into the club and the other civic projects that the Gin Girls embraced. Thank God, Peter and I didn't have any children. That would have been the custody battle of the ages. He was the ultimate gold digger, lusting after my parents' fortune. I was much better off without him in my life. It was a bitter, bitter divorce, I can tell you. Mother made sure he got the short end of everything, and I'm quite sure he deeply resented her for that."

Wendy had not heard this litany of regret about Peter Markham before but listened politely without comment. She had the feeling she was hearing something of significance.

"Peter was a controlled-substance addict, you know," Stella continued, her voice tinged with anger. "Not just one pill, but whatever he could get his hands on. Lortab, oxycodone, even morphine. He toyed with them all, and being a pharmacist, he could get away with it without being discovered. That's the main reason I decided to divorce him. I knew things were only going to get a lot worse between us if I tried to tough it out. Once an addict, always an addict."

Wendy filed away the tidbits of information: Peter Markham. Pharmacist. Drug addict with access to drugs of all kinds. Had he been far gone enough to kill Miz Liddie with potassium cyanide out of spite, and even further twisted enough not to care if he took the others along with her? Then Wendy decided to make her move regarding her newspaper feature.

"If I might take this opportunity, I wanted to tell you that Mr. Hemmings has assigned me a series of articles on all of the Gin Girls. He wants me to tell their family stories and what they all meant to Rosalie. I hope you don't think I'm being too forward in bringing this up now, but if we could set up a time and place to talk, I'd be so very grateful to hear what you have to say."

Stella brightened immediately—even seeming to sober up a bit. "That's a lovely idea. Maybe it would help some of us with our grief. Dalton Hemmings was always good to my mother. She'd call him up all the time for publicity regarding whatever event she had going, and he never let her down. I'm glad you'll be writing the article, too. You've done a wonderful job these past few years with the social column. Everyone constantly raves about how thorough and accurate you are."

Wendy thought quickly on her feet and decided to tell the truth. It was her studied opinion that most anyone with an ounce of organizational skills could do her job. "Thank you for the compliment, but my main claim to fame is typing efficiently, I'm afraid. As far as I'm concerned, what I create is simply rote stuff."

"Don't be so modest. Your social tidbits have all been

charmingly written. They must be in every scrapbook in Rosalie."

"You're too kind." Wendy paused just the right length of time, not wishing to appear too aggressive. "So, when do you think I might interview you about your mother and your family?"

"Would this Saturday do at my house?" Stella said. "Say around three-ish? I'd enjoy the company."

Wendy agreed to the time and place and then decided to press about the others. "What kind of reception do you think I'll get from Beau and Charley Lewis talking about Miz Hanna and Sherry Herrold about Miz Sicily?"

Stella sat back in her chair, sighed, and thought for a moment. "Sherry will cooperate with you—she's an intelligent girl, although a bit mousy and a total shopping addict. She'd want to make sure her mother gets her due and that everything is accurate. I know Miz Sicily would be pleased that you're doing this article, too."

"That sounds promising."

Then Stella leaned forward, speaking softly as if divulging a secret. "But I wouldn't count on getting too much out of the Lewis Brothers. They didn't get along with their mother at all because of that so-called exercise guru she was seeing. Rumor had it Beau and Charley thought he was a gold digger and that Miz Hanna was using up too much of their inheritance on him—buying him things right and left. Even a new SUV and a condo. Mighty expensive gifts. But if you ask me, the Lewis Brothers have always been ne'er-do-wells, themselves. Divorced playboys, both of 'em. Of course, their worries are over now that Miz Hanna is no longer with us. She can't spend any more money on that Hermes Caliban character with all his muscles and tattoos up to his neck. A disgusting specimen of humanity, if you ask me."

More tidbits for Wendy to put away safely in her brain:

Lewis Brothers worried about inheritance from their mother, Hanna. Would they go as far as to poison her to prevent her further extravagances? But if so, why would they kill the others? Did they lack any trace of a conscience?

"Wendy?" Stella was saying. "Is something wrong?"

Wendy came to with a gracious smile. "Oh, I was just thinking about what you just told me. Mr. Hemmings has already said he wants me to put the Gin Girls and their families in the best possible light. There's to be no dirty laundry aired. I know you'll appreciate hearing that."

"Yes, I'm delighted. That's good to know. That would be very important to my mother—and to me as well." Stella craned her neck and pointed across the room. "There they are—Beau and Charley—guzzling punch and rubbing up against the curvaceous Laurel and Karie Baker. Doesn't look like those boys miss their mother one iota to me. They're always on the prowl, those two. Miz Hanna used to complain all the time to Mother about how often they played around on their wives. But I give those women and myself some credit. Once we all found out we were married to randy devils without zippers, we cut our losses."

Wendy observed the two men in the midst of their somewhat corny routine, flashing their teeth and even winking at their targets now and then. They were indeed big, strapping men, perhaps getting a bit long in the tooth for carefree bachelorhood but still boasting flowing manes of dark hair, trim physiques, and a flair for well-fitted, custom-made suits. They might have even been mistaken for twins were it not for the fact that Charley's face had been somewhat rearranged in a bad car wreck as a result of his being mightily under the influence. His once-patrician nose was now somewhat crooked, and there was a large scar right underneath his hairline. Still, he remained as attractive to women as his pristine-featured brother, surely because of being blessed with a conspicuous bank account.

"I see what you mean. Their body language is definitely—well, on the make," Wendy said after a little time had passed. "This could be one of those singles bars, the way they're acting."

"You can try to get them to talk to you, though I wouldn't even think of it now with their minds on other things," Stella continued, her voice dripping with sarcasm. "But you'll have to use all your journalistic skills to get your foot in the door. What I've told you is maybe all you'll get."

"Thanks for the heads-up. I did have another question to ask you, though. Since Miz Bethany was childless, is there anyone left in Rosalie I could interview about her and her family?"

Stella screwed up her mouth and then shook her head emphatically. "Afraid not. But Miz Sicily and Miz Bethany were pretty close. They often traveled abroad together. Sherry could probably tell you a few things about the Morrisseys. Look at it this way: when you visit with her, you'd get two interviews for the price of one."

Wendy marveled at how glib and gossipy Stella had become over the last five minutes or so, particularly about the Lewis Brothers. Perhaps it was just the tonic she needed to get her mind off her mother's death. Wendy had been there, recalling how crazy and all-over-the-map emotionally she had become when her own mother, Valerie, had died of pneumonia when she was just a teenager. She felt as if her soul had fallen to her feet, leaving her hollow. There was no accounting for the way people handled grief; and if it had not been for her father's counsel and fortitude, she doubted she could have even returned to her high school life with any hope of success. She would have been too much of a mess, and her friends wouldn't have understood. After all, they were all immersed in pep rallies, going out on movie dates, and exchanging each other's class rings. As it was, she moved away from the few girlfriends she had cultivated and became somewhat of a loner, on the outside looking in. None of them had lost a parent, and she chose not to talk about it to them, even when they told her they would be there for her to listen. From that point forward, however, her father's advice was paramount among her priorities, and it had always served her well.

"I think I want to be a writer, Daddy," she had told him near the end of her senior year in high school. By then, the pain of her mother's departure had eased somewhat, and she had regained some of her equilibrium.

"What kind of writer do you want to be?" Bax had asked her. "There are all different kinds."

"I'd like to be an investigative journalist. I'd like digging into things the way you've done all these years as a police officer. The hidden things, the mysteries, the whys and the whos. Only, I don't want to join the police force. I'm not crazy about guns. I think I'd be so nervous, I'd probably end up shooting myself. Maybe a newspaper reporter with the right beat would suit me more."

Bax had suggested she apply to attend the University of Missouri, well-known for its journalism department. He revealed that he had once dated a girl who was studying there herself. "That was a few years before I met your mother, you understand," he had added quickly with a wink. "In fact, I never mentioned her to your mother. A man is always wise not to bring up his former crushes to his wife. She'll remember them and use them against him at the most inopportune times."

Wendy had come away from it all with the conviction that she just might have been fortunate enough to have inherited her father's investigative talents. There were those who said you either had that X-plus factor or you didn't. Then she would combine them with the journalism skills she would learn at Missouri and perhaps work her way up to a position at the *Washington Post* or *The New York Times* or some iconic paper like one of those. Her name would become synonymous with tough, ruthless reporting—she would be the equal of any man out there pounding the pavements for a story.

Then reality had kicked in. Writing the social column for her hometown paper was merely treading water, if that. She was drowning in sickly sweet syrup. She just had to make this Gin Girls assignment work and escape to words that carried some weight. She had to get the inside information on the families, including tidbits that had never come to light. She might even have to breach Mr. Hemmings's caveat not to shine a flashlight here and there into too many dark corners of their lives. She envisioned herself plopping the printed document down on his desk and saying something like, "You asked for it, you got it."

Then there would probably be a fevered battle of words after he had read it and taken it all in.

"I assume you realize we can't print some of this," he would say, looking at her with disdain. Maybe he would even pound his fist on his desk as he had been known to do from time to time.

"Even if it's the truth?" she would answer, leaning in with all the fierceness she could muster.

"Offended people mean canceled subscriptions," he would return. "Even our online ones. I've been in this bid'ness a lot longer than you, my girl."

But she would not be put off in her mission to make her mark. "Interesting and compelling reading means new subscribers."

They would go back and forth until she prevailed, and the series on the Gin Girls would even win a prize of some kind. It would be the real beginning of her astounding career.

Wendy surfaced from her feisty fantasy when Stella gently poked her arm. "I was asking you if you needed anything further from me until we talk Saturday. You were off somewhere in space."

"Oh . . . I was . . . no, I don't think so." Wendy took her hand and looked into her eyes. "I just wanted to say again how much I appreciate you taking the time to meet with me during this terrible ordeal. If there's anything I can do for you, please don't hesitate to get in touch with me."

The two women embraced, and Stella said, "I'll do that. But I think you giving me the chance to tell Mother's story will be all the therapy I need right now. It couldn't come at a better time. And if you'd like for me to put in a good word for you with Sherry, I will. I've been kind of a mentor to her. I'd do it now, but I don't see her around anywhere. She may have left early."

Perhaps she had, but Dalton Hemmings had not, and he caught up with Wendy just as she was about to exit the Parish House after she and Stella had said their goodbyes. "I see you're already at work, Miz Winchester. I saw you talking to Stella Markham," he told her while holding the door open for her.

"More or less," she said, as he followed her quickly down the front steps.

"Just be careful not to cross that line," he reminded her.

She bristled at his patronizing tone but managed a weak smile. "Yes, I'll be on my toes."

As she walked to her car, however, she realized how worked up she'd gotten in her head over presenting the finished article to Hemmings. There it was again: the desire to succeed and make a name for herself versus the private grief of families who had just suffered the trauma of death by foul play. She knew quite well she was being manipulated by Hemmings, but she had to find a way to make it all work and not have everyone want to run her out of town as the "sweet little society columnist who had turned into a tabloid monster." After all, she had no experience whatsoever with being perceived as the *bad guy.*

CHAPTER 6

That evening, Wendy and Ross got together for the first time since their canceled dinner at the Bluff City Bistro the day of the murders. They decided against eating out. Instead, Wendy suggested that she cook for them in her little starter bungalow with a front screen porch out on Lower Kingston Road a few miles south of Rosalie. She'd managed to decorate it with finds at flea markets and the cheaper antique stores on Harper Street in Rosalie, plus a few of her mother's paintings. Her father had given her the down payment to take on the mortgage the same year he'd given her the Impala, and she realized how far ahead of the game she was financially as a result. Others were struggling with the economy the way it was—but not Wendy.

In the fifteen years she and her mother had interacted closely and lovingly, she had also learned the basics of being a halfway-decent cook, something Valerie Winchester had embraced with great pride. Wendy had improved exponentially over the intervening ten years and frequently had her father over to test new recipes. As for Ross—not so much. On this particular occasion, however, she intended to wine and dine him, then compare notes ever so subtly, and she figured he would be none the wiser for it under her spell.

"So how was the service?" Ross said as they sat down to her dinner of roasted pork tenderloin, green beans almandine, garlic new potatoes, and what would be more than one glass of Merlot for each of them to sip. He had planned on coming to St. Mark's originally, but a robbery at a convenience store on the north side of town had sent him in the opposite direction at the last minute.

"Kinda weird," Wendy told him. "Reverend Blough was equal parts respectable rector and shocking stand-up comedian. It got a bit uncomfortable for a while there near the end. He seemed to have forgotten the service was not all about him and his anecdotes. But there really was quite a turnout for the ladies. Just about everybody in Rosalie was there, except you and Daddy."

"Yeah, your father wanted to follow us out to the store, since his old friend, Huzzy Noonan, owns it."

"Yes, Daddy texted me. I remember Mr. Huzzy when I was growing up," Wendy said, looking somewhat nostalgic. "Biggest ears in the universe sticking out from the sides of his head. He would come over to the house from time to time, and he and Daddy would play chess and drink beer until they could barely move the pieces around. I can see why Daddy would be concerned, but he said Mr. Huzzy was okay. He's a tough old bird."

Ross swallowed a bite of meat and nodded. "Yeah, he's fine. Just a little shaken. No one likes looking down the barrel of a gun. The cash register got emptied pretty good, but that was all the damage that was done."

"Perish the thought of anything happening to that dear man," Wendy said, after a sip of her wine. "So, any leads on the robbery?"

"Not yet. A tall man wearing a hoodie and a stocking over his face is pretty much all we have in the way of a description. Mr. Noonan couldn't even tell what race he was since he was wearing gloves. About the only thing we can hope for is a trace of his DNA somewhere."

Then came Wendy's seamless segue. She figured the generous amount of wine they'd enjoyed so far would get her some results. "How is the investigation for the murders going?"

"It's picking up a bit. I'll be interviewing Miz Selena Chalk and Miz Crystal Forrest soon. Merleece said they'd both had a row with Miz Liddie this last week. . . ." He paused, putting down his forkful of green beans. "Well, I guess you know I'm not supposed to be telling you this kind of stuff, Wendy." He stared at his wineglass for a moment and grinned. "I see what you're up to."

She pressed her thumb and index finger together and moved them quickly across her lips while giving him a wide-eyed stare. "I'm completely locked and sealed, I promise you."

Ross seemed to relax a bit and resumed eating. "When do you begin your interviews about the Gin Girls?"

"Saturday," she told him. "I'm starting off with Stella Markham. She and I have always gotten along as underling members of the bridge club. I've learned a tidbit or two that might interest you, by the way."

He looked up from his plate. "Yeah?"

"It's about Beau and Charley Lewis—and also Peter Markham."

"I'm listening."

"Miz Hanna Lewis's sons, and Stella Markham's ex-husband. Seems Beau and Charley were quite antsy about their mother's money being frittered away by her on her muscular boyfriend, and Peter Markham, who is a pharmacist, was using and had access to all kinds of drugs, according to his ex-wife. Stella says that's why she divorced him, and not only that, there was really bad blood between him and Miz Liddie as well. Stella says her mother made sure he didn't get a cent of their money in the messy divorce settlement."

Ross put down his fork and wiped the corners of his mouth with his napkin. He enjoyed his food and was not exactly a dainty eater. "Sounds like you're doing some good work. Your trusty Rosalie CID will follow up."

"Could we compare notes later?"

He firmly shook his head. "No can do." He thought for a moment and then backed off a bit. "Well, you can tell me everything you find out like you just did, but I have to keep my end private for the time being. Your daddy wouldn't want me to leak a whole lotta things—even to you."

She leaned in and gave him her best smile, making sure it went all the way up into her eyes. "Even though he used to leak things to me every now and then? You'd be surprised how often he did just that. I think what he was doing at that point was to try to get me to become a policewoman. I mean, I can't prove it, but it wouldn't surprise me if that's what he was really hoping for."

"Yeah, I can see how father and daughter might get all mixed-up in each other like that. Kind of an ego thing both ways."

Wendy was still smiling. "It's what made me think investigating things would be a thrilling thing to do. But really, never as police work, just as a writer. I wanted to be cerebral more than physical."

They resumed eating for a while; then Ross finally spoke up, looking slightly guilty. "Okay, look, about all I can tell you at this point is that Merleece Maxique and Arden Wilson are our primary suspects, especially Merleece. She admits she put the sugar in the coffee cups. It remains to be seen who put the potassium cyanide in the sugar. But both Merleece and Arden had access to it, and both of 'em are bending over backward to incriminate the other. I appreciate you telling me what you learned about the Lewis Brothers and Peter Markham."

"Do you have enough to arrest Merleece or Arden Wilson?"

Ross couldn't help but smile. "You are one persistent woman, aren't you?"

Wendy clasped her hands together prayerfully, her eyes directed heavenward. "Persistent should have been my middle name."

"It doesn't look all that good for Merleece at this point," he told her. "We could get a warrant for probable cause anytime we wanted based on the evidence so far. So could the D.A. But the investigation is far from closed. There are still too many loose ends and too many people still to question."

The alarm clearly registered in Wendy's voice. "But why just Merleece? Why not Arden Wilson? Merleece was always complaining about him every time I visited for a bridge club luncheon. She told me he had all kinds of chemicals out in the gardening shed. Including some for killing butterflies. She thought he was so creepy to do something like that. So what about Arden and his potassium cyanide that somehow ended up in the sugar bowl?"

"He's not off the hook by a long shot, but we have reason to believe that Merleece's motive was the money she mentioned Miz Liddie may have left her in her will. I'm not going to say anything more."

"I understand completely," Wendy said, more than satisfied with what she'd squeezed out of him.

After a dessert of blueberry tartlets and whipped cream garnished with a mint leaf, Ross beckoned Wendy to the two-seater sofa she'd had reupholstered in flamingo pink after rescuing it from its dowdy last stand and impending death at the flea market. "Come over here and let me thank you for that wonderful dinner, sweetheart. You could run your own restaurant."

Although she obeyed and was soon by his side and in his sturdy arms, the all-too-fresh memory of Dalton Hemmings winking while telling her to pursue "undercover" action to get what she wanted for her story brought her up short. Then, too, Ross had called her sweetheart many times before, but she had never said it back to him. She wasn't offended by it—far from it. She'd just stuck with calling him plain old Ross. Nice, dependable Ross. The one-sidedness of the relationship had remained intact no matter how many more months had passed and despite the intimacy they had enjoyed now and then.

When he delivered his usual skillful, tender kiss to her on this particular night, she felt the usual stirrings but did not want to indulge them any further. Yet it was quite clear by the wandering of his hands over her body that he wanted, perhaps even expected, more.

"Wait," she said, gently untangling herself and pulling away. "Just give me a minute, please."

Startled, he stumbled over his words. "Did . . . did I . . . did I do something wrong, sweetheart? Huh?"

"No, it's not you, it's me."

He put more distance between them and sat up straight. "I don't think I'm going to like what you're getting ready to say to me. Seems like we've gotten off track lately."

"There's probably some truth to that. You were the one who canceled our last dinner date, remember?"

He had a disappointed look on his face as he shook his head. "Yeah, in case you've forgotten, that was the day of the murders. Everybody's world kinda got turned upside down, didn't it? The station and the crime scene were both madhouses, and I had to take care of business." He leaned in again, completely unable to turn on his trademark smile that had always worked so well for him at work and play. "I think I have to ask right about now—where are we exactly in this on-again, off-again relationship of ours, Wendy?"

She wanted to lie to him so he could save face, but she couldn't bring herself to do it. "We aren't on the same page, Ross. Not yet. You have to understand. I need to prove myself with this assignment on the Gin Girls. I don't want to be stuck forever doing wedding write-ups and descriptions of baby showers. I've got to concentrate now, and maybe I just don't have the time for the kind of relationship you want. The last thing I'd want to do is disappoint you. But that doesn't mean that we don't have a future together."

He rose from the couch, exhaling what sounded like every molecule of air in the room. "Okay. I get it. I do. Tonight's not the time and place. I've got enough sense not to be pushy."

"Don't be mad. Just . . . just be patient with me," she said, trying her best to soften her tone.

At the door, he turned and kissed her on the cheek, sounding more philosophical. "We both have a lot of work ahead of us, so I can't begrudge you what's on your plate. I guess we could both make a name for ourselves by getting to the bottom of these murders. I should know the kind of drive you have by now. You want in on this in the worst way, don't you? I could tell by the professional interrogation you gave me over dinner."

Her laugh was spontaneous and carefree. "And here all this time I thought I was being so subtle."

This time, he kissed her on the lips lightly, drew back, and flashed one of his smiles. "Hey, I figured what was the harm in giving you a few tidbits to run with? I want you to succeed at this, you know. Then maybe we can both get a lot more serious about our relationship."

"I like the sound of that."

After Ross had left, Wendy padded into her cramped little

kitchen to face the dinner dishes she'd piled in the sink. He'd taken her turning him down tonight awfully well, and for that, he'd earned more respect for himself. It had not been her intention to run him off—just to slow him down. Neither one of them had said anything they would regret later. Mission accomplished for the time being.

Meanwhile, the inside info Ross had given her on Merleece's status as a suspect disturbed her greatly. She just knew at her very core that Merleece could not possibly be guilty of murdering Miz Liddie and the other ladies, and was relieved to hear that other suspects had emerged.

But there was a growing sense of urgency. First thing she would be doing tomorrow would be to reach out to Merleece and question her in even greater depth, hoping to uncover something that had been overlooked and that might turn suspicions away from her and shed light upon the identity of the actual murderer.

CHAPTER 7

Wendy had imagined that Merleece would be living in a bit more upscale house than she was. Not that the small, one-story bungalow wasn't perfectly respectable with its white clapboard, green shutters, and screened-in front porch. Her own house on Lower Kingston Road wasn't much bigger or fancier. But Merleece's could have used a new coat of paint all-around, and the neighborhood surrounding it had more than its share of what could only be termed "shacks." Scattered among them were empty lots full of weeds and a rusted-out car chassis or two. North River Street had never been a prestige location, not even in its heyday. But over the past fifty or so years, it had deteriorated further, and the crime statistics that had been hanging over it like a threatening thundercloud had become record-setting of late. The City of Rosalie was trying to help turn things around with Habitat for Humanity and other low-income housing projects, but progress was exceedingly slow. To make things worse, there were public figures like District Attorney Harry Keller—a former city alderman—who had always taken a dim view of concepts like "urban renewal" and "neighborhood revitalization." Unless they were in his "white" district, and there had been a bit of gerrymandering done to create it in the first place.

As she walked onto the porch and knocked at the front door, Wendy wondered why Merleece had never tried to escape the neighborhood and move on to something safer. Perhaps Miz Liddie had not paid her as much as everyone thought, or as much as Merleece had always claimed she had. Or had Arden Wilson been telling the truth about her son sucking her dry? At any rate, it was Wendy's intention to begin in earnest her career as an investigative journalist and even amateur sleuth when that door finally opened.

Merleece greeted her with a warm smile and a hug, then invited her in, leading the way to a small but comfortable living room furnished with a blue afghan-covered sofa and a couple of butt-sprung armchairs facing a TV set that had been born long before the days of flat screens with high-definition capability. There was a circular throw rug in the center of the room that closely matched the design and color of the afghan. The fragrant essence of apples and cinnamon hung in the air, which added a welcoming note. No matter what else might be lacking, food always did the trick.

"I just pulled me one a' my applesauce pies out the oven, and I thought maybe you and me could sit and have a piece after it cool down a bit. Meanwhile, you want some coffee or some wine or somethin'?"

Wendy thought for a moment but couldn't seem to decide. "Well, what are you having?"

"Some wine, Strawberry, some wine. I always go to the grape when I need to feel comfortable in my skin. Lemme tell ya—it work every time."

"I'll have whatever you're having, then. I've been a little tense myself lately," Wendy said, taking her seat on the sofa.

A minute or two later, they were sitting side by side holding mason jars full of dry muscadine wine—a vintage that had been grown, crushed, and bottled by The Old Rosalie Wine Factory, south of town. It hadn't gotten much play outside of Rosalie, but all the locals swore by it.

"I don't like that fancy stuff," Merleece said, making a face. "Just gimme what they put up right here in Rosalie."

"I agree," Wendy told her. "We hold our own with our spirits here in this town. We're the only city of our size in the country that has a winery, a brewery, and a rum distillery. Must be our proximity to the river, I always say. We do like our cocktails of whatever kind. We've been hard-drinking since we were founded. Our waterfront was a pretty rough and tumble place back then, and nobody paid any attention to what went on down there."

Merleece settled back against the afghan and sighed deeply. "I know that's right."

Wendy let a couple of sips course through her veins before she got down to business. "Well, as I told you over the phone, I wanted to talk to you to see if I could help do something more about all these suspicions surrounding you. Neither of us likes all this finger-pointing in your direction."

Merleece turned and lifted her jar as if she were about to make a toast. "I know I can use all the help I can get."

They actually clinked rims for the fun of it, and then Wendy continued. "And I know you couldn't possibly have done this horrible thing, but evidence is evidence. That's the way the police are looking at it. They always do."

"I already told 'em who did it."

"I know you did. Arden Wilson, right? But do you really think it's as simple as that?"

Merleece pointed to the ceiling with authority. "I swear to God, I know he did it, and you don't have to have a reason to do somethin' like that when you crazy to start with. If you not right in the head, you capable of anything." Then she put a finger to her temple. "I'm tellin' you, that boy ain't right."

Wendy nodded and then reached over to put her jar down on a nearby end table. It contained a small lamp with a shade that nearly matched the blue of the afghan and a framed picture of a young black man sporting Merleece's high cheekbones, minus the warm smile. In fact, it was easy to imagine from the pose that he might just have a big chip on his shoulder.

"Well, I know for a fact Arden is still under suspicion just like you are," Wendy said finally. "But forget him for a moment. What can you tell me about yourself and Miz Liddie and her friends that might help us turn this thing around for you?"

Merleece looked puzzled, then perfectly blank. "Cain't think a' nothin' right now."

"There must be something. What I mean is, can you think of something strange or different that went on at Don Jose's Retreat in recent days? It could be any little thing. Something you've forgotten about or don't think is significant, but it might turn out to be."

Wendy could see Merleece searching her brain as her eyes moved back and forth. "Well, I did tell you 'bout Miz Selena Chalk and Miz Crystal Forrest comin' up in her house and raisin' holy hell. All that fightin' make Miz Liddie take to her bed for one a' her naps."

"Can you remember anything else like that? Anything out of the ordinary?"

"Cain't say I do."

Wendy decided to try a different approach. She'd used similar tactics when trying to squeeze something remotely interesting out of baby showers and engagement parties from some of the most boring, pedantic people in Rosalie. "Okay, then. Let's get specific. What about Miz Liddie herself? Obviously, someone wanted her and the other ladies out of the way. Did you ever get the sense that she was worried about something? Because I have the very strong feeling that this somehow revolves around Miz Liddie more than the others."

After a huge swig of her wine, Merleece's face seemed bathed in the light of sudden recognition. "You know, they was a coupla things, now that I look back. They was . . . well, it was the mirrors and the makeup."

Wendy felt a strong surge of adrenaline that gave her the impression she had a second brain working for her in such hormones. "Mirrors and makeup? Please explain that to me."

Merleece settled back and began her story, enjoying the self-importance she had felt when Ross Rierson had questioned her before about any and everything. "Well, it was a few months back, I b'lieve. Miz Liddie seem to look at herself every time she pass a mirror in the house, and they's plenty of 'em. She didd'n know I spy her doin' it a coupla times. She never used to do that, I know for a fact. She never used to primp thataway, turnin' right and left like some teenage girl worried 'bout a pimple. 'Cause she way beyond that foolishness now. And then she started puttin' on lots more makeup than she used to. And checkin' it all the time when she pass the mirrors, takin' out her compact and powderin' her nose. I never seen anything like it. That lady, she never was a primper. Used to be, when she walk away from her bedroom vanity, she ready to greet the world. She never look back that I can remember."

Wendy's excitement rose another notch. "Did she ever say anything at all to you about any of that?"

"No, it was just somethin' that I happen to notice all of a sudden. I did mention it in private to her daughter, Miz Stella, one time when she took Miz Liddie place at the bridge table, and Miz Stella say that her mother just tryin' out some new makeup to look younger and that she gettin' vainer and vainer every year—and what can you do 'bout that? I figure that if Miz Stella not worried 'bout it, then I shoudd'n be, either."

"So you think that was all there was to it?"

Merleece raised her eyebrows. "Seem to make some sense to me at the time. Guess it still do."

"Is there anything else you can think of? You may not think it's important, but it could be."

"I don't like to speak ill a' the dead, you know what I'm sayin'?" Merleece added. "But Miz Liddie was 'bout as mean-tempered as I ever seen her these past few months. Ever since she stop poofin' up her hair and go to bangs. Now, why should a new hairstyle make you cranky? And she just not snappin' at me. She go outside and snap at the mailman if the mail was late. She worse than some dog barkin' and tryin' to bite him. I never remember her bein' like that, long as I work for her. She never easy to work for, but I got around her by learnin' to do everything perfeck. But they was times recently I thought to myself, 'A different person got to be inside her body.' It was like that science-fiction movie where them pods come down from outer space or somewhere to take over the world, one person at a time. Now you know I could'n go round sayin' that to people here in Rosalie, so I kep' it all to myself. Until right this second tellin' it to you, Strawberry."

Wendy pressed further, believing she was on to something. "What about any of the other ladies? Was there anything different about them? Did they have any concerns they expressed to you?"

"Now you want me to tell you 'bout the rest of 'em?" Merleece said, unable to suppress her laughter. "I didd'n work for the rest of 'em. I didd'n vacuum they carpets or polish they silver or sometime fix they food and leave it in the fridge for 'em to eat at they leisure after I leave. I only see 'em when they come here to play bridge. Or when they used to come here." Merleece paused and teared up slightly.

"I'm tellin' you, they is days I don't wanna get up 'cause a' what happen to the ladies like it did. What a normal, decent person s'pose to do with that? I go to church right away—

I mean, that evenin' after it happen I went—and I get down on my knees to find me some answers, but I cain't see any sense to this. I got nothin'. Whoever commit these horrible murders, they beyond help. They headed to a bad, bad place in my opinion."

"I understand how you feel," Wendy said, not wishing to upset her friend further. "I was just wondering if there might have been anything going on between any of the Gin Girls that could be described as of a hostile nature. It doesn't have to be physical, you understand. Maybe some very harsh words—that sort of thing. Even an old-fashioned catfight."

"Now that, I can tell you 'bout. They was always bad blood between Miz Liddie and Miz Hanna. I think it go all the way back from they childhood. Miz Hanna resent the way Miz Liddie tell everyone what to do all the time. She tell me so herself one time when she come into my kitchen feelin' no pain, if you know what I'm sayin'? 'Course, they all feelin' no pain by the time they get to the end of every bridge game with all that drinkin'." Merleece caught her breath long enough to down some more wine. "And that last time when they was murdered, Miz Liddie kep' on remindin' me of things like it was the first time I was doin' 'em. I couldn' make good sense of it. I been with her twenty years and I got everything down pat to the last detail, I promise you that. Nobody have to tell Merleece Maxique anything twice."

"I'm sure that's true," Wendy said. "I saw you in action several times while I was trying to learn the art of the *finesse* looking over Miz Liddie's shoulder. She never would let me sit behind the others. She really did want to control everything and everyone when it came to the bridge club. It was almost like she thought she and she alone had invented the game."

"Strawberry, I don't know 'bout that, but I had her bell-ringin' routine down to a science. I work out just how long to cool that coffee down and all the rest of it. That last time when Miz Liddie and her friends get murdered, I know it was all perfeck. It was all set up for they toast with the coffee and they bridge game just like always. Well, they made the toast okay 'cause I was there to see it, but they never did get to play. The hands, Miz Liddie say they all dealt out and waitin' in the other room, but that was the only time they never got to play 'em. That police detective say the cards now just evidence down at the police station, but like I say to him and tell you last time, how can they be evidence if they didn't play 'em? That don't make the least bit a' sense."

"I see your point, but maybe it was just a police technicality for the fingerprints and the DNA that were on them," Wendy said.

Then Merleece rose up dramatically from her sofa cushion and briefly put a finger to her lips. "All them times you sat in on the bridge games at the luncheons, did Miz Liddie tell you 'bout playin' with new decks?"

"What?"

Merleece smiled and drew herself up farther. She adored being the storyteller. "You not gone b'lieve this. Miz Liddie use a new deck every time she play a game a' bridge. Don't axe me why. But she got a coupla dozen decks a' cards stored away in the chest a' draws in the room where they play bridge. She tell me once, 'I think it's bad luck to play with worn cards, so I use a brand-new deck every time.' It was expensive, but b'lieve me, she had the money to do that kind a' thing."

Thoroughly fascinated, Wendy said, "What did she do with the decks after she'd used them once?"

"Threw 'em away in the trash. She axe me once if I want any of 'em. But I don't b'lieve in card-playin' of any kind. It can lead to gamblin', you know. And then, that can lead to worse things."

"Did the ladies ever bet money on the game?"

"No, not that I know of. But they might could have. I

mean, who know what go on under the table? The ladies, they all have deep purses. Or is it s'pose to be deep pockets?"

Wendy had to suppress her laughter. "Probably pockets. But I catch your drift. And to answer your original question, no, Miz Liddie didn't say a word to me about using new decks all the time, Merleece. That sure was a lot of wasted cards."

"Yes, indeed. The other ladies—they knew 'bout it. But I guess Miz Liddie wudd'n gone tell you 'til you get in the club officially. Not that you could've change anything if it bother you."

Wendy decided to move on. "The police think that money left in the will may have been your motive, but I know they're dead wrong, of course."

"You bet they wrong!" Then Merleece gave out a cute little gasp. "Oh, the pie. You want that piece I promise you? Bound to be cool by now. You in for a treat, if I do say so myself."

Wendy said yes, of course she wanted it, and soon they were both back on the sofa savoring forkfuls of buttery applesauce pie bursting with the flavors of cinnamon, nutmeg, ginger, and cloves.

Wendy's taste buds had all they could handle, and she just had to rave. "Why haven't I ever tasted this before, Merleece? Didn't you ever serve this at one of the bridge luncheons? I would think all the ladies would have loved it and wanted you to fix it for them every time."

"They never get the chance to taste it 'cause Miz Liddie didn't like it. She say it was too sweet. She the only one that ever say anything like that to me."

"That's a shame," Wendy said, then wondering if she dared. "Now, do you jealously guard the recipe or what?"

"I'm makin' uh exception for you, Strawberry. But you gotta promise me you won't tell nobody else."

"I promise."

When Wendy finished with her pie and put the plate down on the end table, she focused on the picture of the young man again. "He has your cheekbones," she said, turning to Merleece with a smile.

"Yes. My son, my only chile, Hyram Ray. I wish he had more a' me in him than that, though. I thought I bring him up right, but he have other ideas. He roam around the country doin' just what he please now. I hear from him mostly when he need money, and the mother in me, well, she cain't turn him down. When you become a mother, you gone understand what I'm talkin' 'bout."

"I'm sure I will, but don't beat yourself up too much. I'm sure you did your very best."

Merleece hung her head, looking down into her lap and her plate full of crumbs and one irregular chunk of crust. "I musta done somethin' wrong, though. Now, I know I took him to church, but it didd'n take. He so disrespectful to his girlfriends, and I know I didd'n teach him that. Maybe one day soon he be comin' home and show he love his mama and do the right thing by me. I hope so."

Wendy reached over and took Merleece's hand, giving it a squeeze. "Don't give up on him yet, Merleece. People can always grow up. Maybe when you least expect it, he'll be there at your door."

"Could be. You a sweet girl to keep my hope up like that. Wish I had a daughter like you." The two women embraced; then Merleece pulled back, looking Wendy straight in the eye. "They's one thing I wanna know, though. Why you think it'd be easy to learn bridge with the likes a' Miz Liddie and her friends sittin' around the table drinkin' all the time like they did? Seem to me like they's gotta be a better way to do it than that."

Wendy smiled at first, but then went all sheepish in the face. There were times when she had wondered the same thing, but then there was that old bugaboo about hindsight. Why couldn't it ever come first? She briefly amused herself with that thought and then continued.

"The truth is, I had no idea what I was getting into. Daddy and his friends had always played chess when I was growing up, and I learned almost by osmosis, just by watching. So I thought I could do the same thing with bridge, and The Rosalie Bridge Club was the best around. Once I'd gotten in—and I was totally surprised that that actually happened—I realized that the ladies really weren't about playing bridge. They were much more about taking things out on each other. It's my opinion they weren't very kind, despite all the charity work they did."

"You figure all that out mighty quick, I gotta say," Merleece said. "It take me a whole lot longer to realize they still holdin' grudges against each other for all kinda things that happen a while back. That swingin' door between the kitchen and the dinin' room, it wudd'n all that thick. 'Course I know I should'n a' been listenin' in, and I speck that make me a eavesdroppin' sinner."

Wendy seized the opportunity to draw Merleece out further. Perhaps it was even important to develop a "rhythm" of sorts when interrogating people. "I wouldn't worry about it too much if I were you. Did you overhear anything that really sticks out in your mind?"

Merleece pursed her lips briefly, clearly in the midst of conflict. "What I don't wanna do is get it all wrong, you see. I could'n tell they voices apart sometime 'cause they all talk at once, but what I can tell you is somebody slep' with somebody else husband. I know that got brought up once."

"But you can't say who the voices belonged to? Were they loud enough for you to distinguish?"

"If I was to guess, I'd have to say it was between Miz Liddie and Miz Hanna 'cause they always arguin', and one time

Miz Hanna did storm out the house in the middle of a game. I do remember that like it was yesterday. I told you they was bad blood between 'em."

"Did that happen recently? I mean the part about Miz Hanna storming out of the house?"

Merleece laughed out loud and clasped a hand to her chest. "Lord no, Strawberry. That was way back when I first start workin' for Miz Liddie. Them walls at that house, they full a' secrets, I can tell you that. They know what went on."

Wendy suddenly realized she had left her notepad and pen in the car and needed to write a few things down—phrases, names, and words that would trigger other ideas that were forming in her head. She was too used to doing little more than copying, editing, and romancing announcements for her column. Puff piece work. These goals she had set for herself—investigative journalism and detective work—were going to require a lot more attention to detail in a different way. Instead of descriptions of gowns, cakes, and floral arrangements, she was going to have to put pieces of puzzles together, and nothing was going to be handed to her on a silver salver anymore. The many passes she had been given because of who she was and what she was writing about had come home to roost. She was about to face the acid test.

After excusing herself and quickly returning with the tools of her trade, however, she found Merleece gently rubbing her temples with the tips of her fingers. "While you gone, somethin' flash in my head. But then it flash right out again. I hate that, you know. They's somethin' you tryin' to reach back and pull out, but you just cain't do it no matter how hard you try."

"Something about Miz Liddie or the others? Maybe secrets? That's what we were talking about before I left," Wendy said, sitting back down on the sofa with a hopeful expression on her face.

"No, it wudd'n a secret. Just let me think a little bit more and maybe it finally come to me."

"I want you to take your time. I need to write a few things down anyway, and I don't want to be rushed."

The next few minutes were spent in silence as both women concentrated on their tasks at hand. Finally, Merleece snapped her fingers, abruptly halting Wendy's stream of note-taking. "I got it back now, Strawberry."

Wendy turned to a blank page in her notepad with her pen poised. "Great. Tell me what you got."

"It was Miz Liddie goin' away now and then these last few months. What I mean is, that house'd have to be on fire for her to miss a bridge game. I think maybe she miss two in all them years since I start workin' for her. But Miz Stella have to sit in for her maybe four or five times lately. Miz Liddie say she goin' to visit relatives somewhere, but she never say where. I tell her maybe she should write out where she goin' and leave me a number in case anybody call or they's an emergency, but she just shrug and say don't worry about it. So if we wanted to reach her for anything, we could'n do it."

Wendy finished up a quick note and said, "Yes, I remember those games when Miz Stella sat in for her. I hate to say it, but we all had a better time when Miz Liddie wasn't there. The other ladies seemed far more relaxed. Not that they drank any less, but they were . . . well, they were nicer to each other."

"I heard that. But what I'm tryin' to say to you is Miz Liddie never do anything like that up until these last few months, and she never talk 'bout the relatives when she get back. Not even a picture to show me 'bout her travels. Not my place to get nosy 'bout it, either. Miz Stella always say not to worry 'bout anything her mother do these days, so I don't. But they's three things that really have change recently, and now I told you 'bout all of 'em—mirrors, makeup, and missin' bridge games."

This visit with Merleece was bearing fruit. Pieces of the puzzle had been handed to her, but she had many others to pick up and try to position to compose "the big picture." Clearly her visit with Stella Markham the next day could not be coming at a better time. It might be the breakthrough she needed.

But Merleece was not finished yet. "They was still somethin' else I was tryin' to pull outta my head for you, but I cain't seem to do it."

"You can always call me when you remember," Wendy said. "Most people pull it up out of nowhere in the middle of the night."

"You think I did myself any good today talkin' to you? I see you writin' everything down like you writin' a novel."

Wendy closed up her notepad and put the pen in her purse before taking Merleece's hand once again. "You definitely did. And I promise you, I'm going to work very hard to take you off the board as a suspect."

"Strawberry, like I say, you the daughter I never had. Instead, I got Hyram to carry on when I'm gone, sorry to say."

There was another heartfelt hug; then Wendy said, "That was the best pie I've ever had."

"Wait," Merleece said, giving her own cheek a light slap. "You wantin' that recipe. Come on, let's us go into my kitchen, and I write it down for you. Do you wanna take another piece home?"

Wendy's anticipation caused her entire face to light up, and for a moment, all was right with her world. "Sounds like a plan all around."

CHAPTER 8

Merleece cautiously peered out her kitchen window to make sure Wendy's car had driven away after their long visit. Then she sat down at the kitchen table, where a few minutes earlier she had shared her jealously guarded recipe for applesauce pie. Things had almost seemed normal during that brief period of time, but her reality was a universe away from that. Yes, Strawberry was out to help her, perhaps as no one else could. She was a sweet and smart girl, but would she be enough? Did she have the smarts to get her out of this mess? After all, she herself had stirred the sugar into the coffee cups as she always did, and Arden had seen her do it. There was no way out of that part. Even though she remained convinced that Arden was the one who had put the potassium cyanide in the sugar bowl for his own insane, tightly wound, man-bun-wearing reasons. Or perhaps he had done it on someone else's orders. The idea of a hired assassin was not foreign to her—she had seen it on many TV shows and in movies over the years. Had it now come to Rosalie, or was she just being naïve?

Meanwhile, her fingerprints and DNA were all over everything, no matter how diligently she had wiped and polished over the years. She was frightened to the core by the way the evidence was piling up against her, and other than Strawberry, she had no one to turn to in Rosalie. She knew only too well her position: she was a black domestic servant, and that wasn't very high in the pecking order of the world she had inhabited all her life. Yes, she had survived and made an adequate living taking orders from very wealthy white folks, but that still meant that the deck was stacked against her in a town like Rosalie.

But there was an alternative—reckless as it might be—and she was giving it more serious consideration now as her worries began to weigh so heavily upon her that she could hardly breathe at times. She did not like the fact that she had lied to both Strawberry and the police about Hyram. Despite the disappointment he had turned out to be and had brought into her life in so many ways for so long, he was still her only flesh and blood. That still counted for something in this life she was living. What was more, she knew where he was now and even had a vague idea of what he was up to. She dared not let the police know any of that, or her "son of so many vices and flaws" might be in serious jeopardy for the same reasons she was. This was no time for her to dwell on his mistakes of the past, not with the way everything and everyone was closing in on her.

Resolutely, she stood up and trudged over to the kitchen phone. She punched in a number and waited patiently. She made a clucking noise with her tongue with each ring. Finally came the "Hello?" she needed to hear.

"Hyram, baby, we got to talk," she said, forgetting all formalities as her voice went all high-pitched on her. "I think maybe we got to go on and do what we say we might have to do last time we talk. I don't like how this goin' one bit and how they treatin' me. I could be railroaded."

There was silence at the other end for a long period of time. Too long. It seemed like Hyram would never answer her. But he finally did. "I believe you, Mama. I got outta there a long time ago for things like that goin' on all the time. So, when you wanna do this?"

"Yesterday not soon enough for me," Merleece told him, sounding even more desperate.

Then the words that brought her the sense of relief she needed to keep from falling apart completely: "I'll do it for you, Mama."

"God bless you, son," she told him, her tears welling up.

Wendy knew that she didn't need to coordinate anything with Ross on the matter of her interviews, whether they were with suspects or survivors of the murdered ladies. As he had pointed out, his CID had their methods and priorities apart from anything she did. She would wing it and develop hers as she saw fit, and she decided that visiting the Lewis Brothers would be her next move that afternoon. When she spoke to Beau Lewis over the phone to set up an appointment, he seemed to know who she was and cheerfully agreed to see her. She could only hope he would be that forthcoming with his answers to her questions.

After an uneventful, paper sack lunch of a homemade tuna sandwich and sparkling water in her cubicle at the paper, Wendy drove to their cookie-cutter condo in the upscale Rosalie suburb of Whiteapple Village. The only thing that distinguished it from the many others lined up all in a row was a small front yard that was woefully unsightly. Most of the St. Augustine sod had turned brown, and ungainly, opportunistic weeds had shot up here and there as a result. There were also a couple of dried-out, dead azaleas on either side of the front door. By contrast, the other yards were well-mowed, bright with greenery, and blooming with late-spring flowers. There were even a couple of sprinklers hard at work spreading their life-giving water around on the fussiest of the mini-landscapes.

The brothers were hospitable enough as they welcomed Wendy at the door in their Bermuda shorts and pastel polo shirts. Then in perhaps an overly friendly manner, they offered her a choice of booze that they suggested she could guzzle along with them as they talked. To which she quickly replied with a smirk, "I shouldn't drink on the job, fellas, even if this is Rosalie."

Both men laughed, and Beau said, "You got that right. Rosalie makes its own rules. Please have a seat, won't you?"

"First, as I said over the phone, I want both of you to know how sorry I am for your loss. I know this must be a very difficult thing to deal with. Thanks for agreeing to talk with me. While the CID is doing its official investigation, I'm preparing an article on the ladies and their families," Wendy said, arranging herself in a huge, leopard-print armchair and taking out her notepad. As she did so, the thought occurred to her that Elvis's decorator must still be afoot and imposing himself upon the unwary and unsophisticated.

"Yeah. Shocker about Mom, isn't it?" Beau said, taking a big swig of his beer from his spot next to his brother on the endlessly sprawling, black leather sofa. But it sounded like he was saying, "Do you happen to know what time it is?"

It was not lost on Wendy that neither brother looked or sounded remotely distressed. That in itself was a bit confounding. "Do you know of anyone who would want to do harm to your mother? Even commit murder?"

Charley exchanged glances furtively with Beau and shrugged. "Nobody we can think of."

"What about the other ladies? Did you have much contact with them? How well did you know them?"

This time, it was Beau who shrugged, followed by contemptuous laughter. "They were Mom's bridge biddies, that's all. She called 'em buddies. We called 'em biddies. We got it right, you know. Everything they did revolved around playing bridge—and drinking too much."

"You didn't approve?"

"Wasn't any of our business, really."

"Have you ever been in Miz Liddie's house?"

Beau looked profoundly puzzled. "Sure. Been to a party there a coupla times. Had a good time."

"Seen her beautiful gardens?"

"Of course," Beau said. "We both have. I think pretty much everybody in Rosalie has at one time or another."

"Ever met Miz Liddie's gardener, Arden Wilson?"

Charley answered that one with a smirk of recognition. "We both met him once. Had a beer or two with him. Knew his father a whole lot better, though. That was Mr. Brent Wilson."

"Did Mr. Arden Wilson ever show you around his gardening shed and all the chemicals that were in it?"

Charley's laugh had an air of disbelief about it. "Yeah, like it was on the Spring Historic Tours or something. It was just something in the background you saw whenever you went over there. No big deal."

"So that's a no?"

Charley nodded and went back to his whiskey on the rocks, staring at it as if it were liquid gold.

Wendy decided she needed to go at this in a different way. The two were clearly in their eternal bachelor comfort zone, and why not? Their spacious den had suggestions of dorm room meets Playboy Mansion about it. There were collegiate and professional sports team pictures all over the walls—some of athletes, others of stadiums and arenas. Scattered here and there were also photos, drawings, and paintings of voluptuous and rather scantily-clad young women. An enormous marble-topped wet bar in the center of the room made another indelible statement about their hedonistic lifestyle. Finally, there were two huge trophy game heads centered above the large brick fireplace and hearth—one of a rhinoceros and the other of a tiger. That was one of Wendy's pet peeves—people who bought or sold wild animal parts, especially those of creatures on the endangered species list. But she decided not to ask them if they had actually killed the animals on the wall. The fact that they displayed them proudly as décor told her all she needed to know.

"Why don't you fellas tell me what you think about Mr. Hermes Caliban?" she said next, going in for the kill.

The expressions on their faces changed to sneers immediately, and Beau said, "He is a dirty, sweaty con man and a stinking gigolo for starters. Do you really want me to go on?"

"He tried to take Mom in for all she was worth," Charley added. "And he would've continued to milk her dry if she hadn't been—" He came to an abrupt halt and scratched the back of his head. "Well, you know . . ."

"Conveniently murdered?"

"Yeah . . . no, you just put words in my mouth."

Wendy gave him a big smile, pleased with the way things were going. "If you guys don't mind me saying so, you don't seem to be taking the loss of your mother too hard. I lost my dear mother to pneumonia when I was fifteen, and I was shaken down to my roots."

Beau spoke up, the anger rising in his voice. "I know what you're saying, but we haven't gotten along with our mom since forever, okay? She didn't like the way we were spending the money Dad left us. Too bad, but it was ours, not hers. She didn't like the way we treated our wives before we got divorced and told us all the time we had an obligation to give her grandchildren. Many, many grandchildren. Yeah, right. An obligation. She wanted to run our lives forever, but she couldn't do it anymore after we got our inheritance from Dad. When he died, we gained our freedom, and I want you to know, I'm not exaggerating."

"You better believe it," Charley added. "We can do anything we want to do now, and that means forever."

Wendy gestured broadly to the room-at-large with her hand. "I can see that."

"Hey, it's the way we choose to live," Beau said. "So it never fit in with Mom's vaunted social agenda, but we didn't think she looked too respectable running around with that hunk of gaudy ground beef and his jumping jack routines, either. Even her bridge girlfriends thought it made her look ridiculous."

Wendy pounced immediately. "But I believe you told me you didn't know too much about the ladies."

"We don't," Beau said, bristling. "Mom sometimes called them North, South, and West. That's not a helluva lot to go on. If you wanna know the truth, I think Mom had a love-hate relationship going on with the entire group. I think there were times she wanted to break away, but she just couldn't."

Wendy decided to play devil's advocate. "But death is the ultimate exit."

"Please tell me you aren't implying our mother was behind this," Beau said, sounding as disagreeable as possible.

"I'm just tossing out some possibilities. But it sure sounds to me like you might have overheard a conversation at a bridge game or two. Or gotten information from someone on the inside about various opinions. Am I wrong?"

"If you're accusing us of something, Miz Winchester," Beau said, "go ahead and do it. Say what you gotta say right now. Otherwise, I think you've overextended your welcome."

"I'm not accusing you of anything, fellas. I'm sorry if you thought so—I'm just having a conversation with you about this terrible thing that happened to your mother and maybe trying to shed a little light on it, and I want to be fair to you and your family. You've got to admit, it's a puzzler."

The awkward silence was finally broken by Beau. "Okay, look. If you want a little emotion about Mom, here it is. Maybe we haven't wrapped our brains around this whole thing yet. We went to the memorial service and heard a dictionary full of words from people who told us how sorry they were for our loss and how awful this whole thing was. But they were just words. They rang hollow. People mean well. But they don't know us. They didn't even know Mom. They just thought they did."

Finally. Something genuine out of one of the Lewis Brothers. Wendy proceeded cautiously.

"Care to elaborate on that?"

Something akin to silent agreement passed between the brothers in the form of a mutual nod, and Beau said, "Mom held grudges. Against us. Against her biddy friends if they'd done something to hurt or displease her. Against everyone, really. She was a very intense person. You should have seen how she went for the jugular when she played tennis at the Rosalie Country Club—or the testicles if it was mixed doubles. I mean, that was a big ouch to watch from the stands. Hey, she wore us out with all her expectations by the time we got into college. She pushed us and pushed us until we didn't have any room to breathe. We couldn't wait to get away from her, and that's why we feel the way we do. But I don't think there was anything more to it than that. I certainly don't think she was capable of murder—or of killing herself."

"But did you ever think of your mother as a violent person? Did she have a quick temper?"

Beau's lip quivered just a tad bit. "On the tennis courts sometimes. She always wanted to win, but she'd take her own sweet time during a match, waiting for the right opportunity to slam the ball down her opponent's throat. Then she'd move in for the kill at the net."

"Interesting way of putting it."

"Don't read too much into that. A very poor choice of words," Beau said. "I'm strictly talking tennis here. That's how she took out all her frustrations. No knife, no gun, no poison, just a tightly strung tennis racket. I really think you should leave it at that."

"Fair enough," Wendy said. "By the way, where were you guys on the day and time of the murders?"

"We need alibis now?" Beau said. "Should we be lawyering up? 'Cause we gotta good one who's never let us down."

"Probably not. Just tell me where you were."

"No big deal. With a couple of girls at the Rosalie Country Club eating lunch and playing tennis," Beau said, clearly annoyed. "The Baker sisters. You can call 'em up anytime."

"I'm sure the police will do that after they've interrogated you."

Unexpectedly, Beau's tone became conciliatory. "So, how's the investigation going? Do they have any idea who did this and why?"

"I'm sure I don't know. It's early yet."

Beau looked perplexed. "Aren't there just thousands of unsolved crimes all over the place? Don't people get away with murder all the time? Seems to me I've read articles about that before."

"Unfortunately, yes, you're right. But I have the feeling this won't be one of them."

Beau exhaled noisily and sat up straighter. "Look, for what it's worth, we both hope you find out who did this. Even if we had lots of issues with Mom—and we had plenty, believe me—no one deserves to go out like that. You've observed that we haven't been showing much emotion today, but Mom's pretty much responsible for that. You shouldn't interpret that as an indication of our guilt, though."

"I didn't say I did," Wendy told them. "I also want to assure you that I think there's something unspeakable and unhinged about the way this was done. Four people at once. We're not dealing with an ordinary criminal here. I believe we'll all have to think outside the box for the who and the why of this one."

CHAPTER 9

Whatever else Wendy had expected of her Saturday visit to Stella Markham's restored Queen Anne cottage on Dulcimer Street, it was certainly not an interminable PowerPoint presentation of the history of the Gin Girls from high school through the formation of The Rosalie Bridge Club and beyond. Stella seemed to have made it her particular calling in life to preserve all photographic evidence of the unparalleled relationship the four women had with one another, and Wendy was quick to observe that the effort was far from Academy Award–worthy. Stella's narration, in particular, droned on and on without taking into consideration the possibility that she might be the only person in the world who was *that* invested in the exploits of her mother and her three childhood friends.

After an extensive tour of the tastefully appointed house, which included much Belter furniture, many Savonnerie rugs, and Waterford crystal chandeliers—not to mention a display of the Langston and Rose Families' coats of arms hanging on the walls—Wendy found herself nursing a mimosa on the sofa in the darkened living room. Occasionally, she made polite comments to show she was paying attention. The truth was, it wasn't so much pictures Wendy needed for her series of articles—although a couple would certainly be useful—it was stories. Lots of them—exaggerated, poignant, endearing, humorous, whatever was available that might provide valuable insights into these four unusual ladies who had lived their entire lives—minus college—in Rosalie. And perhaps clues to their murders as a result.

"Now here's one of the four of them at the sorority house the day before Homecoming in 1969," Stella was saying. "Look at what they wore back then. Isn't it a hoot? Still, they definitely all filled out those sweaters in the Ole Miss school colors quite well, didn't they? They all had good figures and never hesitated to show them off. Mother said that everywhere they went, they got plenty of whistles."

"They sure look attractive to me," Wendy said, wondering if she sounded at all convincing.

Stella moved on. "This one was taken on Bourbon Street on New Year's Day in 1970. They'd had a few at this point, Mother told me. Not that it's any stretch to believe her. They'd all gone down for the Sugar Bowl when Archie Manning single-handedly beat Arkansas. I mean, he scrambled and scrambled around and did it all by himself. Will you look at that obnoxious Razorback fan putting up donkey ears behind Mother's head? Ha—Ole Miss got the last laugh, though. We were the ones who did all the partying into the wee hours on Bourbon Street, and there wasn't a Razorback fan in sight. They'd all gone back to their hotel rooms to cry into their beers."

"That looks like fun, but I was never much of a football fan. I went to Missouri and buried my head in all my journalism classes. Maybe some people would've called me a nerd or a geek."

Stella let the remark pass without a comment or a smile, and there was the slightest hint of judgment in her stoic expression, which Wendy could not even begin to see in the darkness.

"I wasn't much of a party girl," Wendy added to break the silence. "I stayed in the dorm and studied a lot. I knew what I wanted to accomplish, and what I'm doing now is my passion."

"And I hope you can bring that to these articles about the Gin Girls and the club," Stella said.

Wendy steeled herself as picture after picture appeared before her. The ladies always practiced the same pose, lining up by height from left to right, and they were always smiling big, looking perfectly composed. But what were they thinking? What was behind all that surface sunshine and perfect spacing? That was what Wendy needed to uncover.

Stella's narration became particularly animated when a picture of the ladies in front of St. Mark's Orphanage appeared. "They weren't just about having a good time with cards and gin, though," she was saying. "If it hadn't been for them, the orphanage would have closed its doors long ago. Mother was responsible for getting everyone in the club to donate a substantial amount of their money to keep it going. Later, they helped the Senior Center out, too. I think those were their finest hours. That's why I can't imagine Reverend Blough going on the way he did with all those anecdotes at what should have been a completely dignified occasion. I thought about saying something to him after the service, but there just didn't seem to be a moment when he wasn't surrounded by parishioners and such who were praising him for this or that part of the eulogy. Obviously, I wonder how many of them were lying through their teeth just to be polite and keep the peace."

"Some people have a strange sense of humor," Wendy said, but she felt awkward even as she was saying it. She had no answer for Stella's obsession with the Episcopal rector of long standing.

When Stella came to a photo in which Bethany was missing from the usual lineup and no one was smiling, she said, "This was one of the few sad occasions the ladies bothered to capture for posterity. Mother, Miz Hanna, and Miz Sicily had just visited Miz Bethany in the hospital after one of her miscarriages. She had quite a few and was never able to carry to term. Such a tragedy, but I know for a fact that her friendship with the others helped her get through all that."

"That's a wonderful human interest story. I'll make it a point to weave it into my article."

"That's why I told you about it," Stella said, clearly pleased with herself. "I think we need pathos for these articles, not hearsay and gossip."

Finally, and later rather than sooner, the presentation ended, and Stella flicked on the lights. Wendy could not help but notice that she seemed transformed by her efforts, her eyes alive with pride, her face almost glowing.

"Isn't it remarkable that they all stayed together that long? It dwarfs the time Peter and I were together, but don't get me started on that. Just think about all the changes in society they lived through. Such a volatile period of history," Stella said, moving to sit beside her guest on the sofa. "Over fifty years by my calculations. I have their slogan memorized, of course."

"Slogan?"

Stella chuckled and patted Wendy's hand a couple of times as if she were a small child. "That's what I've been calling it all this time. I know *slogan* makes it sound like a business. Maybe it was more like a motto. Yes, I should think of it that way, really. Anyway, Mother said that when they were in high school and decided to name themselves the Gin Girls, they came up with these words that they claimed would carve out a place for themselves in the universe. It was really like a poem, except it didn't rhyme:

Raising hell in high school,
Raising hell in college,
Raising hell in marriage,
Raising hell in Heaven.

"Isn't that outrageously marvelous? People tend to think of Southern belles as all sweetness and light and batting their eyelashes, but the Gin Girls had their jalapeño peppery side, if you'll excuse my made-up expression. They could make other people sweat. They even made each other sweat at times. They all knew things they shouldn't have known. Of course, wouldn't you know it? Miz Hanna Lewis wanted the motto or the poem or whatever you want to call it to rhyme, and she even insisted they all take a vote on it. Her version was:

Raising hell in high school,
Raising hell in college,
Raising hell in marriage,
All for love and knowledge.

"I like it," Wendy said. "But I'm going to assume the vote didn't go Miz Hanna's way?"

"No, it didn't," Stella said. "Mother told me all she had to do was glare long and hard at Miz Sicily and Miz Bethany, and the vote was three to one in favor of Mother's original version."

Wendy perked up and took her notepad and pen out of her purse. Now this was more like it. "I'd have been happy with either version if I'd been in the group. Do you mind if I take notes now that the lights are on? This is the kind of thing that will help me with my feature."

"Please. Go right ahead. I hope you enjoyed my presentation, and it didn't drag too much. Maybe I get carried away at times. But I felt it would set the mood for you to truly understand what the Gin Girls were all about. I feel I've been more or less entrusted with their legacy. I don't think the Lewis Brothers really care about it at all, Sherry Herrold has always deferred to me, and there's nothing left of the Morrisseys, so it's all up to me."

"I understand completely," Wendy said. "The presentation was very thorough. I felt I was almost back in college at a lecture, and I'm thoroughly prepared to take plenty of notes."

Stella appeared pleased, straightened up, and took a deep breath. "Good. If you don't mind, I've written down a few notes and thoughts I know will be helpful to you in preparing your articles for the paper." Stella dug into her pocket, sat down, handed over a sheet of paper, and gave Wendy some time to scan it. "I'll be happy to expand on it, if you'd like," she added after a while.

Wendy looked up and nodded. "Certainly. Go right ahead."

Stella gently rubbed her eyes with her fingertips and then folded her hands in her lap. "As you've noted from looking that over briefly, Mother had become very concerned lately about the activities of both Merleece and Arden Wilson. Once, she looked out the window and saw them huddling near the gardening shed. Then she said they went in together, and she couldn't figure out for the life of her what they were doing in there like that. They never got along, but she said they looked perfectly comfortable with each other that time. She believed they were genuinely up to something, but she said she let it go. It's my belief that she made a huge mistake by not questioning them then and there."

Wendy dutifully made her notes, but she was not liking what she was hearing. It appeared to be more evidence against

Merleece, even if Arden had been involved as well. Still, she had to maintain her objectivity. "So your interpretation is?"

"That they were plotting something, and they were up to no good. I can't prove it, of course. But you need to know what Mother saw and suspected, even if she misinterpreted it. Mother had told me some years back that she knew Merleece was drinking up her liquor on the sly. And then there were a few things that went missing from time to time. In the end I guess Mother didn't do anything about it because good help is so hard to get, you know. But Mother was trusting Merleece less and less."

Wendy put down her notepad, speaking calmly even though she was agitated on the inside. "I always do my own cleaning, though. And so did my mother when I was growing up."

Stella reached over and patted Wendy's hand. "Well, you just keep those notes, and you might even want to share them with the police. Aren't you seeing that detective, Ross Rierson?"

"Off and on," Wendy said, not caring to explain further. "But maybe we could get back to talking about the Gin Girls?"

"Certainly. Would you like to know how Mother and her friends ended up with gin as their choice of poison?" Stella gasped loudly and covered her mouth. "Poison. I can't believe I just said that. I guess I'm still a bit in shock. Please don't write down that I said that. Please."

"Of course I won't. That just came out the wrong way," Wendy told her, almost in a whisper.

After a deep breath, Stella continued. "Well, it happened one weekend when Grandma and Grandpa Langston were away on a trip to New Orleans. Ole Miss and Tulane were playing football, and half of Rosalie must have been there partying on Bourbon Street. Mother was told she could invite some of her friends for a sleepover, so naturally she invited Sicily, Hanna, and Bethany. At one point, Mother said they got bored with all their boyfriend talk and pillow fights and wanted to do something more exciting. So Mother proposed they get into the liquor cabinet and see what they had in store for themselves there. She reached in and the first bottle she pulled out was a fifth of Gilbey's. She said you've never seen such sick teenagers in your life after they'd downed a few jiggers. Of course, we had to do quite a bit of cleaning up after ourselves, too."

Wendy was smiling and puzzled at the same time. "So how did they ever stick with gin after that? I would've thought they would have avoided it like the plague after all that."

"It was the *raising hell* thing that they all felt they had to live up to," Stella said. "They were all determined to conquer the gin because of it, Mother said. From then on, they found ways to get their hands on it through older friends, and they learned how to drink it and tame it. By the time they got to Ole Miss, the Gin Girls were all-around pros."

"Great stuff," Wendy said, busy taking notes. "Do you mind if I work it into the piece?"

But Stella was shaking her head. "That was just meant for you, though, Wendy. I don't think it would cast a very good light on Mother and her friends. Maybe it would be best to leave out the part about sneaking into the liquor cabinet, don't you agree with me on that?"

"Maybe so," Wendy told her. But she was not about to agree to have her content controlled by her sources. She felt Stella was being way too sensitive about things she had volunteered in the first place. Perhaps the best thing to do would be to move on quickly, so she again consulted her notepad. "This might seem like a strange question, but were there cliques within the Gin Girls?"

"You mean who liked who better, and who hung around

with who more?" Stella's laugh seemed almost girlish. "That one's easy. Miz Bethany and Miz Sicily were pretty close and did a lot of traveling together. Mother liked everyone well enough, except she and Miz Hanna had some disagreements from time to time. But not enough to break up their friendship. Everyone stayed in the group no matter what. When they called truces among themselves, they stuck to them."

"Why do you think that was?" Wendy continued. "What kept them together all those years?"

Stella's carefree demeanor disappeared quickly. "Alcohol and all that it leads to, in my opinion."

"That's a bit cryptic, don't you think? Or are you just being clinical here?"

"I didn't mean it to be either one. All I meant was that gin brought them together and kept them together. They liked having a good time, getting a buzz and beyond, living it up, you name it. No matter how old they got, they still had that same devilish spark they first displayed to everyone when they were in high school and staying out late, worrying their parents to death. They were small-town, patrician celebrities, and everyone followed their activities from the get-go. Who they were dating, where they were going to college, when they got into town for the holidays and all that. Later on, it became when they were getting married, when they were pregnant, where they were going on vacation. They loved the attention, and I really think the town of Rosalie had an outright love affair with them."

"I could easily tell that from the turnout at the memorial service," Wendy said, nodding. "Was your mother responsible for the formation of The Rosalie Bridge Club as well?"

"Yes, she was. They had played informally off and on before, including at the sorority house at Ole Miss. Mother's original idea once they all returned to Rosalie and settled down with their husbands was to create an exclusive social club built around bridge. As time went on, she had intended to expand the membership. But I think she realized she would be watering down the nature of the Gin Girls in doing so. Even when Miz Hanna or one of the others had nominated someone for membership, she would turn them down, since only one negative vote was necessary to blackball people. It was their sorority days all over again. Mother was the president of that, too, you know. I don't think there was anything they belonged to that she didn't run."

"I'll make a note of that. So what kind of bad feelings did the blackballing cause?" Wendy continued.

"No, no, let's not dwell on the petty stuff. Back to the important things."

Wendy saw her chance for an effortless segue. "Which reminds me, Stella, I have a few things I hope you can clear up for me. Merleece told me recently that your mother had developed a few new affectations and behaviors, and missing bridge games was one of them."

Stella's face went sour. "I wouldn't be surprised by anything that Merleece told you about my mother. What all did she say besides the obvious fact that Mother missed out on a few games?"

"She said that your mother had started posing in mirrors all the time, as well as wearing a lot more makeup than she had before. Can you shed some light on any of that?"

Stella's laugh was surprising, even startling. "Oh, I see what's happened. It's all a misunderstanding. Mother was a very private person in some ways, and despite what Merleece would have you think, she did not share some very personal aspects of her life with the help. Langstons simply have never done that sort of thing, you understand. That would be beyond the pale. The unfortunate fact is that Mother had developed rosacea and was horribly embarrassed by the condition. All those red spots and broken capillaries on her cheeks and nose. She'd never had so much as a pimple growing up, so she didn't react well at all. She took great pride in her skin. So she was mortified. You can understand that, I'm sure."

"Of course I can," Wendy said, putting her fingertips on her fair, lightly freckled cheeks that had been prone to sunburn all her life.

"So what was Mother to do? She decided to go out of town several times to consult various specialists in hopes of improvement or even finding a miracle cure. She didn't want anything to slip out about it with local doctors and nurses, of course. There are some that simply don't respect the doctor-patient confidentiality, sad to say. But in the end she was left with medication to take and makeup to try and cover it up the best she could. She never told any of the Gin Girls about it. Merleece must have seen her checking her makeup from time to time, especially when the ladies were coming over for a bridge game. Mother didn't like feeling insecure one bit, but the rosacea did the trick for her for the very first time in her life, unfortunately."

Strangely, Wendy felt disappointed by the rational explanation. She had expected something more sinister or something that might give her a clue to the murders. But this revelation hardly seemed to qualify. Not that rosacea wasn't to be taken seriously. She devoutly hoped she never developed anything like that in her lifetime. "And there was nothing more to what Merleece said than that?"

"Nothing, I can assure you. I'm pleased you'll be doing these features on Mother and her friends because it's important that their legacy be preserved. I hope you'll take the high road. Perhaps in my enthusiasm I've let a few things slip that I shouldn't have, but those biographies on all the ladies I put together for you should also help you a lot. It's all accurate—down to their birthdates. I suppose it's acceptable to reveal their ages now that they're all gone."

Wendy glanced across the room to where Stella had placed the stack of papers atop a mahogany plantation desk; then Dalton Hemmings's warnings to be circumspect flashed into her head again. "I definitely want to be accurate and fair. I know you need all of this for closure. I still can't imagine what you're going through."

Stella was staring off into a corner of the room, her voice trailing off there at the end. "No, there's no way you could possibly imagine."

Wendy gently rubbed Stella's arm and then checked her notepad again where the single word *hair?* appeared at the bottom of her list. "Merleece said that your mother changed her hairdo a while back. Was there any significance to that, or was it just a stylish whim?"

"Just more of her rosacea strategy, actually," Stella said, sounding almost flippant about it. "There were some break-outs on her forehead. She felt the bangs would help cover them and draw attention away from the extra makeup at the same time. She felt the conversation around the bridge table would be about the hairdo when the ladies saw it. And she was right, as it turned out. Mother said it generated more conversation about how they all styled their hair than they'd had in years."

The two laughed genuinely for the first time during the interview. Wendy knew quite well that many women in Rosalie and elsewhere bonded over their hair.

"It seems your mother wasn't so much of a mystery after all. This was just about bad skin showing up at the wrong time," Wendy said, sensing it was time to leave and rising from the sofa.

"She had the mystery that all great beauties have, though," Stella said, joining her on her feet. "Men wanted to find out what was behind those delicate features, and in addition she had the advantage of her great height. Mother always said to me, 'A man has to stand up tall to meet my expectations. Only one man ever did—and that was your father, Murray Rose.' "

At the door, Wendy turned and said, "If there's anything of significance you want to add about your family that we didn't cover today, you know how to reach me. We'll be publishing your mother's story first, of course, but it might be a few more days before we go to press with it. I have a lot more interviewing to do among all the family members."

Stella acknowledged the comment with a nod of her head and said, "I certainly hope you don't get writer's block."

CHAPTER 10

Ross had not been looking forward to interrogating Selena Chalk at headquarters. But the time had finally come, and he had no choice but to bear down and do his job even if he had a soft spot in his heart for her. There was simply no room for that kind of subjectivity in detective work. She had sounded puzzled when he had called her up and asked her if she would come down to answer a few questions about her recent visit to Miz Liddie's house.

"I can't imagine why you want to know about that," she had told him forthrightly. "But because you are such a loyal customer of mine, I will gladly do you the courtesy. Besides, I have nothing to hide."

So now they were face-to-face in the interrogation room with its institutional green walls, and after a few ordinary pleasantries, Ross turned up the charm even more. "I expect our conversation to be brief, Miz Chalk. The sooner to get you back to managing that wonderful restaurant of yours overlooking the river. I tell ya, you're a godsend to a hungry detective like me who wants something to sink his teeth into."

Selena looked smug, patting her hair triumphantly. "I wish everyone thought like you did."

"That's what I want to address today with you. I'm well aware of that letter that Miz Liddie and her friends wrote to the *Citizen* about your bistro. Let me say here and now that I completely disagreed with it. I thought it was a hatchet piece, and I was very disappointed in Dalton Hemmings for publishing it."

"Thank you," she said, managing a sincere smile. "You're a true Southern gentleman. How do I clone you, though?"

"I don't know how you can do that, but I do know that letter from the ladies didn't do you any favors."

"That's an understatement. You've probably noticed for yourself all the times you've come in since. More and more empty tables."

"Sorry to say I have," he told her. "But I intend to keep comin' around for your delicious food. That said, I do need to ask you about your visit to Miz Liddie's house. The housekeeper says you made threats to her and her friends. In fact, she says you threatened to kill them all. In view of what subsequently happened to them, I'm sure you can understand why we need to interrogate you. So the first thing I need to confirm is—did you actually threaten to kill them for writing that letter on that visit? We have an eyewitness that you did."

Selena was anything but prompt with her answer. It was Ross's experience that such delay tactics were typical of someone calculating a response and not necessarily prepared to tell the truth. Finally, she said, "If I did, it was in the heat of the moment. Miz Liddie and that maid of hers were actually pushing me out the door there at the end. It took the both of them to do it, by the way. I admit it—I'm a large woman who likes to eat the food I prepare and sell." She stood up and briefly pointed to her bulk the way a game-show spokesmodel might.

"Not necessary, Miz Selena," Ross said as politely as possible. "You can sit back down."

"You should know right here and now that I'm not the least bit ashamed of my size. Big can be just as beautiful, you know," Selena continued. "My maiden name was Kohl. I'm of hearty German stock. As a result, the dresses I wear may be formless, but at least they're comfortable. I do not care about clothes one iota. I only care about food. I take great pride in my restaurant. I know what I'm doing. I believe Miz Liddie and her friends gave me a raw deal for whatever reasons, and I went over to her house to ask for a printed retraction. I thought it was the least she could do to be fair. She dismissed me like I was some random stranger off the street. I will readily admit that I have a temper, and that Miz Liddie brought out the worst in me once I had her in my sights. But you have to believe me, I had no intention of killing those ladies, even though they've practically killed off my business. Why, I wouldn't even begin to know how to go about such a thing."

"I suppose you've read about how they were killed," Ross said.

"Some poison or other, I believe. Was it cyanide?"

"A type, yes."

"How awful." She put a finger to her lips. "Is it cyanide or arsenic in the rat bait we put out behind the store in the alley where they pick up the garbage? I forget. At any rate, that's the only thing I even remotely know about poison. I've always thought it was a yucky thing to deal with for any reason whatsoever."

Ross shrugged, made a mental note, and then changed the subject abruptly. "Where were you on the day of the murders?"

"At the restaurant running things, of course. All of my employees can readily vouch for that."

"I'm sure they can. Did you go to the memorial service?"

Contempt fairly shot out from Selena's eyes. "Indeed, I did not. I owed those ladies absolutely nothing. They gave me no respect at all, so I gave them none in return. Had they been regular customers, I would have sent flowers, of course. But I'm quite sure you understand why I didn't. You reap what you sow."

"That's straightforward enough. I'd like you to do me a favor now and give us a sample of your DNA and your fingerprints."

"You don't actually think I killed them, do you?"

"It doesn't matter what I think, unless we're talking about your food," Ross told her. "The evidence will help to clear you quickly enough."

Selena seemed both delighted and relieved. "Are you going to put one of those cotton swabs in my mouth? I see them do that all the time on all the TV shows."

"You got it."

Ross efficiently tended to his duties and then said, "Meanwhile, I wanted to tell you that I'm continuing my campaign here at headquarters to get every man and woman on the force to drop by and try your food whenever they're in the neighborhood. I'll keep on doing what I can to help out."

Selena gave him a great double chin of a grin. "I'll see what I can do about a discount for y'all."

"No, no, no. You charge us full price. You don't need to be giving away your margins. Now, a free cup of coffee here and there probably won't hurt your bottom line too much."

"You're right about that," she said, looking at him shrewdly. "If you ever get tired of leading the policeman's life, I could use you as my business manager. I need all the help I can get."

Ross laughed good-naturedly. "I'll keep that in mind for a rainy day. I did take a few college courses in accounting before I decided that law enforcement was actually where my heart was. In the end, numbers really didn't do it for me, but hitting the bull's-eyes in target practice did."

* * *

With her nose in the air, Crystal Forrest sat down across from Ross in the interrogation room, which somewhat contorted her ordinarily pleasant features. "What's that camera for up there in the corner?"

"We tape everything in here so we can review it at any time," he told her. "We're a small-town operation on a budget. No two-way mirrors like they have on all the TV shows."

"Thanks for the warning," Crystal said. "I don't promise I have anything of interest to tell you during this little audition."

At the moment Ross was fascinated by her dangling sapphire earrings that swayed back and forth like a metronome every time the woman moved a muscle. They matched exactly the expensive blue dress and shoes she was wearing. A dramatic, upswept hairdo with no signs of gray completed her conspicuous consumption ensemble.

"Let us be the judge of that, please."

"Don't worry, Detective Rierson. I've always taken a stand to cooperate with the authorities." She pronounced *stand* to rhyme with *wand,* as in magic, as in fairy godmother.

Ross found the woman's "accent" both distracting and off-putting. She talked through her nose and appeared to be trying to strain everything through a "British" sieve, as if viewing Ross as a venerable inspector from Scotland Yard. It was all the more odd because she had made a huge to-do when she had first arrived in Rosalie of the fact that she was from Al-*benn-y,* Georgia. "The accent is on the second syllable," she was always reminding everyone, almost all of whom could not have cared less. She had not been the first to arrive in Rosalie trying to buy friendship and acceptance with an extremely stout checkbook.

"We're always glad to have the cooperation of our Rosalie citizens," Ross managed. "I hope you'll continue in that spirit as I question you." Then he paused for a second. Was he subconsciously phrasing his words to match her British-y shtick? Without thinking any further, he reworded his sentence. "What I mean is, let's get down to business."

"I should certainly hope so," Crystal said, working her earrings in a dizzying fashion.

Ross literally had to avert his eyes to focus. She could have hypnotized a room with those things.

"I need to ask you about a recent call you made on Miz Liddie Rose at her house on Minor Street. Do you recall that visit?"

Crystal adopted a pose that was nothing short of regal, proudly lifting up her chin. Any second now, she might start a begloved waving in slow motion at the crowd gathered below her at Buckingham Palace. "Indeed, I do. It was of a social nature, although we did have a spot of business to conduct. We'd both been concerned about those noisy carriages going up and down Minor Street at all bloody hours of the day. There was simply no relief in sight. We wanted to petition the city to restrict them, you understand."

"And that was all that was discussed?" Ross continued.

"Yes," Crystal told him. "Other than the weather, of course. Everyone likes to chatter a spot about that." Here, Crystal had chosen to make *chatter* rhyme with *blotter,* as in ink.

"Yes, they do," Ross said. "But it seems Miz Liddie's maid, Merleece Maxique, has reported to us that you made an offer to Miz Liddie that she definitely could refuse, if you'll pardon the cliché. She also told us that you threatened Miz Liddie with bodily harm."

Crystal's face went blank, and her earrings were stilled. "I've no idea what you're getting at, dear boy."

"Don't you? You didn't offer to pay Miz Liddie to join her Rosalie Bridge Club? In fact, to pay a substantial amount if she would take you in?"

"I've never heard such nonsense in my life," Crystal told him, sounding more like an angry Southerner than a subject of the British Crown for the first time since the beginning of their interview.

"Then you're saying that Miz Maxique was lying?"

"I *cahn't* believe you'd take the word of a servant over mine," Crystal said. "Consider the source."

"Then you deny ever having made such an offer to Miz Liddie? Or threatening her in any way?"

"Of course I do. I've no earthly idea what that housekeeper was up to. I under*stahnd* she was a witness to the whole thing and was in the house at the time according to the *Citizen*. Perhaps she was diverting suspicion away from herself with made-up tales about law-abiding citizens such as myself. Have you considered that possibility? I should think her motives would be obvious to anyone within a fifty-mile radius who was drawing a breath."

"In that case Merleece would have to be psychic since your visit took place before the murders."

Crystal leaned in smartly, suggesting a model showing off accessories for the camera. "She wouldn't have to be psychic if she were planning the murders all along, now would she? I think you're missing a surefire bet as to the identity of the culprit. It's my view that you can never trust servants anyway. They'll steal you blind if you let them. I've had to fire them right and left over the years, and it always pained me to do so. I pay generously and give a decent amount of time off. And for that, I still find little pieces of my property missing."

"You seem to have given this a lot of thought. It occurs to me that you could be trying to divert attention from yourself and onto Miz Maxique."

"Nonsense." Crystal practically spat out the word.

"Perhaps. By the way, where were you on the day of the murders?"

"I was having a luncheon of my own at Old Concord Manor. Any of my friends can verify that. There were at least two dozen in attendance. You know, I give the very best parties and only invite the most important people in Rosalie."

"I'm sure they'll all give their very best cooperation to us. And would you mind giving us a sample of your DNA and your fingerprints?"

"I *cahn't* believe you think I'm a suspect. Don't you think that's beyond the pale? I do."

"Your prints and DNA should take care of that, Miz Forrest. It's the easiest way to remove suspicion. At least on the surface."

Crystal reluctantly agreed to his requests and then seemed to regain her form. "You haven't given me the opportunity to express to you how sick at heart I've been about these murders."

"Even though you were denied entry into The Rosalie Bridge Club? With a fee, no less."

"I told you before, Detective. That never happened. I don't even play bridge. It's a silly game for bored housewives, and I am anything but. I am a civic leader who lovingly restored one of Rosalie's greatest treasures. Why, it was on its *lahst* leg before I stepped in. The roof had caved in, there were squirrels and raccoons scampering around, and it was about ready to be condemned."

Ross immediately returned to his lengthy interrogation of Merleece, who had described Crystal Forrest's confrontation with her Miz Liddie in great detail. He had already gotten Selena Chalk to admit to her showdown the week of the murders, which Merleece had also revealed to him. At the moment, Ross was inclined to believe that Merleece had been telling the truth about both encounters.

"Yes, everyone knows what you did for Concord Manor. But on the subject of bridge, all those women and men around the country who play the game seriously and even manage to win championships for money will be astonished to learn of your description of the game they love so well," Ross said, feeling as if he were in the midst of a fencing match and had just scored a touché.

"Make fun of me all you want, Detective. I told you why I paid a visit to Miz Liddie. She was thoroughly sympathetic to my idea about restricting the carriage rides. We parted on perfectly splendid terms intending to follow through with the city. Now it looks as if I'll have to take that on all by myself with her untimely departure. Isn't that always the way?"

Ross proceeded calmly. "Interesting. We have two entirely different versions of what went on between you and Miz Liddie that day. One of them has to be a lie."

"You're the one who's made me come off a spot defensive since you've been treating me like a person of interest."

Ross perked up. "I see you know that term."

Crystal seemed to light up as well, and her earrings took on new life. "My late husband, Rogers Forrest, was a barrister, you know. He shared his most interesting cases with me. I know the legal angles on just about everything, particularly how people can get out of all kinds of bloody sticky messes."

"A barrister, huh? Did your husband practice in the UK?" Ross said, unable to help himself.

"Why, no. He practiced in Al-*benn-y* until his death. Years ago, he and I had traveled to Rosalie for the Spring Tours, and we both thought it would be a delightful place to retire when the time came. It was on our bucket list. I just didn't think when I accomplished it, I would be a widow."

Ross let the British dig go since she apparently didn't pick up on it. "We will want you to stay here in Rosalie while our investigation is ongoing, Miz Forrest. I'm sure you'll cooperate."

"I fully intend to," she said. "I have everything to lose

by abandoning my dear home on Minor Street. I have sunk a fortune into it, and I intend it to be my legacy. And by the way, I will continue to pursue getting the city to restrict those bloody carriages to reasonable hours. I had a legitimate complaint, and I don't intend to give up until I get satisfaction."

"That's your right as a tax-paying citizen," Ross added.

Crystal's terse response summed up her histrionic performance perfectly. "It jolly well is."

CHAPTER 11

Sherry Groves Herrold spent most of the first few minutes of her interview with Wendy dabbing at her eyes and wiping her nose with a white linen handkerchief. Alone among the survivors of The Grand Slam Murders, she seemed to have blown an emotional gasket that the others had managed to repair to some extent.

"I'm sorry to be like this," she was saying to Wendy as the two of them sat at Sherry's cozy kitchen table with the nearby pastel window treatments keeping the morning sun out of their eyes. They were sipping cups of green tea, and there were also fresh-baked croissants for the taking. "I wake up every morning, and for a few seconds I'm fine. But then when I remember what happened to Mommy and the others, I just fall apart. I don't think I'll ever get over it no matter how long I live. My two children came home from college for the service and have gone back, and yes, they were upset about losing their grandmother the way they did, but they're not taking it like I am. They seem so much more resilient, and I don't know how they do it. As for my husband, he cut short one of his business trips to New York to attend the service, but he's right back on the road as usual. He and Mommy never did get along, so I didn't press him about hanging around any longer than he had to."

"I understand completely how you feel," Wendy told her. "I lost my mother when I was in high school due to a case of pneumonia that crept up on her practically overnight. I never did get a chance to say goodbye. I felt like I was underwater for so long and that I'd never break the surface again. Teenagers just aren't equipped to handle that kind of trauma."

"How long did it take you to get back to normal?" Sherry asked, still full of sniffles.

Her demeanor and tone of voice made her come off like a little girl, even though she was firmly middle-aged. Her taste in fashion was too young for her as well. There was about her in general an air of never having quite grown up, of constantly being distracted by the most inconsequential things. Even the fly that had been buzzing around the room earlier had pulled her focus completely. She had not rested until she had retrieved a swatter, followed it about, and squashed it into oblivion.

"It never really quite happened. But I learned to live with it. I wish I could give you a timetable, but I think it would be doing you a huge disfavor. No two people are alike when it comes to grief." Wendy reached over and patted Sherry's hand. "But, listen, if you aren't up to this, I could easily come back another time. My deadline is very flexible."

Sherry sat up straight for the first time, and a certain determination entered her voice. Even the incessant sniffles seemed to have been chased away. "No, you stay right where you are. Mommy would want me to tell you everything about her and our family and set the record straight."

Wendy let the last sentence sink in a bit. Had there been some great misunderstanding about her mother that had not been addressed for some time? "You go right ahead and tell me whatever you'd like."

Sherry put her handkerchief down on the table and then did a double take. "Oh, there's a water ring right here. Now, how did that happen? I'll have to polish it after you're gone." She looked up. "Where were we?"

"You were going to tell me about your mother and your family, I believe."

Sherry narrowed her eyes until she'd located her mental bookmark. "Oh, yes, my family and my mother. It's the redhead thing, you know. Something I never had to face because of this mousy-brown hair I unfortunately inherited from my father. There were times when I thought of dyeing my hair, but in the end it just seemed . . . well, sorta pathetic. Like I was trying to be my mother—which I could never be."

"Talk to me more about the redhead thing." As a breathtaking strawberry-blonde, Wendy's interest was definitely piqued.

"Mommy was the only redhead in the group. Practically the only one in Rosalie when you get right down to it. I don't count Molly Joan Preston because her hair is that orange peel color that never fades. Really, I have no idea why anyone considers that to be red. But back to Mommy. I really think the others were jealous of her hair. She got dates that they didn't get because she said men were fascinated by, umm . . ." Sherry lowered her head and blushed a bright pink.

"Say no more," Wendy told her with a wink and a hint of a grin and then glanced at her notepad. "But I'm not sure I can go there in print. I can just see my editor's face right now."

"No, I suppose you can't go there."

"So tell me something I *can* publish."

Sherry took her time and then quietly gasped. "Well, Mommy told me that she went along with all the gin drinking from the beginning because she wanted to fit in. Then once she saw all the attention it was getting her—even getting the entire group—she couldn't walk away from it. There was that article in the *Citizen* that made local celebrities out of them decades and decades ago. Then they all decided to go to Ole Miss together, and that's when they took the partying to another level. Ole Miss is well-known for being a party school, and the Gin Girls fit right in. As long as we're on the subject, Rosalie girls always fit in at Ole Miss."

"I hope you don't mind my asking, but didn't your mother and Bethany Morrissey get kicked out?"

Sherry seemed to take no offense at the question and was even smiling. "Yes, they did. Once Mommy decided to do something, she went all out. She got Bethany to climb up with her on the sorority roof one night, and they sat up there drinking straight gin and singing 'Forward, Rebels,' the Ole Miss fight song, quite loudly. They woke up the whole house and even most of the sorority next door. Naturally, the housemother ordered them to come down at once, but they refused. So, they were sent home to Rosalie to sober up, so to speak. Mommy said seeing the housemother storming out in her bathrobe and curlers made it all worthwhile. She was a busybody named Miz Crowe, and they all hated her. She was so horribly strict and a teetotaler to boot. Imagine that, a teetotaler at Ole Miss running a sorority house. Boy, did she have the wrong job in the wrong place. Don't know how she stayed on as long as she did."

"Would you mind if I used that anecdote in my feature?"

"I think Mommy would probably approve of that one," Sherry said. "Just not the part about Miz Crowe being a busybody."

Wendy nodded enthusiastically as she made more notes. "Gotcha." When she had finally finished, she said, "Tell me more about Miz Bethany Morrissey, if you wouldn't mind."

Sherry's expression seemed almost exalted. "Personally, I loved Miz Bethany. She was so cute, and she never seemed to gain an ounce. I can look at a picture of a piece of cake and gain two pounds. Mommy was her favorite traveling partner abroad. I don't think there was a part of Eastern Europe they didn't visit at one time or another. I never did know why Eastern Europe, though."

Sherry's smile suddenly diminished. "The only thing was . . . well, of the four ladies, Miz Bethany could drink them all under the table, and who would have guessed it being as small as she was? And she never gave up smoking, either. Even after all the information came out about it being bad for you. Especially if you were pregnant. Mommy would get after her all the time to stop every time she got pregnant. But Miz Bethany wouldn't listen, and she kept having miscarriage after miscarriage. She didn't make the connection, she was so stubborn. It just broke Mommy's heart. Mine too. If she'd had children, I would have grown up with them. We would have been playmates. Instead, I had to settle for the imaginary kind, but I can't even remember their names now."

"That's funny," Wendy said, putting down her pen. "Mine was an elf I named Puh-ray-shah-day."

Sherry returned her laughter. "What's the story behind that?"

"It was my mother's fault. She was such a stickler for buying things like milk that would go bad if you didn't pay attention to such things. She'd let me ride in the shopping cart when I was little and she went for groceries, of course. Back then, you could, you know. Today, there are signs in both English and Spanish that warn customers not to let children ride in the buggies or whatever. Anyway, it seemed to me that all I ever heard from my mother during these expeditions were comments about the *expiration date* of this and that. She practically ignored me, except to take me in and out of the cart. So my five-year-old brain invented Puh-ray-shah-day to keep me company, and guess what—she even came home with me and entertained me for hours. She still hangs out in my refrigerator, of course."

It was difficult to say who was laughing louder, but suddenly, Wendy realized that she was telling Sherry stories instead of the other way around. How had she let that happen? She needed to return to her investigative mission disguised as a puff piece. "If you don't mind, I'd like to ask you a question or two about the period of time leading up to that terrible day. Can you recall your mother mentioning anything unusual or different that occurred among the four ladies in recent months? Perhaps even a fight or disagreement of some sort that stood out?"

Sherry looked thoughtful and then shook her head. "No, they just played bridge as usual as far as I know. There was nothing earth-shaking that I recall Mommy mentioning to me." There was a significant pause. "Except . . ."

Ah, there it was. Wendy's instincts as an aspiring investigative journalist and detective in the making had always leaned toward the proposition that people knew far more than they thought they knew. All they needed was a little prodding, and they would tell you everything without even knowing they had.

"Except?" Wendy repeated.

"I do remember Mommy saying that she thought there was something strange about Miz Liddie recently. She just didn't seem herself. She changed her hairdo and started wearing more makeup than she ever used to. Mommy always used to say that Miz Liddie was blessed with such perfect features that she really didn't need makeup at all. Then all of a sudden, she was laying it on thick. I have to say that it really wasn't all that attractive. She should have left a good thing alone."

Wendy's heart sank. She already knew about the rosacea cover-up. This was old news, and it was obvious that Miz Liddie had concealed her condition from her companions quite well. They had not guessed even though some of them had commented on the "new look." But perhaps there was more to learn anyway if she just persisted.

"Was there any other information your mother passed along to you?"

Sherry practically blurted it out. "Temper. I forgot all about that. Mommy said Miz Liddie had suddenly developed a terrible temper. It was different than it was before. She had always run the bridge club like a dictator, and the ladies all went along with it, more or less. But this was different. Mommy said that there had always been an element of patronizing patience in Miz Liddie's manner before. If you trumped a perfectly good trick, she would point it out to you and ask you not to do it again. Lately, though, she couldn't seem to stand a mistake of any kind. Her patience seemed completely at an end."

Wendy remembered that Merleece had described Miz Liddie almost in terms of "being another person inside that body." Could rosacea have done a number on her self-esteem that much? Or was there something else going on? Something that might have a bearing on the ghastly murders.

"How often did you get to see Miz Liddie?" Wendy said.

"Every other month or so," Sherry told her. "I wasn't much on bridge like Stella Markham is, so I never did pressure Mommy to get me into the club. I'm afraid I would have been a huge disappointment to everyone. But I did come to the parties Miz Liddie threw now and then. Those, I did like. Plenty to drink and eat and lots of gossip floating around."

"Was there one you came to in the past few months?"

"Yes, there was," Sherry said. "Miz Liddie had just gotten back from one of those trips where Stella sat in for her at the bridge table. I remember thinking at the time, 'Is that the same woman Mommy and I have known all these years?' And it wasn't just the makeup and the hairdo. There was something else that was different, but I swear I can't put my finger on it to save my soul."

"Possibly the temper thing?"

Sherry frowned for a moment. "That might have been part of it, but there was something else physical that was different. It wasn't quite right, but I do remember saying to myself that it was probably just the makeup and the new hairdo after all. Maybe my imagination was working overtime."

Taking notes furiously now, Wendy finally looked up for a breather. "Did your mother feel the same way regarding this other thing that seemed different about Miz Liddie as you did?"

"Yes, I think she did. She said something to the effect that she knew good and well they were all way past menopause, so that couldn't be it. I guess we'll never know now, though."

Wendy was just itching to say something like, "Perhaps we will if I stay on the case," but thought better of it. Instead, she said, "Stella Markham gave me some wonderful biographies of all the ladies, as well as some background information on all the families in general. I have them all folded in my purse if you'd like to check yours out as a courtesy to you."

Sherry declined immediately with a wave of her hand. "I know all about those. I helped Stella put them together, so I know everything that pertains to my family is accurate."

"That's good to know. I'm going to try and blend who was born where and who got married when with the more lighthearted material. I hope to do all the ladies justice by the time I've got it all pieced together."

"I'm sure you will," Sherry said. "Stella told me you were very attentive to her slide-show presentation and understood how important it was to put the Gin Girls and The Rosalie Bridge Club in the proper light. Although sometimes it seems to me that Stella worries way too much about image, so to speak."

Wendy was listening intently now. "Can you give me a good example?"

Sherry hesitated while biting her lip but finally opened up. "Well, there was this thing that Stella says Miz Liddie came up with all by herself up at Ole Miss. My opinion is that if Stella didn't want us to know about it, she shouldn't have told us. I think she'd probably had a few too many gin and tonics the day she did tell us several years ago. Anyway, Miz Liddie supposedly rounded up the Gin Girls and told them they were all going to attend a party over at the Baptist Student Union. She loved to mess with the heads of Baptists, Mommy told me. Miz Liddie thought they were such stick-in-the-muds, claiming they never drank anything, but then sneaking around all the time and doing it anyway behind everybody's backs. So she had all the girls smuggle in bottles of gin inside their purses, and they spiked the fruit punch when no one was looking." Sherry's eyes widened, and she had a guilty look on her face.

"What happened then?" Wendy said.

"Well, according to Stella, you've never seen so many teetotaling Baptists throwing up and staggering around the floor, bumping up against each other like they were playing blindman's bluff. She said Miz Liddie and the others thought it was the funniest thing ever and made their exit giggling to themselves without anyone ever suspecting the source of the so-called party pollution." Sherry suddenly put her hand over her mouth. "Maybe you shouldn't write that story down. I don't think Stella wanted me to tell it. I just kinda forgot myself there for a minute."

"I'll take it under consideration," Wendy said. What she did not say was that neither Dalton Hemmings nor Stella Markham nor the Lewis Brothers nor any of the other family members she had interviewed would be the ultimate arbiter of what she created at the computer. This was her moment, her shot at the main chance. She was bound and determined that this was going to be her watershed project, and she was not going to go back to churning out mind-numbing engagement announcements and obsequious gossip just to pick up a paycheck. Not to mention that she remained convinced Merleece could not possibly be the murderer, and it might just be up to her to prove it.

CHAPTER 12

On the way back from her interview with Sherry Herrold, Wendy's thought processes were all over the map. Both Merleece and Sicily Groves had expressed the idea that Miz Liddie had been almost a different person in recent months; that there was something more involved than the hair and the makeup and the outbursts of temper; that they couldn't isolate exactly what that *something extra* was. Wendy continued her mental gymnastics. What if it were as plain as the nose on your face? What if it were hiding in plain sight? Perhaps she needed to go there instead of trying to make this too difficult. But where to start?

Familiar Rosalie landmarks whizzed by, but they might as well have been part of a dream as Wendy remained lost in thought at the steering wheel. And then she had the idea she knew would not let her down. It had been at least three weeks since she'd had her father over for dinner, what with everything that had happened. A session with sturdy, dependable Captain Bax never failed to uplift her, or calm her down or whatever else she needed to have freshly supplied. When she finally got home, she would call him up and ask him what his "teeth were tickling for." Ha! That was his expression, and it had always made her laugh from the time she was a little girl. She remembered the routine as if it were yesterday.

"My teeth are tickling for some pot roast today, Valerie," he would say to her mother before he left for the police station. "You think you could pull it off by the time I get home, sweetie?"

"I don't see why not," she would tell him with a smile before sending him off with a kiss.

As long as her Captain Bax didn't want her to simmer a pot roast all day, Wendy was certain she could throw together whatever he wanted, even one of his favorite desserts like coffee ice cream with bittersweet chocolate pieces sprinkled all over and whipped cream on top. She had all those ingredients waiting for her in her kitchen at this very moment, mostly in the fridge alongside her ever-faithful imaginary companion, Puh-ray-shah-day.

More importantly, Wendy needed her father's counsel on her current project. He would be able to tell her if she might be veering off track, concentrating on this too much and not paying enough attention to that. She could bounce her ideas off of him and see if he gave her his seal of approval. Because she was becoming more and more concerned that no matter how many questions she asked of however many people, the evidence that pointed to Merleece was still there. It was never going to go away. Yet, she could simply not imagine herself being "played" by Merleece, either. Sooner or later, something had to give, and her father might be just the person to give it an enlightening shove.

Bax showed up at Wendy's house carrying Dalton Hemmings's interview with Harry Keller in the *Citizen* all rolled up in one hand like he might just shout through it the way cheerleaders do with their megaphones; then he promptly plopped himself down at the kitchen table, spread it out, and started reading excerpts out loud in a tone that was equal parts mocking and outrage:

> Hemmings: Don't you think a tragedy like this demands the utmost attention from our law enforcement officials? Why, if little old ladies aren't safe playing cards in their parlors, then who among us is?
>
> Keller: That's an excellent point. Rosalie cannot and must not put up with evil thuggery. There's an element in this community that doesn't play by the rules. All they want to do is play the victim because of past history. Well, we can't change the past, but we can go after those who commit crimes because they resent the money, power, and success that others have and have had for generations. And let me say here and now that color does indeed have something to do with it. In this case, the color of money. All four of these ladies were quite wealthy. I'm confident that the culprit or culprits who committed these dastardly murders will be found out and dealt with accordingly. I expect our law enforcement officers to act quickly when the evidence clearly points to the perpetrator. As I understand it, that moment may already be close at hand.

Bax's face was getting redder and redder as his blood pressure rose, so he stopped reading. But not before banging his fist on the table. "Code words. Victims because of the past. Thuggery. He won't come right out and put it in terms of black and white, but that's what he means by it all. He's gotten wind of the evidence against Merleece, and he wants to run with it. He's running it up the flagpole knowing his constituency will eat it up."

Wendy walked over to where her father was sitting and stared at the picture of Hemmings and Keller sitting across from each other at the editor's desk. Harry Keller was one of those mature politicians who never seemed to age any further. Devoted to three-piece suits even in the blazing heat of Rosalie summers, he probably dyed his hair to keep even one strand of gray out of it; perhaps he'd even had some nipping and tucking done to avoid a turkey neck for all anyone knew. Whatever the case, both his politics and physical appearance remained constants—dependable for some, deplorable for others.

"When I was a teenager," Wendy said, pointing to the photo, "I actually shook the man's hand as he was moving through the crowd at one of his rallies. By accident, of course. I must have been about fifteen, and I couldn't even vote. But he was snaking his way around all of us, and he just happened to reach out and grab my hand. It was sweaty and limp, and it made me cringe. It was like he couldn't be bothered to take the time to offer a firm handshake. He was all about touching as many people as he could, no matter how creepy it felt. *'Preeshate ya vote . . . Preeshate ya vote . . . Preeshate ya vote.'* That's all he ever said to anyone while he was making contact, as if those were the only three words in the English language. And we all know his vocabulary hasn't improved all that much since."

"Yep, that mentality is what we're dealing with," Bax said, making a big paper ball out of the article and then craning his neck to locate the trash can.

"It's right over there at the end of the counter," she told him.

"Think I can sink it?"

"Sure."

Bax compressed the ball further and then took aim quickly, disdaining a practice shot. "Three-pointer," he said, raising both hands in triumph even before it went in.

"The trash can is where it belongs," Wendy said, smirking. "Anyway, I'm ready to put dinner on the table. You hungry?"

"You bet. I was beginning to think you'd lost my phone number," he said as she produced two Caesar salads with Parmesan croutons out of the fridge.

"Never," she told him, placing the first course on the table. "And you're exaggerating as usual."

"It's just that you've got your mother's touch as a cook. I'd like to enjoy it a little more."

"Well, I have to be perfectly honest with you," she began, taking a bite of her salad. "I'm feeding you a home-cooked meal in hopes that I can pick your brain about The Grand Slam Murders. In exchange I do K.P. duty. Fair exchange?"

"Sounds like a good deal to me, and you know I'm putty in your hands anyway." Bax dug into his salad with relish, and it did not take him long to finish it. Then he sat back in his chair a bit, clearly satisfied with what he had just eaten.

He was remarkably fit for a man in his early fifties, still as sturdy and formidable a specimen as he had been in his twenties starting out on the force. He worked out regularly at the gym, maintaining his impressive physique. Only patches of gray around his temples and expression lines across his forehead hinted at his maturity. Yet there was little of his physical profile in Wendy. She favored her late mother, Valerie, in that respect, except that no one could figure out where the strawberry-blond hair had come from. It was a genetic wild card, but one that Wendy was always grateful she had drawn from the deck. Furthermore, she had never minded the attention it had brought her throughout her life.

Over the main course of rosemary baked chicken, roasted Brussels sprouts with lardons, and al dente wild rice, Wendy began to throw her thoughts around. "I don't see why these murders had to happen, Daddy. It seems like they came out of nowhere to strike the most unlikely people. Sometimes I think I've lost my mind just contemplating it all. Does that make any sense?"

Bax speared a Brussels sprout and made short work of it. "Murder never comes out of nowhere, daughter a' mine. Even if it's a crime of passion. There are always reasons that drive people to do such things. The reasons aren't always logical, and they're certainly never justified according to the moral code we live by."

"But these murders especially seem so insane," Wendy said, taking a sip of water. "To kill four people at once like that. Is it possible that only one person was meant to be killed and the rest were in the wrong place at the wrong time?"

"That's possible. If that's the case, then the next question is: which one of the ladies was the primary target?" Bax speared another Brussels sprout and chewed on it thoughtfully. "You would think it would have to be Miz Liddie because it happened in her house, wouldn't you? I don't think it's any secret that her personality could be more than overbearing at times, either."

"I've been leaning toward Miz Liddie being the primary victim all along, and I have feedback from more than one person to back me up. Plus, they've all mentioned the fact that they thought something was different about her lately that they couldn't put their finger on, and they weren't talking about the fact that she'd changed her hairdo and started wearing more makeup. Her daughter, Stella, told me that she'd developed rosacea and was trying to cover it up. The others never knew about it, but it explains those changes well enough. Even so, there was something else."

Bax manfully dug into his chicken with his knife and fork as if it needed to be taught a lesson, put a healthy slice of it in his mouth, and changed the subject. "You haven't lost your touch with this rosemary chicken, sweetie."

"Thanks. I kinda like to save it for special occasions like this. For my one and only sweet daddy."

Bax gave her a fond little wink. "Back to the murders, though. What if the primary target wasn't Miz Liddie? Which one of the ladies would come in second on the victim list in your mind?"

Wendy didn't have to think twice. "If you pushed me to the wall, I'd have to say Miz Hanna Lewis."

"Interesting that you would say that. Ross has gotten some interesting vibes from his interview with the Lewis Brothers. Mother and sons were adversaries, it seems. Why do *you* think Miz Hanna might have been the target?"

"Well, I got those same vibes that Ross got. I know Miz Hanna spoke her mind about the bridge club and the way it was run, and there was a fierce competition between Miz Liddie and Miz Hanna, Merleece told me."

Bax swallowed more of his chicken and said, "So a lot of what you think you know about these ladies has been coming from Merleece, is that right? Maybe you should consider your source."

"Some of it has come from her, yes. But not just Merleece, though. I've had in-depth interviews with Stella Markham and Sherry Herrold. Who better to know their mothers than their own daughters?"

"On the other hand, who better to go out of their way to protect their mothers than their daughters? And fathers can go out of their way to protect daughters, too. I've done a bit of that myself."

"I never looked at it that way," Wendy said, gazing at her father affectionately. Then, she mentally kicked herself. She was going to have to get a lot better at this detective stuff.

Bax leaned in and lowered his voice, speaking calmly. "I'm

not supposed to share this at this point in the investigation, but I will because I know you'll keep it to yourself. I'm not just chapped because of Harry Keller's interview in the paper, he actually called me up yesterday. He's doing something that's rarely done in bypassing us here at the department. He's just about ready to have Judge Lahey issue a warrant for Merleece's arrest. The lab confirms that the only DNA and prints found in Miz Liddie's house were from her, the three other ladies, Merleece, and Arden Wilson. Ross has just about made the rounds with other possible suspects, and their DNA is not showing up. If Keller has his way as his coded interview indicates, Merleece will take the fall for this. If she did it, well, justice will be served. If she didn't, something needs to come to light quickly to prevent that from happening. The first thing you should do is share with Ross everything you've learned from the people you've interviewed. I mean tell him everything. You never know what incidental fact or comment might end up revealing the truth."

Wendy put down her fork as her appetite quickly waned. "When will the arrest warrant be issued?"

"I can quote Harry exactly on that. He said to me, 'It's in the works now, Bax. I'm not messing around with this.' "

"Poor Merleece."

Bax's expression was grim. "I told Harry to stop throwing his weight around and go through us for a warrant at the proper time, but he and Lahey have always been in on all sorts of schemes together. Of course, we all know the public is outraged about the murders and wants to see something done quickly. That interview in this morning's paper just stirred the pot even more. I can vouch for the fact that people keep calling the station all the time asking for the details we can't give them. 'Why haven't you arrested someone by now?' 'Rosalie's not a safe place anymore.' 'Do something.' That sort of thing. Now, I'm making an exception about telling you a few things because . . . well, I'm your father and I've leaked a few things to you before and no one has to know about it but you and me and Ross."

Wendy couldn't help herself, allowing her adrenaline to flow freely. "Thanks, Daddy, you know I'll keep your confidence. I was completely disgusted by that interview with Keller. There are times when I seriously doubt I want to go on working for the *Citizen,* even though Dalton Hemmings can't live forever. That's what I keep holding on to. But the article gave Keller the perfect platform to demagogue the issue. All that stuff later in the interview about our culture falling apart as crime from undesirable elements takes over our daily lives. It was all a bunch of code words, as you just said. Are we talking about a lynch mob mentality developing here in Rosalie because Merleece is black? The scenario is all too familiar. Are we going back to those days again? And we all know how Harry Keller comes down on the white privilege thing. The man is a throwback to the Jim Crow mentality if there ever was one."

"Daughter a' mine," Bax said, careful to keep the affection in his voice, "I don't care for the man's politics any more than you do. He's what I'd call a slick, upscale version of a racist wearing a carnation in his lapel and a three-piece suit for the photo ops. He belongs to all the right clubs and says all the right things to all the right people, and very few of them are black. But the fact remains that no matter how you feel about her personally, Merleece Maxique admitted to stirring that sugar into the cups of all those ladies, and Arden Wilson is the eyewitness. That's more than probable cause for her arrest at this point to someone like Keller."

"I don't know how stupid she would have to be to think she could get away with something like that right out in the open. It had to be a setup, Daddy. Somebody framed Merleece, I'm sure of it. Probably Arden Wilson. Or somebody could have paid him to do it."

"But you'd have to prove that. You'd have to make it stick, and you'd be in a helluva fix yourself if you couldn't. And besides that, Merleece admitted to Ross that she was pretty certain Miz Liddie was going to leave her something in her will. There you have it—motive, opportunity, and a gardening shed full of potassium cyanide at her disposal. That's the case Harry Keller will make if it goes to trial."

Wendy picked up her water glass for a couple of frowning, yet thoughtful sips. "Has the will been read yet? Does anyone know that for certain?"

"Didn't you say you'd talked to Stella Markham recently? She would know," Bax said. "Usually, these things take a little time, though. Could actually be a matter of months."

"True. I'll get back to her on it," Wendy said, picking up her fork and returning to her food.

Bax joined her, and the two of them ate in silence for a minute or two. Then he took a deep breath. "You know, a lot of times the obvious solution is the right one. But it's been my experience over the years that a percentage of cases just don't follow form. They are out there all by themselves on a limb. It's the gifted detective that can sift through everything and find that crazy explanation out of left field. Did I ever tell you about Miz Thelma Foster's death? It happened way back when I had first joined the force."

Wendy stopped chewing and squinted for a moment. Her father had told her so many stories since she was a little girl that it was sometimes difficult to sort them all out. "No, I don't think you did."

"Well, Miz Thelma was a dear, retired schoolteacher who lived alone. She'd taught me first grade, as a matter of fact, and I thought she was just wonderful. I remember coming home from school and telling your grandmother about the funny clicking noises she made when she spoke. Gran-Gran explained that Miz Thelma's dentures didn't fit, but she never would do anything about them."

They both chuckled, and Bax continued. "Which is far from the point of the story. One fateful day she was found laid out in her backyard stone-cold dead with a big bruise on her throat and a big lump on her scalp. Nearby were a dead raccoon and a shovel. Well, everyone was dumbfounded at first, to say the least. What kind of foul play was this, and what could the motive possibly have been? There was no sign of theft in her house, though the back door was unlocked. Then one of our detectives, Bill Harbour—who's long since gone to his reward—pointed out that there was a clothesline out there near that random collection of items. The marks on Miz Thelma's neck matched the clothesline cord, and her trash bags were scattered all over the place. It gets better—or worse, as far as dear Miz Thelma was concerned. Bill envisioned a comedy of errors that had turned into a tragedy because that raccoon had probably been rummaging through the trash, and Miz Thelma had gotten after him with a shovel, chasing him all over the place. She must have landed a fatal blow at one point, but she also must have run into the clothesline at full speed at about the same time, fallen to the ground, hit her head, and that was what did her in. What was left for the police to discover made no sense until Bill Harbour thought way outside the box and put all the pieces together."

"What a bizarre and unlikely way to go," Wendy said, putting a hand to her chest to steady herself.

"Yes, it is. But the point is that sometimes the obvious and easiest solution is way off base. Any number of diverse components can come together to create tragic circumstances. If we all believe that Merleece is not the obvious and easy solution, then you and I and Ross and the rest of the department must come up with something equivalent to Miz Thelma chasing a raccoon with a shovel and running into the clothesline."

Wendy tried hard but could not suppress a hint of a grin. "I know it's not the least bit funny, but imagine all that being brought up in court."

Bax remained stoic, however. "No, murder is never funny. But it can be devilishly clever—sometimes even inspired. And I think that's what we're dealing with here. Ross and I have discussed it several times down at headquarters as we've reviewed the various tapes of everyone who's come in so far. As you've said, it just doesn't add up. How could Merleece, or Arden Wilson, hope to get away with something like that? They had to know they'd be the first ones suspected, and even though they've loudly accused each other of the murders, Ross and I don't believe either one of them did it. We've concluded that we're looking in the wrong places for all the wrong reasons. Perhaps we should just go ahead and widen our net somewhat."

Wendy was more perplexed than ever. "Are you saying that someone outside of Rosalie could have done this for an unknown motive?" Immediately, Merleece's framed picture of Hyram flashed into her head, but she was so conflicted that she chose not to say anything to her father for the moment.

"It's possible."

"Who else does Ross have left to interrogate and when?" Wendy said, eager to change the subject.

"Tomorrow he sees Peter Markham, that pharmacist fella who Stella Markham divorced, and Miz Hanna's exercise boyfriend—or whatever he was to her—with the ridiculous name."

Wendy and her father exchanged wry glances and she said, "Hermes . . . uh, Caliban, I believe he goes by. Does Ross think . . . scratch that . . . do you think they're viable suspects? I told Ross what Stella had said about her husband being a drug addict, but I didn't know whether he would follow up or not."

"He's going to, of course, but they're both long shots in my book," Bax told her. "Still, you never know in this bid'ness. Sometimes people who aren't really suspects reveal some little thing that leads to the real culprit. Don't ask me how it works, but it does often enough not to dismiss it. At any rate, we don't have any time to lose if we're gonna get Merleece off the hook. If I didn't say so before, I totally agree with you that she didn't do it. Or at least she didn't know what she was doing when she stirred that sugar into those cups. Ross and I have gone over her tape many times, and we see a decent woman who's outraged that she's been accused of such a heinous crime. We don't see someone who's holding anything back."

"How did Arden Wilson come off on his tape?"

Bax stopped short of rolling his eyes but did make mini-circles with his index finger around his right temple. "One of the strangest and cockiest young men I've ever come across in my career—and not just because of the butterfly thing. You could tell he was playing to the camera all the way during his interrogation. Ross had the same impression of him at headquarters and each time we watched the tape, as if the guy knew he was golden all the way and—"

"But there wouldn't even have been any potassium cyanide around if it hadn't been for him," Wendy interrupted.

"Yeah, you're right, and he could have put it in the sugar as easily as Merleece could have, but if he did, he was clever enough to cover his tracks. His DNA and prints were nowhere near the sugar bowl or any of the coffee service. Hers were. And he says Merleece made up the story about him smoking grass in the shed. We didn't find any evidence of the stuff out there. If he was rolling doobies, he wasn't doing it on Miz Liddie's time, and it wasn't in his system, either. So it looks like Merleece was trying to finger him because they didn't get along. That doesn't look good for her."

Wendy looked annoyed. "But she could be telling the truth."

Bax acknowledged her with a terse little nod, and said, "Yes, but I guarantee you this—Harry Keller will make a case against Merleece long before he'll turn on Arden Wilson, and you and I both know why. It'll satisfy those visceral feelings that go back hundreds of years in this part of the country. Even Hemmings got in on the act. As he said in that interview in the paper, 'Why, if little old ladies aren't safe playing cards in their parlors, then who among us is?' It was the perfect setup for Keller, and believe me, Harry'll wring every ounce of political capital out of it. They say he's got his eye on Congress down the line."

Despite her distaste for the quote, Wendy maintained a deadpan pose and posture as she thought once again about Hyram Maxique and the idea of an "outsider" being responsible for the murders. Was he somehow the key to this horrendous quagmire? Did that imply that Merleece was involved, playing her for the fool after all?

"Well, I can tell you that they couldn't pay me a million dollars to vote for Harry Keller for dogcatcher," Wendy said, returning to her father's diatribe on the man.

Bax grinned, sat back in his chair, and gave his daughter a proud, fatherly gaze. "You know, I have a strange feeling about your interest in this case. And I mean that in the most positive way."

"And why is that?"

"You may not remember," he began, "but your mother and I were sitting at the dining room table putting together a jigsaw puzzle when you were about seven years old. I think it was a huge one of the Mississippi River at Rosalie. We were having trouble finding the right pieces, and you just walked up and found them immediately. It was almost as if you had a sixth sense about it. You'd point here and there, and your mother and I would pick up that particular piece, and it would always be the right one. We both thought that was remarkable because so many of those pieces looked exactly the same. They were all just part of the muddy water that occupied most of the puzzle. But that didn't bother you one bit."

Wendy looked as if she'd just had the epiphany of her life. "Oh, yeah. I do remember that now. You mean I was never wrong about any of the pieces?"

"Never. You had a gift. And not only that, you continued to be terrific at problem solving at other levels. You didn't have to point to puzzle pieces, but you aced all your math courses in high school and college. You seemed to have this island of knowledge when it came to thinking outside the box."

"Now, this island of knowledge thing, Daddy. You're not implying I'm a savant of some kind, are you?"

Bax's thoughtful expression looked as if he might be seriously considering the possibility. "Who knows? Some people can sit down and play the piano without a single lesson. They never do learn to read music. For instance, Jerry Lee Lewis was born across the river from Rosalie over in Ferriday, Louisiana, and he was rockin' and rollin' without a single lesson. I believe Miz Trigg at the Trigg School of Music tried to teach him, but she couldn't. He didn't need that sort of training. He was a prodigy, pure and simple."

The mention of Jerry Lee Lewis brought a smile to Wendy's face. "Miz Trigg did manage to teach me the scales, though."

Bax laughed heartily. "And then you got bored and quit before your first recital. Your mother and I were very disappointed, but we didn't want to force you to do something you didn't like. Anyway, there are others who can shatter glass with their singing voices without any training. Maybe your gift is to see the puzzle—any puzzle, whatever it is—completed and not be distracted by the pieces that don't seem to fit."

Wendy leaned over and patted her father's arm. "I'm highly flattered by your analysis, of course. On the other hand, that's a lot of pressure to live up to. But regarding problem solving, I have to admit that there was a time at Mizzou that I briefly considered majoring in math. But then I thought, what could I possibly do with it other than teach—unless I got a job with NASA."

They both enjoyed a good laugh, and Bax said, "Not totally out of the realm of possibilities. Anyway, that's why I think it's a good thing that you're in on this case. Maybe that wonderfully curious brain of yours will cause you to point us to the solution when we least expect it."

Then, out of nowhere, Bax took his phone from his pocket and started texting. "Speaking of dessert, you're not the only one who loves your coffee ice-cream dessert with the bittersweet thingies, by the way."

"That's a non sequitur if I ever heard one. Dessert? What are you doing? We haven't even finished dinner yet."

"We have no time to lose. I want you to talk to Ross tonight about your interviews with Stella Markham, Sherry Herrold, and the Lewis Brothers. He's talked to all four of them, too. You can compare notes. He's on his way here now, and, hey, three heads are better than one."

Wendy gave him a quick, sideways glance. Father and daughter had been there before. "Still trying to get us together?"

"This is strictly professional."

"Uh-huh."

He altered his tone just enough to let her know she should take him seriously. "If we're going to bend the rules for you and what you might bring to the table, we might as well go all in. My gut feeling is, between the three of us we're going to solve this case for sure."

The dam had burst. Nothing Dalton Hemmings had said to her at the beginning of the assignment was going to faze Wendy now. Here she was huddling at her kitchen table with two experienced law enforcement officers who were treating her as their contemporaries, and the feeling was nothing short of exhilarating. It was also putting Ross in a more favorable light, relieving somewhat the pressure her father had been applying for some time now regarding their future together. His putting extra helpings of Ross on her plate did not make her want to sample more.

"Did Stella Markham tell you about Miz Liddie's rosacea?" Wendy was saying in between spoonfuls of her ice cream. Their discussions of various persons of interest and otherwise had been going on for some time now.

Ross did not sound particularly concerned. "I don't believe she did. Tell me all about it."

Wendy revealed Stella's explanation of what Merleece had told her about the mirrors and the makeup; then Bax added, "Miz Liddie always was something of a prima donna. I can see why she'd be devastated by a condition like rosacea. All the Langstons were prima donnas and divas, of course. When Miz Liddie married Murray Rose, a lot of Rosalieans frankly thought it would never work. All the Roses had big egos like the Langstons over matters such as which family got to Rosalie first and who had contributed the most to the city over the centuries. But the marriage lasted for a long time, and it even produced one daughter."

"Just be glad Stella Markham didn't show you that interminable slide show of hers," Wendy told Ross. "She goes a bit overboard when she talks about her family, the Gin Girls, and The Rosalie Bridge Club. It's all a bit much to sit through. What was your take on her?"

"The same as yours," Ross said, trying to arrange his dessert so there was a last bite of whipped cream to go with the last bite of ice cream. "Maybe a bit of a snob where her family is concerned, but she has every right to want justice pursued where her mother's murder is concerned. She seemed convinced that both Merleece and Arden Wilson were somehow involved in it together. That doesn't seem all that out of line when both Merleece and Arden confirmed that Miz Liddie pointed at them accusingly and said, 'You!' when they came running into the room."

Then Bax stepped up, having finished off his dessert. "So what do we really make of that, kids? Is it what it really appears to be?"

Wendy frowned at her father. "Isn't it sort of straightforward?"

"Is it? There are any number of possible interpretations," Bax continued. "Miz Liddie could have meant Merleece when she pointed her finger and said, 'You!' Or she could have meant Arden. Or both of them. Or *neither.*"

Wendy remained puzzled but definitely intrigued. "Please. Explain the neither, Daddy."

"Suppose Miz Liddie had intended to say more," Bax began, "but she wasn't able to because she . . . well, she just died and that was the last word she ever said. What if she was going to say something like, 'You . . . two help me,' or 'You . . . two call 9-1-1,' or something like that?"

"That puts it all in an entirely different light," Ross said, nodding in Bax's general direction.

"But what about Stella Markham saying that her mother had the impression Merleece and Arden were up to something? Not that I wanted them to be up to something, especially Merleece."

Bax leaned forward in his chair and put his hands on the table. It gave him an even more authoritative air than he normally had. "Unfortunately, Miz Liddie having an impression about something and mentioning it to her daughter is no proof of anything. Some people have overactive imaginations. But we do have the admission by both Merleece and Arden that she said that one word and pointed at them. My purpose in bringing all of this up is to suggest that appearances and even words can be deceiving when taken out of context. They can be very misleading."

The three of them sat with that for a few moments until Wendy glanced down at something she'd written in her notepad. "I guess we can revisit that. Meanwhile, what was your opinion of Sherry Herrold?" she said, turning to Ross.

"A bit of an emotional mess," Ross said, right after licking his dessert spoon clean. "Given the great respect and devotion both Stella and Sherry had for their mothers, I don't see much that helps us in either of our sessions with them."

Wendy noticed his empty bowl and smiled. "Want another scoop? I can fix you up in no time. What about you, Daddy?" Both men politely refused, and she added, "Okay. How about I clear the dishes later and we continue the discussion?"

"Great," Ross said. "I interrogated both Miz Selena Chalk and Miz Crystal Forrest, and my gut feeling is that Miz Selena was telling the truth about getting into a shouting match with Miz Liddie concerning the Gin Girls' bad review of her restaurant. I had to struggle to keep my objectivity about that one, since I think the Bluff City Bistro is a great place to eat."

"I like it, too," Bax said.

"On the other hand," Ross continued, "I believe Miz

Crystal was lying about not offering to pay Miz Liddie to let her join The Rosalie Bridge Club. I think Miz Crystal was too embarrassed to admit it and was trying to save face by denying it when I questioned her. How she comes off to others is very important to her—she kept primping for the camera in the interrogation room once she knew it was there—whereas I believe Miz Selena is chiefly concerned with the success of her restaurant and could not care less about her personal appearance."

"But the restaurant is her livelihood," Wendy said. "If she ends up going out of business because of that letter the Gin Girls wrote to the newspaper, she can't make a living."

"Point well-taken," Bax said. "Both women have invested huge sums of money in their lives here in Rosalie. One in a restaurant, the other in restoring a Rosalie historic treasure. If they both felt threatened enough, I suppose they might be motivated to murder. But it goes against my instincts."

"Please tell me you don't think women aren't capable of murdering other women, Daddy."

Bax smiled, nodding his head gently. "To the contrary. The record shows that women are capable of murdering anyone, just like men are."

"What about the idea that either Miz Selena or Miz Crystal could have had someone do it for them? Doesn't that happen sometimes?" Wendy said. "My candidate for that would be Arden Wilson."

"But again, we have the burden of proof upon us. Difficult if there's no paper or DNA trail," Bax added. "Ross and I both feel the Gin Girls did a great disservice to Miz Selena, but Miz Crystal did a great disservice to herself by lying, no matter what she says to the contrary. We don't see any reason for Merleece to make up either story about Miz Liddie's confrontations during the week leading up to the murders. Both women confirm they met with Miz Liddie, so it just comes down to who you believe as to what actually took place. They also have alibis on the day and time of the murders. So do the Lewis Brothers, Stella Markham, and Sherry Herrold. Again, the only people other than the victims who were actually present in that house at the time of the murders were Merleece and Arden Wilson. Which is not to say that the cyanide couldn't have been placed in the sugar by someone at some other time—even on another day. If you look at it that way, these murders were just sitting around waiting to happen after being planned well in advance. That said, an alibi's an alibi."

Wendy pushed away slightly from the table and sighed. "So what have we accomplished this evening? I know I fixed some good food for us, but I don't think we've narrowed things down much. Merleece, for instance, is still very much on the front burner of the suspects. Seems like we're just spinning our wheels. Are investigations always frustrating like this, or am I just showing my impatience as a novice?"

"Maybe a little bit of both, but don't beat yourself up too much. I actually didn't expect things to change all that much, but it's always a good idea to understand the cast of characters when you're trying to figure things out one way or another," Ross said, rising from the table.

"I think it's fascinating, and I'm determined to help with the solution," Wendy told him.

Ross adopted a thoughtful pose. "Just keep on with your input. Meanwhile, I have Peter Markham and that Hermes dude who was involved with Miz Hanna Lewis to interview tomorrow. That may give us something unexpected to chew on—or then again, maybe nothing at all. Sometimes this profession is a crapshoot, but I definitely like the challenge and taking the risks."

"Well, let's sleep on it, kids, why don't we?" Bax said, getting to his feet alongside Ross.

Wendy would ordinarily have been suspicious of such a

statement coming from her dear father where Ross was concerned, but on this occasion, she did no reading between the lines. She had already decided that if her on-again, off-again boyfriend wanted to stay the night with her, she was going to let it happen this time around. And if he didn't ask, she was going to take the initiative herself. Wasn't he going to be the lucky lad tonight?

Furthermore, Dalton Hemmings might not be ready to treat her as an equal, but on this particular evening, Ross Rierson had; he had also complimented her on her cooking without making her sound like she represented "the little barefoot and pregnant woman in the kitchen feeding her man" stereotype or some other misogynistic concept that some men still loved to cling to to make themselves feel superior.

But that wasn't Ross. He had come off as genuine and respectful of her ideas—listening to her intently without interrupting—and he could have no idea just how much good he had done himself. This was the sort of man she definitely wanted in her life over the long haul.

After Bax had conveniently left, in fact, Wendy and Ross retired to her "flea market find" sofa with the flamingo-colored cushions. It sat right up against a large wall full of Valerie Winchester's bright, acrylic primitives, which gave that particular room a unique, pastoral aura.

It would turn out to be an evening for reasoned conversation, rich food, and a bit of hanky-panky.

CHAPTER 13

Peter Markham had made a long, rambling to-do of carving out ten or fifteen minutes for Ross's interview on his midday lunch hour at Markham's Superior Drug Store on Locust Street. In fact, he made it sound more like he was President of the United States, and the entire Free World depended upon his presence and judgment on any issue that might come across his desk regarding the universe of pharmaceuticals. Why, one wrong move and there might be a pandemic of unimaginable proportions. In fact, Peter's advertising slogan summed it up precisely: MARKHAM'S—THE SUPERIOR CHOICE IN DRUGS.

"You have no way of knowing this, but my employees can't get through the day without me," he had told Ross over the phone in that rapid-fire style of his. "I've built my pharmacy from scratch. When I took it over, it was just a failing specialty store selling bath salts, perfumes, aspirin, laxatives, and Whitman's Samplers. It may be my imagination, but sometimes I think I can still smell those bath salts. Maybe the molecules are stuck in the walls. But now Markham's is stocked with oval and circular miracles from top shelf to bottom. And I'm the only one who really knows where everything goes and when new supplies come in what day of the week. These interns from the college think they know what they're doing, but they really don't. I have to hold their hands half the time. Plus, you've got to know how to dismiss the pharmaceutical reps that you simply don't want to deal with. They'll take up half your day if you let them. And, believe me, my time is far too valuable to spend listening to spiels of any kind."

Given such an exhausting buildup, it was no surprise to Ross that Peter Markham shook his hand rather quickly and then ushered him into a cluttered office with no windows behind the main prescription counter, where the line was currently lengthy. Everything about this gangly man seemed harried—his complexion was flushed, his thinning hair was not particularly well-groomed, and his eyes seemed unable to focus on any one object in the room. Instead, they shifted back and forth and up and down like he was trying to track annoying floaters clouding his inner field of vision. Despite all that, he was not an altogether unpleasant-looking man. When he chose to smile, the overall impression of being frantic faded somewhat, and glimpses of the human being behind the busy façade emerged.

"So you wanted to talk to me about my late mother-in-law and her demise, right?" Peter said, once the two of them had settled in across his desk. "I don't mind telling you here and now that I have nothing good to say about her, and I don't intend to pull any punches."

Ross did not blink, his smile firmly affixed. He knew exactly where he was going. "And your ex-wife?"

"I make no bones about it," Peter continued. "I married the wrong woman and had no idea what I was getting into when I fell in love with her for some hidden perverse reason that I will probably never figure out."

"Are you referring to the Gin Girls or The Rosalie Bridge Club when you say you had no idea what you were getting into?"

Peter's laugh was a surprise. He was shaking his head all the while, and there was a decided air of regret about it all. "That was part of it, of course. Stella turned out to be a poor enough choice, but that mother of hers—Miz Liddie—she was sent from Hell below."

"I'd say that's quite a vicious little description there, sir," Ross said. "Would you care to elaborate further?"

Peter was staring at a smudge on the wall and absent-mindedly fiddling with the lapel of his lab coat while managing to keep the temper out of his tone. "Where to begin? For starters, Miz Liddie felt I wasn't good enough for her daughter. I was just a common druggist. A doctor would have sufficed, but never an ordinary pill pusher. She also felt that the Markhams were far beneath the Langstons and the Roses. That's what she did, you know. Miz Liddie played these games about whose genes were superior to whose in Rosalie. That was the exact phrase I heard her use once when she'd had a few too many of her gin drinks at one of her parties. She and Stella were very much alike in that respect. They both truly felt that just about everyone else in the town of Rosalie was beneath them."

"Would that include the other Gin Girls?" Ross said.

Peter's "pinball" eyes were at it again. "I don't think Stella felt that way. She always referred to her mother's friends as Miz Sicily, Miz Bethany, and Miz Hanna. She maintained a degree of respect for all of them. But as for Miz Liddie, I don't think there was a person in the known universe she felt was anywhere close to being her equal. I've never seen anything like it. Maybe that kind of arrogance comes along once every other generation."

"So I gather you weren't particularly sorry to see Miz Liddie leave us in such an untimely manner?"

Peter almost seemed to be shuddering. "I wouldn't describe death by potassium cyanide as untimely. I'd call it downright gruesome."

"Being an experienced pharmacist, you would be well aware of that outcome, of course."

"Yes, sometimes you have to shudder to maintain your objectivity." There was a prolonged silence, and Peter seemed unable to look up from his lap. To say that he personified an impression of guilt was an understatement.

"I'm going on the assumption that you have an alibi on the day of the murders, of course."

Peter nodded, and instantly there was a great deal of confidence in his voice. "I was working here the whole time as usual. It's my greatest flaw—I'm a workaholic. Always have been. I have no superior in that regard."

"You seem to be obsessed with the concept of superiority," Ross said. "You even incorporated it into the name of your pharmacy and your advertising slogan."

"Believe me, I could never outdo Miz Liddie in that regard, no matter how hard I tried."

Ross sounded almost amused. "So in addition to being a workaholic, do you have any other flaws?"

"Such as?"

"Drug addiction. Your wife says that's why she divorced you."

Finally, Peter's eyes snapped to attention, and the intensity of the gaze darting out from them was somewhat alarming to behold. It was as if some unknown force had taken control of his body. "What!?"

"She says your habit, so to speak, was what drove you apart."

"She . . . didn't . . . dare," Peter said, finally allowing a nearly palpable anger to ooze into the words coming from between his gritted teeth.

"What are you saying?"

"I'm saying that back when we were first married, the DEA hadn't yet come down as strong on controlled substances as they do now," Peter began. "Not by a mile. People were overprescribed shamefully. We tried to get pregnant over and over again in those early years when things were still tolerable between us, but Stella couldn't conceive. She said she needed something to help with all the stress and anxiety, and I admit to slipping her an extra prescription or two that I probably shouldn't have. But you gotta understand, Mr. Rierson, *she* was the one who developed the habit. I happen to know that she was forging prescriptions there at the end. But I didn't turn her in. I gave her a break. Yes, she was flat out of control, so I willingly gave her the divorce. We just called it *irreconcilable differences* and left it at that."

"Offhand, I'd say you and your wife had irreconcilable *stories,*" Ross told him. "Both accusing the other of being the addict. So, you had no interest at all in the money that Miz Liddie and her daughter had more than plenty of to throw around until the end of time?"

"I'm sure Stella told you that I was a gold digger," Peter said. "But the truth is, I'm a self-made man. I built Markham's Superior Drug Store up from nothing. It didn't bother me in the least that Miz Liddie got in her gin cups one night and told me in no uncertain terms that I'd never get a cent of her money, so I'd better give up the ghost or give up her daughter. Those were her exact words."

"So you're saying you had no motive to take her out with a little sprinkling of cyanide, then?"

Peter was presenting his most superior look now. "Just the opposite. She blamed me for getting Stella 'hooked,' as she called it. It was Miz Liddie who talked all the time about wanting to take *me* out. That's what made the divorce so nasty. It wasn't about money at all. It was about Miz Liddie seeing to it that her precious legacy and reputation were preserved at all costs. She perceived that I stood in the way of that, so I consider myself lucky that she didn't put out a hit on me or that I didn't swallow one of her gin cocktails laced with cyanide."

Ross leaned forward, pulling no punches. "That sounds slightly paranoid to me, but, anyhow, do you think Miz Liddie was right? Do you think that you got your wife hooked?"

Peter was emphatic, his eyes focusing once again. "No, she has an addictive personality. There are such types, you know. Sometimes it's liquor, sometimes drugs, even gambling, food, and sex. I didn't find out for quite some time that Stella was forging prescriptions when I tried to cut her off before she ended up getting arrested and in way over her head. I did everything I could to get her off and succeeded. But Miz Liddie kept blaming me until the very end. She was the stereotypical monster mother-in-law. You may have heard it elsewhere around Rosalie, but you never wanted to get on the bad side of Liddie Langston Rose."

"Yes, I think I'd certainly believe that," Ross said. "That's not the first time I've heard it."

Peter checked his watch and squirmed in his seat a bit. "Have we just about wound this up, Detective? I have to grab lunch and then get back to the aches and pains of this world. Or at least of Rosalie. There are times I think that Rosalie is the world leader in aches and pains, by the way."

"One last question, I think," Ross said, mildly amused. "We know Miz Liddie didn't kill you because you're sitting right here breathing and carrying on this conversation with me. But who do you think killed her?"

Peter played around one last time with his eyes. "From what I've read and heard—and particularly after that interview in the paper with the D.A.—I'd say Merleece Maxique is trying to pull a fast one. But I don't think she'll get away with it. I don't think she can hide in plain sight forever."

"So you're a fan of Harry Keller's, are you?"

Peter's frown lasted a brief second, then morphed into a twisted smile. "I'm not a great fan of his, no. I see through the way he manipulates people for his political career. He's in the grand tradition of Theodore Bilbo, Ross Barnett, George Wallace, and Huey Long—the populists and the racists. But in this particular lulu of a case, I think you have to double back to get at the right answer. I believe it was left in the dust from the get-go."

Peter's last remarks were branded upon Ross's brain immediately: "Double back to get at the right answer." "Left in the dust from the get-go." He somehow sensed that there were inklings of the truth there that he should not ignore. Particularly if Peter Markham was trying to divert attention from himself.

For some reason Wendy decided to skip lunch in the break room, even though she had brought a thermos of her homemade vegetable soup to refuel herself. Ever since she had embarked upon her special assignment, however, she was finding her appetite replaced more and more by her excitement over the prospect of obtaining the job of her dreams and even coming up with the solution to The Grand Slam Murders.

Instead of eating, she opted for some exercise, walking from her office to the Bluff Park overlooking the Mississippi River a mere three blocks away. There she sometimes sat on one of the benches under the moss-draped oaks to clear her head and take stock, weather permitting. Along the way, she could do a bit of window-shopping or even stop to read the specials on the sidewalk chalkboards of other restaurants. Today, the Toast of Rosalie was featuring shrimp and grits, and for a few moments, she was tempted to give in to her fondness for the dish. As it happened, that was all the time she needed to spot Arden Wilson at a table inside through the huge front window, having lunch with a well-dressed matron. The two of them were sipping on cocktails and engaged in what appeared to be very lively conversation.

Not wishing to be as gauche as to press her nose to the glass, Wendy stepped back and then resumed her progress toward the park. At first the identity of the woman would not come to her. But by the time she had settled in on one of the benches, everything clicked. The woman was Crystal Forrest. There couldn't be anyone in Rosalie who hadn't seen her picture in the paper hundreds of times since she'd moved to town and saved Concord Manor from certain demolition. Like Miz Liddie, Crystal apparently had had Dalton Hemmings wound around her little finger when it came to scrounging up publicity for her civic works.

Wendy was temporarily distracted by a squirrel scampering along a particularly muscular oak limb across the way, but the recent conversation she had had with her father and Ross about the possibility of someone paying Arden to off Miz Liddie and her friends soon dominated her thoughts. Had Crystal Forrest been that someone? If so, the two of them were being awfully brazen to appear together in public like they were an item. Wouldn't it be prudent for them to lay low?

Wendy wondered if her speculation happened to be way off base. She thought it almost had to be. What woman in her right mind would take up with such a wildly unkempt, hygiene-challenged specimen like Arden? Of course there was always the older woman–younger man thing. Wendy grimaced. She was glad she hadn't had anything to eat for lunch. But she made a note to mention the pairing to Ross the next time they got together.

* * *

It was Ross's observation that Hanna Lewis's two randy sons had certainly been right in their assessment of their mother's generosity toward Hermes Caliban. The Whiteapple Village condo that she had allegedly given him "for services rendered" was a mini-palace of contemporary and abstract treasures, more impeccably tasteful by far than the digs of the Lewis Brothers, which were about a mile away. Enormous paintings with vibrant splotches of primary colors on the walls and great panes of glass overlooking the carefully landscaped hues of nature gracing the small front yard and backyard set the upscale tone.

"I *am* the personal trainer to the stars . . . of Rosalie, that is, and Hanna Lewis happened to be one of them. She will be sorely missed, I can assure you," Hermes told him as the two of them sat down at his butcher block kitchen table. It featured a strange welded centerpiece that most closely resembled a shot-putter in the midst of competition. But it might well have represented something else entirely considering the unbridled, avant-garde décor everywhere present.

Also as advertised was the man, himself. A red tank top barely restrained a pair of pecs that might have been chiseled out of stone, Mt. Rushmore–style. But his tattooed biceps and neck were the stars of the steroid show. The beefy left bicep featured a bouquet of red roses with green stems and thorns, which were emphasized far more than the flowers; the matching-in-size right bicep displayed the gaping maw of a great white shark with all of its fearsome, predatory teeth; and the neck could easily have won an inking trophy with its two symmetrical rainbows flowing upward from the collarbone to just behind the ears on either side of the jawline. The face, itself, was tanned or stained to a bronze finish, as was all the visible skin of most bodybuilders. It was not a particularly handsome face because of the sharp, chemically engineered angles, but it offered an intensity that was nonetheless arresting. Particularly to lonely, vulnerable females, almost all of them with money to spend.

"I gather you and Miz Hanna enjoyed a friendship that was quite profitable for you," Ross said, continuing to survey the premises. He was more a fan of old-fashioned furniture and decorating, imagining that he and Wendy would someday live in such a house.

"She paid me well for my services, and I took a genuine interest in her," Hermes said. "And contrary to the rumors which I know you've likely heard from the busybody survivors of all the families, I did not lobby Hanna for this condo or the car I drive. She offered them to me on her own. She was that pleased with me, and I'm *that* good. It was a win-win for both of us."

"And you did not refuse these gifts, I see."

"Why should I? I'll tell you something, Mr. Rierson. There are lots of lonely, wealthy ladies here in Rosalie, and I see nothing wrong with bringing a little good circulation and companionship to their lives. No one forces their hand. They need something, and I provide it skillfully."

"I would agree with you there," Ross said. "We all want . . . good circulation and companionship." Then came one of Ross's specialty pauses. "Tell me about Beau and Charley Lewis, please. From your own special point of view, of course. Please speak your mind."

Hermes finally dropped the somewhat blasé façade. "You'll never meet two lazier men if you live to be as old as Methuselah." There followed an unexpectedly long silence.

"Is that all you have to say?"

Hermes pointed down in the direction of his belly. "Well, they both hated my guts, and they weren't all that fond of their mother, either. I think it was a shame, really. I wouldn't put it past them to have committed those horrible murders out of pure greed. If they did do it, I hope they will be punished accordingly. The idea of matricide gives me the creeps."

"Do you think they had a reason to kill the other ladies? What did they have against Miz Liddie, for instance?"

Hermes leaned in with a somber countenance. "You'd be surprised what you learn when you live the life of a personal trainer. You're like a psychiatrist with some exercise and sweat thrown in for good measure. Instead of having our patients lie down, we administer our therapy through sit-ups and jumping jacks and all the rest of it. In fact, I think we learn more than psychiatrists do that way. Especially in the 'cool-down' moments. Toweling off is definitely a 'come clean' process for some of them."

Several depictions of "cool-down" moments flitted across Ross's mind, but he had to shut down his speculation quickly. The prospect of other people's private lives made him a bit queasy. "So tell me what you might have learned or observed in those so-called moments from Miz Hanna that might shed some light on the Lewis Brothers or these murders?"

"I know for a fact that Hanna and Miz Liddie had a really nasty feud going on beneath the surface of their polite club activities," Hermes began. "Hanna told me that Miz Liddie had had an affair with her husband many years ago, and that the two ladies had had a knockdown, drag-out confrontation about it when it first came to light. The upshot was that Miz Liddie told Hanna she'd slept with her husband *because she could*. That Miz Liddie thought she could have any man she wanted in Rosalie and anywhere else and never had to settle for no. The way Hanna talked about it in her most private, pillow talk moments with me—and, yes, we had them—I'm not sure she ever forgave Miz Liddie for that."

Ross's expression was skeptical at first, then amused. "You just gave me a plausible explanation for why Miz Hanna might have wanted to murder Miz Liddie. But it doesn't explain why she would also take herself out along with the other ladies, and it doesn't address the Lewis Brothers much."

"Doesn't it? Well, suppose they were about getting revenge on behalf of their mother?"

"A mother they weren't all that fond of by their own admission to me? And it still wouldn't explain why *they* would want to kill the other ladies. That part just doesn't compute."

"You're the detective, not me," Hermes said, back to his flippant ways. "But my guess would be that they were afraid their mother was going to run through their inheritance before she died. So they put a stop to that ever happening for good and didn't much care about the fallout, meaning the other ladies."

"I've heard that theory before," Ross said, matching the flippant tone. "So let's get back to you now. Do you know if Miz Hanna was going to leave you anything substantial in her will? That would certainly give you a viable motive to kill her if you had a mind to."

Hermes looked alarmed; then a fierceness crept into his face that had not been there before. "I find that very offensive. Seems like you're going out of your way to treat me like a suspect now. You told me this was just going to be a friendly conversation on behalf of the investigation. I agreed to talk to you out of respect for Hanna and the other ladies. It was an unbelievable thing that happened to them, and I guess there's a part of me that's still in denial, but I have nothing to hide. You're beginning to make me feel like I need a lawyer. Should I get on the phone and call one up right now?"

Ross remained perfectly calm. "You have a right to one, no matter what, of course. I have to explore all possibilities and then hopefully arrive at the right conclusion. So you and Miz Hanna never discussed her will, then?"

"No, we didn't," Hermes said, relaxing somewhat. "You already know that she gave me this condo and the SUV I drive. I admit that, but I never put any pressure on her in her financial matters, no matter what those sons of hers have said. Her generosity pretty much blew me away."

"All right, then. We'll move on. I have to ask you where you were on the day and time of the murders."

"With another of my ladies," Hermes said. "Mrs. Helen Hope Williamson on Wensel Street. She's trying desperately to lose some weight before her fiftieth class reunion. I don't have the vaguest idea why, since most of the people she'll see there live right here around her and know very well how big she's gotten recently. But I'm sure she'll be happy to verify our vigorous efforts together on that day and also at the time of the murders."

"Ah, yes. The redoubtable Miz Helen Hope, as all of Rosalie knows her. I'm sure we'll ask her that very question. Meanwhile, would you mind giving us a swab of your DNA and your fingerprints?"

Hermes seemed unperturbed and quickly complied with the request. "I wish I could have been more help to you," he said afterward, rising from the table.

"You've been plenty of help," Ross told him, getting to his feet as well. "Every little piece of the puzzle is appreciated."

"I'm happy to hear that. I hope justice is done. I really will miss Hanna Lewis. Among all of my ladies, she was exceptional in so many ways. She was already in great shape when she came to me. After that, she just got better and better. I let her know that in so many different ways that she appreciated."

"Yes, I've heard about your prowess at . . . tennis," Ross said, smiling as they headed toward the front door. "Of course, the department will want you to stay in town. You never know about breaking developments and how they might affect the big picture. Things have a way of changing drastically in this business."

"I'm not going anywhere," Hermes told him with some

authority. "I have my appointments with my other ladies as we melt the pounds and inches away with physical activities of every imaginable sort."

"I *can* just imagine, believe it or not."

Ross had already headed out when he thought of something and turned at the last second. "Would you mind if I asked you a question about your name? You have to admit it's quite unusual."

Hermes laughed like a little boy who had just cracked a joke successfully for the first time in the company of adults. "You like it, huh? I haven't told anyone else this, but I think I can trust you to keep a confidence."

"Yes, you definitely can."

After a huge intake of air that inflated his impressive chest even farther, Hermes began. "The truth of the matter is that no one is going to hire a personal trainer by the name of Melvin Norman Schrift, Jr. It just doesn't fly if you're going by the name alone when you're thumbing through the phone book or something. Sounds like a nerd with a slide rule in his pocket and a pair of thick glasses. I'm a college-educated man, though, so I dug into mythology and Shakespeare and came up with something much more dynamic like Hermes Caliban. I guess it's a bit over the top, but I coupled that name with my revealing advertising campaign full of my muscular body shots and discovered I was suddenly in business big-time. I mean, maybe the body alone would have done the trick nicely, but I decided to take no chances and go all out for the win. 'WORK OUT WITH HERMES' sounds a helluva lot more appealing than 'WORK OUT WITH MELVIN,' don't you agree?"

"I'm cool with it. Whatever works for you," Ross said, giving him a little salute of a goodbye.

As Ross walked down the sidewalk to his car, he pushed aside his most recent interview and all of its implications and began contemplating his own name. *Ross Rierson.* Would he ever consider changing it for any reason whatsoever? No, it had a nice, masculine, alliterative ring to it that he knew he should just leave alone. Besides, Wendy was the only person he really needed to impress, and he felt things were heading in the right direction on the romantic front once again. Even if he had long ago admitted to himself that Wendy Winchester was a high-maintenance woman.

Wendy was looking forward to a second straight romantic evening with Ross, although she was just as interested in hearing anything he chose to reveal to her about his interviews with Peter Markham and Hermes Caliban. *Chose* being the operative word here. He was under no obligation to share anything uncovered in the ongoing investigation with her. Nor was her father. Yet both of them had bent the rules because they both wanted to give her every advantage in putting together a blockbuster series on the Gin Girls and succeed in her quest to upgrade her position at the *Citizen.* For that she was truly grateful. Now all she needed to do was deliver the goods to Dalton Hemmings and hope for a big dose of fairness from the man for once.

Of course, she still hoped for even more glory by somehow solving the murders herself—that was the ultimate victory of victories—and it would set her apart from all others in Rosalie forever. On the other hand, daydreaming about it as she did while churning out at her computer the pedestrian social announcements that were still her bailiwick was nothing short of counterproductive.

Quitting time finally came at the *Citizen,* however, and Wendy got into her car, heading out to her bungalow with her mind on anything but the gas gauge. Soon enough, however, the low fuel icon popped on in all its burnt orange glory and stubbornly refused to disappear. She could have sworn that she had just filled up, but she also could not deny that she had been completely preoccupied with her upcoming feature articles and all the challenges that The Grand Slam Murders had been presenting to her. As a result, certain mundane but necessary matters were occasionally falling by the wayside. Therefore, Wendy made a mental note to pay greater attention to detail. Even though she had AAA, running out of gas would be a pain in the butt she hardly needed, and no investigative reporter and amateur sleuth worth her typeface and thinking cap should ever let that happen to her.

Wendy's favorite service station was out on the busy, neon-lit, franchise-laden Rosalie bypass. The station's prices were always anywhere from five to ten cents under all the others in town, sometimes even more during the infrequent gas wars that occurred. Every bit as thrifty as her father, she had continued to go out of her way to reward the owner, the gregarious Little Sammy Junkin—who topped out at five foot six—for his consistent discounts by giving him her business exclusively.

After Wendy had pulled up to the gas pump, swiped her credit card, and started filling up, she decided to chastise herself mentally for her lack of attention to detail about getting gas in a timely manner. Accompanied by the smell of the inevitable spillage of thousands of customers before her on the surrounding concrete below, she even began a makeshift mantra: *attention to detail . . . attention to detail . . . attention to detail . . .* Her brain began responding immediately as the mantra faded away. Her eyes wandered to the young man standing opposite her at the next pump over. The first thing she noticed was his sneakers. They were dirty. One of them was untied, and she thought about calling it to his attention but for some reason thought better of it. Why, she did not know, because he could easily trip over the laces and injure himself.

She moved up to his pants. He was wearing badly faded

jeans with no belt. Above them, the tee covering his chest was nondescript and pitch-black. Finally, she moved to his face. Rich brown skin, impossibly high cheekbones, a somewhat sullen expression. The entire package of features was definitely familiar. Where had she seen it all before? She immediately knew she was in one of those situations where she would not rest until she placed it.

The mantra returned briefly as if urging her to contemplate the matter further: *attention to detail . . . attention to detail . . .*

And then the recognition crashed through her studied curiosity like a strike in a bowling alley.

Hyram Maxique.

There he was standing across from her.

Even though Merleece had told her she did not know where her son was, he had leapt from the picture frame on the end table in her living room and landed there in Rosalie, now busily pumping gas as if he had no cares in the world. She could easily have nodded and said hello to him the way people sometimes do in a perfunctory manner while biding their time at such places, but something told her not to go there. And that even if she did, he would not respond in kind. She was more certain than ever that it was the right thing to do not to have mentioned his shoelaces to him.

Instead, the burgeoning amateur sleuth in her quickly put together a plan. She would follow through with it even if it meant denying herself a couple of gallons by stopping the pump a little early and driving off without the receipt she always collected for her monthly expense account report. How to tail a car without being obvious about it was something she and her father had done together for fun one summer when she was home from college her junior year.

"Show me how you do it," she had told him on a whim as they were driving back from lunch at The Silver Rooster,

Bax's favorite "dressed-up burger joint" with a salad bar that went on forever and came free with every order.

"Why the sudden interest?" he had said.

"I don't know," she said. "Maybe I'll change my mind and become a detective instead of a journalist. I've got your genes, after all."

Bax had turned to her with a proud smile on his face. "That'd be an interesting development, daughter a' mine. Keep me posted."

Then he had picked out a car at random, pointing to a white Toyota ahead of them going with the flow of the traffic. "We'll follow that fella with his arm hanging out the window for a while and see what happens. If you're in the surveillance mode and not chasing after someone at the speed of sound, you wanna lay back and cruise slowly like in one of those teenage movies."

Wendy had covered her mouth with her hand and snickered. "But you don't peel rubber, right?"

"Exactly. No pedal to the metal. Obviously no tailgating, and no crazy antics like in those televised car chases that everybody thinks are so cool. But they're not. They're downright dangerous. You're not delivering a traffic ticket, and you're not a Hollywood stuntman. They're paid to risk their lives for entertainment purposes. You can even put a car or two between you and get in a different lane as long as you have a good sight line. Your man can make a sudden move, speeding up or slowing down here and there, but you maintain your pace. Your objective is not to lose him and not to tip him off that he's being followed."

And now, Wendy was about to put that fatherly lesson of a few years back to constructive use.

She waited patiently for Hyram to top off the banged-up looking vehicle he was driving. There was actually a big, ugly wound of a dent in the door just behind the driver's side that was just begging to be repaired. It brought to mind recklessness or lack of insurance, or a host of other scenarios that hinted at chronic immaturity. Fortunately, Wendy was able to fill up and pocket the receipt that the pump spit out before he finished, so she was ready to get going when he was.

As they moved methodically along the bypass in a tandem that was far from obvious, Wendy was overcome with the feeling that this chance encounter with Hyram might just mean she was going to crack open this case all by herself. Her father had told her more than once over the years in their many discussions of his police work, "Sometimes, you just need a bit of luck to solve things. I know I've had it happen to me, and I can't explain why. I just know that it does."

At the same time—and with a sinking feeling that was growing stronger with every mile they traveled—Wendy knew exactly where Hyram was headed. It simply could not be otherwise, and with each turn they made, her conclusion was validated. If she had a dime to her name, it would be North River Street. The wayward son appeared to be going home to his mother for unknown reasons. More importantly, what did that portend for the investigation? And had the culprit of the crimes been an outsider after all, as her father had intimated in one of their recent discussions?

Ten minutes later, Wendy was watching from a distance in her idling car at the top of one of the many undulations that defined winding North River Street. A half mile or so below her, Hyram had pulled into Merleece's driveway, shut off the engine, and hurried into the house through the front door without knocking, totally oblivious to his ongoing surveillance.

Wendy had now reached a crucial juncture. What was her next move? Should she go in and confront Merleece in an attempt to discover what was actually going on? She had to admit she was a bit shaken by what had taken place over the last fifteen or twenty minutes. Or should she report the incident to Ross or her father and let them take it from there? She could do the safe thing and reach either of them on their cell right now if she wanted.

Then, the full-blown, patronizing image of Dalton Hemmings rose up before her across the windshield like a demon in all its bug-splattered glory. As a reflex action, she even found herself turning on the wipers and summoning the twin jets of fluid to banish that stubborn, chauvinistic memory. Then she shut them off quickly and chuckled at herself. No, it was entirely the wrong thing to leave it up to the wipers to do the dirty work and clean up her doubts and fears about her ability to handle things as the men would. She was going to drive down the hill forthrightly, knock on the door, and ask Merleece to level with her about everything this time, since she obviously had not done so before. In a sense, Wendy felt she had already gone out on a limb on Merleece's behalf. She had invested too much to turn back now.

The one thing that apparently did not occur to Wendy as she turned into Merleece's driveway was the possibility that she might be in some sort of physical danger by zealously pursuing things on her own. In that respect, seasoned law enforcement officers had it all over her.

CHAPTER 14

Ross did not understand why Wendy had not responded to any of his casual texts over the past thirty minutes. Their agreement to indulge in a "second straight date of a serious nature"—to use an old-fashioned description that he much preferred to the more graphic versions so typical of the millennium—had been straightforward enough. They were to meet again at her house, and he was getting ready to head out that way from the station. Once there, they were to play the cuisine and intense cuddling by ear. For instance, if they decided to thaw something in the freezer after some heated love, then so be it. On the other hand, if they chose to get dressed again and head back into town for a late dinner somewhere, that would be an option as well. It had been a while since they had felt this at ease with each other. But Wendy had never been one to let any of his texts go unanswered for long. Ross began to worry and returned to his thumbing.

is something wrong?
hey, Wendy girl? r u good?

Five minutes passed and still no response. This was starting to become alarming, but Ross decided not to tell Bax at this point. There might be nothing to the lack of response at all—just some temporary glitch—and any second now, Wendy might be chiming in with one of her playful signature texts. Something like: *all good here, I like New York in June, how about u?*

The last thing Wendy had expected when she entered Merleece's living room this time around was to be looking down the barrel of a gun. But at the moment, Hyram Maxique was providing her with that unnerving, pulse-pounding experience. In retrospect, her insistent knocking at the front door while begging to be let in had been ill-advised. But finally, Merleece had relented, opened a crack, tentatively peered through it, and told her in no uncertain terms, "Strawberry, I need you to go away now."

"It's important that I talk to you, Merleece," Wendy had said for the second time. "You need to explain to me what's going on."

It was at that point that Hyram had flung open the door and strong-armed her inside without saying a word. The gun was doing all his talking. He continued his silence even as he gestured empathically that Wendy find a spot on the sofa and that his mother should join her.

"Wish you hadn't come here, Strawberry," Merleece said, sitting down beside her. "You the last person I expect to see."

Somehow, Wendy found the courage to answer. "And the last person I expected to see at the gas station was your son, Hyram. I recognized him and followed him here to see what was going on."

Hyram spoke up at last, his words oozing with belligerence. "This white girl a cop, Mama?"

"No, she work for the newspaper," Merleece said. "And put that gun down, Hyram. Stop all this actin' like a thug. I've 'bout had enough a' that. You might carry on like that up in Chicago, but this is where I raise you. While you under my roof, you behave like a Christian boy."

Hyram lowered the gun, but not his attitude. "Mama, you gotta be kiddin' me. You wanna get outta here or not?"

Wendy turned and studied Merleece's face. Did she even know who this woman really was? Was Merleece Maxique the kind of person who would consider going on the lam? Or was Hyram twisting her arm?

"Strawberry bein' here now make everything different, though," she told Hyram.

"So, lemme get this straight. You call me up, and I drive all the way down here from Chicago and even get a ticket in a speed trap in one a' these redneck towns on the way to rescue you from this cracker lynch mob you went on about, and you gonna back out now? You crazy or what?"

Merleece flashed on her son. "I'm not sayin' that to you yet, Hyram Ray. Don't put words in my mouth."

"Then what, Mama? Did you get all packed up for nothin'?"

Merleece turned away from him and gave Wendy a motherly gaze. "Whatchoo think about it, Strawberry? Now that you here, you might as well let me know. Go right on ahead."

"Who *is* this white girl you so crazy about, Mama?" Hyram said. "I told you not to let her in."

"A friend, Hyram," she told him. "Don't matter what color she is. Cain't have too many friends, and I think I need to hear what she have to say. Now, you calm down right this minute."

Wendy quickly took advantage of the invitation to speak up. It seemed she had inadvertently been given the opportunity to save Merleece from getting into even worse trouble than she already was. "If I understand this correctly and you were planning to run away, my advice to you is to stay put. Don't you see that leaving town would look like an admission of guilt to the police?"

"Don't listen to her, Mama," Hyram said. "It's no skin off her back if you take the fall or not. You know how things work around here if you got black skin. Your only chance may be to run and hide. The way I see it, we just wastin' time. If she gets here five minutes later, nobody answers the door no matter how many times she knocks. We are flyin' up the interstate on the road to freedom."

Although the gun in Hyram's hand was no longer pointed at her, it still required a bit of bravado for Wendy to argue with him. Who knew if he and the gun might explode at the same time any second now?

"The police have a way of finding you no matter where you go, and I do care about your mother, Hyram. Don't ignore the advice of a true friend," Wendy told him, talking way bigger than she felt. To stay in character and keep her swagger about her, she imagined herself as a female John Wayne in boots and spurs. "And I don't want to see her take that fall you just mentioned. I don't believe she's guilty, and I've been working hard to try and get at the truth."

"Why should she b'lieve you?" Hyram said. "Why should I?"

"She asked for my opinion. I just gave it to her—and to you. Your mother is a suspect because there's strong evidence against her. There's an eyewitness. This will become an open-and-shut case if she tries to leave town. I guarantee you that. I'm giving you the facts, pure and simple."

Hyram refused to back down. "So, we just sit here and wait for the police to come and get you, Mama? Is that it?"

Even though Wendy knew that could possibly happen, she had to convince the two of them otherwise. This was her chance to save the day, and she wasn't going to blow it. "I understand why you came down here, Hyram, but the best way you can help your mother now is to stay here and stick beside her, no matter what. If you love her, have faith that the truth will come out."

Hyram offered up a contemptuous laugh. "Tell that to the ones who ended up hangin' from trees waitin' for the truth to come out."

His angry words made her wince, but Wendy was not about to give up. "I don't deny that. There were lots of things about the past here in the South that were ugly. Some people would say there still are. You have every right to be upset and to want to protect your mother. But leaving town is just not the way to do it. You have to stay here and fight. And trust me, I wouldn't be waving that gun around while you do it."

"Pretty words," Hyram said. "White people always know all the pretty ones, don't they? They got all the sweet talk down pat. And how do I know that if they don't try to pin this on Mama, they won't try to pin it on me? I'm not only black, I'm a man, too, and my gun is my only protection."

"Hyram, stop all this disrespectin' her," Merleece said. "Strawberry just tryin' to help."

"You think so, Mama? How do you know she didn't come here to talk you into giving yourself up?"

"The probabilities that I would meet up with you at the gas station are astronomical," Wendy said. "I don't know why this happened the way it did, but I think we all have to pay attention to it."

"More pretty, fancy talk," Hyram said.

Merleece did not answer at first, obviously lost in thought. She was even gazing back and forth between her son and Wendy. Finally, she said, "Strawberry wouldn't lie to me 'bout the way this come down. But they was too many times I needed to be there for you, Hyram, and I wasn't. But it was the other way around, too. You call me when it suit you and you want somethin' outta me. Seem to me like we been runnin' away from each other all our lives. Maybe we should try and see what we can do together this once."

The studied frown that seemed to be permanently etched in Hyram's face softened, then disappeared completely. He even put the gun down on the end table, apparently signaling some sort of truce between his macho façade and his better nature. "You really want me to stay, Mama? I didn't think you wanted me to after I slapped Charice around like I did. I thought you wanted me gone for good when she pressed charges." His voice grew softer with a hint of sadness. "I . . . didn't feel too good about it myself. I just lost it with her one night when she told me she was leavin' me for that Darius King and she'd been seein' him behind my back."

"I guess we got to stop this runnin' away from trouble. We gotta turn this around," Merleece told him. "Strawberry, she right 'bout this. And she right that they would catch up with us soon enough. So I'm sayin' I'm changin' my mind right here at the last minute. I don't wantchoo to take me up to Chicago and hide me somewhere. That's not my life up in there. I know I would'n like it. Bad as all this mess is with Miz Liddie and the ladies bein' killed, I know I be lost in a big city like that. This is my home, and this all I know."

"Then you'll both agree to stay here?" Wendy said, feeling stirrings of accomplishment.

"Guess so," Merleece said. "But I don't know what I'm s'pose to do next. Do you know, Strawberry?"

"Sit tight," Wendy said. "You and Hyram stay right here in this house. Catch up with each other and find out what you've been missing. You fix him your good food, Merleece. Give him a slice of that applesauce pie. You eat it, Hyram. Something good will come from all that, I just know it."

Hyram was allowing himself a hint of a smile, even though

he was shaking his head. "You white folks all talk like that, don't you?"

Wendy somehow found an answer for him, even if it sounded slightly cryptic. "I don't talk the same way twice."

"What's that s'pose to mean?" Hyram said.

"It means I'm a reporter," she told him. "I mold my words to the story. The story changes every day. I don't think in terms of white or black. I just want to get at the truth."

Hyram shrugged and turned up his nose. "Whatever." Then he focused on his mother. "How long you want me to stay down here, Mama? I got some business to take care of back in Chicago."

"Until this whole thing blow over," Merleece said. "When you think that'll be, Strawberry? 'Cause I got the feelin' I may be runnin' outta time."

"I wish I knew the answer. But I'm determined to see justice served. I feel the solution is just around the corner coming at me out of left field. I just need to concentrate."

"You gone tell that boyfriend a' yours 'bout what almost happen here tonight and what you say to us?"

Wendy took her hand, and both women felt the significant bond between them growing ever stronger. "Nothing happened here tonight. Your son just came to visit you, right, Hyram?"

He did not answer but nodded.

"And you'll stay to support your mother, right?"

This time he spoke up. "Yeah, I . . . will for now. I come all this way, I might as well get somethin' done. But you gotta tell me the truth. You don't think I had anything to do with the murders, do you?"

"No, I don't. The Maxique Family is golden with me. But I do have a tip for you. Be careful with that gun. I wouldn't be pulling it out and threatening people with it unless you're threatened first."

"Lissen to her, Hyram," Merleece said.

"I gotta have it on me, though. I always carry it when I'm up in Chicago. Got to have it on me big-time. In some ways it's worse up in there," Hyram said. "Black on black, you know."

Then Merleece retracted her hand and brought it up to the side of her face with a little gasp. "Strawberry, when you visit me last time, they was somethin' I couldn't seem to remember. Somethin' important. I been tryin' to bring it up from my brain ever since, and it come to me today just 'bout the time Hyram arrive. You need to know 'bout it. They was this time not too long ago—maybe a week or two ago—that I was lookin' out the kitchen window into the yard while I was takin' me a break. And there was them Lewis boys talkin' to Arden Wilson out by the gardenin' shed. Then the three of 'em all go in the shed together. They was in there a good while. Do you think you need to tell that boyfriend a' yours 'bout it?"

"I most certainly do, and I will." Wendy's adrenaline spike was off the charts. Was this the answer? Had the Lewis Brothers paid Arden Wilson to put the potassium cyanide in the sugar for them, knowing Merleece would likely take the blame? Had this been about their greed all along, and were the three of them guilty as sin? Had they simply not given a damn about the other lives they took?

"I'm so glad you finally remembered," Wendy added.

"I don't know how I could forget somethin' like that," Merleece said. "But they has been so much on my mind lately I'm doin' good to remember what day it is. I used to be on Miz Liddie calendar, but now I'm just on mine."

"I understand," Wendy said. "What you've told me is important, and it could end up clearing you in the end."

"I hope so. Since this happen, I been havin' all these nightmares. They's this one that make me crazy 'cause I have it more than once. I'm in Miz Liddie kitchen, and I hear all that racket out in the dining room just after she and her friends drink the coffee, and I rush in screamin' at 'em all, 'Don't drink it, don't drink it!' But it always turn out to be too late."

"That must be awful for you," Wendy said. "I'm sure most everyone in Rosalie has been having nightmares about this. Merleece, do you still think Arden Wilson did this, or that the Lewis Brothers put him up to it for a price?"

"One or the other. Make the most sense to me. You go tell that good-lookin' detective you datin' and see what come of it."

Hyram's abrasive attitude rose again like a phoenix. "So she may not be a cop, but you just said she's datin' one. I think you're playin' with fire, Mama. Maybe you better step back."

"She could be uncovering the truth, Hyram," Wendy said. "I know from my father that successful investigations often revolve around some seemingly insignificant conversation or even a snapshot that's not what it appears to be. I'm sure Ross will find out what those three men were up to, and it could mean you're in the clear when the dust settles. Give it some time."

"Sounds too good to be true to me," Hyram said.

Wendy decided to make one last pitch anyway. "Just promise me you won't run away with your mother, Hyram. Her freedom depends upon both of you staying here in Rosalie. I know what I'm talking about. You don't want to fall into the category of fugitives. It's not tough, it's not glamorous, it's a miserable way to live, and it gets even worse once you get caught."

"You sure do talk like a cop," Hyram said, trying hard to keep the judgment out of his voice.

"I'm the daughter of one. Maybe it's in my genes," she told

him. "And I assure you I'm going to run with the information you gave me about the Lewis Brothers and Arden Wilson. The police department will pursue it as soon as possible."

Wendy could tell Ross was having a hard time believing her story about "just dropping by" Merleece's house for a visit and forgetting to turn on her cell phone. Once a detective, always a detective. But there was more to it than that. She suspected it might be the growing intimacy between them. She couldn't swear to it, but it seemed like there were times he could almost read her mind now. It was a new and puzzling development. Did stirrings of love open a window to the brain? To the soul? Was it impossible to give that much of yourself to someone and not expose things that were routinely kept hidden? At any rate, Ross was voracious in his campaign to uncover information he believed she was withholding from him, and she was uncomfortable.

"You always have your cell on," he was telling her as they sat together on her sofa, holding hands. "You always answer my texts immediately."

"But I'm telling you the truth. I just put it in my purse and turned it off. And I texted you as soon as I realized my mistake."

"Yeah," Ross said, "*oops, didn't mean 2 shut u out.* That has to be the most humorless, un-Wendy-like message you've ever sent me. I think you've been doing some extra detective work I don't know about. If it would help the investigation, you need to tell me about it. Come on, now, this is Ross you're talking to. What really went on tonight? Are you by any chance biting off more than you can chew? Don't forget that someone who murders once won't hesitate to murder again. If nothing else, you've got to develop the habit of looking over your shoulder and growing a pair of eyes in the back of your head."

Wendy was growing impatient with him. Okay, maybe she had been somewhat careless in finding herself being held at gunpoint. But nothing terrible had come of it. She'd talked her way out of it. From her viewpoint, Ross was being a little too solicitous. "Don't patronize me. I thought we were beyond that. Look, what does it matter how Merleece and I got together this evening? I have a lead for you, and you need to act on it right away."

"Why didn't you say so? That's different, then. You shouldn't have made me squeeze it out of you like that."

"You were in the middle of a tantrum about texts," she told him, managing to crack a smile. "I couldn't get a word in edgewise. So are you ready to hear what Merleece said she saw?"

"Shoot."

Then she told him about the Lewis Brothers and Arden Wilson huddling at the gardening shed, followed by spotting Arden having lunch with Crystal Forrest at the Toast of Rosalie. Ross couldn't help but pump his fist. "These may be the breaks we needed to bring this home," he said.

"I admit they're new leads. But do you think Arden Wilson is capable of murder for hire? Would he be that desperate for extra money? Merleece says he was well-paid by Miz Liddie for keeping her gardens in tip-top shape."

"Don't overthink it too much. It's all well and good for you to play devil's advocate here," Ross said. "But those Lewis Brothers left a real bad taste in my mouth last time. I'm kinda looking forward to getting another whack at 'em. This gives me the opportunity, and I can ask them about Miz Crystal, too."

"Good. Glad I could help," she said. "Meanwhile, are you in the mood for eating in or out? The night is still young."

Ross leaned in and kissed her hungrily. "First things first."

She let her hand roam aggressively through the hair on the

back of his head as she returned his passion. "Yes, I'm all for working up an appetite."

There was a small part of her, however, that honestly wondered if she was doing the right thing by keeping the news about Hyram Maxique from him. Was she putting herself—or even Ross—in danger?

CHAPTER 15

Ross had chosen to break up the Lewis Brothers' obfuscation act in the interrogation room down at the station the next morning. It had not escaped him that they had frequently made eye contact and signaled each other with specific body language while he was interviewing them in their condo. Now, he would have them on his turf separately, one-on-one, and that might very well tell the tale. He further decided that Charley would go first. The one with the huge scar on his forehead and the crooked nose would be the easier mark, he reasoned.

"So it's come to our attention that you and your brother were having a nice little visit a while back with Arden Wilson in the vicinity of the gardening shed. I seem to remember that the two of you said you went to a couple of parties at Miz Liddie's but nothing more. Or was it that you had a coupla beers with Arden one time?"

As Ross had predicted, Charley became extraordinarily ill at ease, shifting his weight from side to side in his chair. "I can't remember every little thing that happened over the years. But, yeah, I remember having a beer or two with Arden Wilson. What if I did? What if my brother did?"

"Out by the gardening shed?"

Charley looked around the room as if desperately searching for his brother's face as he had done so often in their condo interview. But he was on his own now and eventually returned to Ross's stare and unsettling smile. "I dunno. I forget. It may have been out there."

"Could your brother have been there, too?"

"Could have."

"What were y'all talking about? Do you remember?"

Charley ran his index finger up and down the bridge of his nose as if trying to straighten it out, and Ross knew instinctively that whatever came out of his mouth next would most certainly be a lie. "Just stuff. Shootin' the bull, you know. Guys do it all the time."

"We were told by a reliable source that the three of you went into the gardening shed together," Ross said.

"Sounds to me like someone was spyin' on us. Who cares if we went into the gardening shed for a few minutes?" Charley told him.

"Your hardworking Rosalie Police Department cares for one," Ross said. "For instance, we would like to know if the subject of potassium cyanide came up during the conversation inside the gardening shed."

Charley went from uncomfortable to indignant in a flash. "It most certainly did not. Why should it?"

"Did any money change hands, by any chance?"

That seemed to shut Charley up entirely.

"You're not gonna answer the question?"

"All I'm gonna tell ya is that Beau said if I was unsure about anything, not to say a word. He said we'd get a lawyer if we needed to."

Ross raised an eyebrow but otherwise seemed completely unperturbed. "In that case it looks like your brother is calling the shots, and I need to speak with him."

"Be my guest. I don't know what you're gettin' at with all this, Mr. Rierson, but my brother and I have nothing to hide. We did not like our mother, but we did not kill her, and he'll tell you the same thing."

"I'll certainly ask him."

"You do that."

Beau Lewis and his middle-aged, yet still chiseled, features were making a grand art of scoffing at Charley's runaround. "You have to understand about my brother. Ever since he had that bad wreck, he's been unsure of himself. He's never really come back from it all the way. He doesn't have the confidence he used to have, including the golden touch with the pretty ladies. He'll say anything to get the pressure off him on most any subject these days."

"Did you tell him you thought the two of you should lawyer up?"

Beau distorted his handsome face for a few seconds. "Kinda. What I mainly told him was not to act like he was guilty."

"Afraid he didn't pull that one off."

Beau's laugh was slightly contemptuous. "Charley's not capable of plotting things, if that's what you're implying. He's a follower, and I'm the one he follows. It's always been like that, ever since we were little boys. Hey, what are big brothers supposed to be for?"

"I figured that out about your brother," Ross said. "So tell me. What did you and Charley and Arden Wilson talk about out there in Miz Liddie's gardening shed that particular day?"

Beau looked perfectly blank. "What day was that? Do you have anything more specific to clue me in with?"

"Don't know the specific date, but it would have been during the past couple of weeks," Ross said. "You were spotted from the window of Miz Liddie's kitchen discussing something both inside and outside the gardening shed."

"I gather by your intensity and all those lines in your forehead that you think this might have something to do with those Grand Slam Murders, is that it?"

Ross nodded. "We're looking into the possibility. But I'm here to get your side of the story."

"Well, there's nothing to look into. The fact is that Charley and I needed Arden's help and quickly, and we paid him good money for that help."

Ross's pulse quickened. Beau Lewis couldn't be that brazen and stupid. "What kind of help was it?"

Beau inflated his manly chest, looking supremely confident. "Mr. Rierson, I'm sure you recall your visit to our condo."

"Of course. The Playboy Mansion lives."

"Very funny. But do you recall our yard when you were walking up to the front door?"

Ross reflected as random images came back to him piecemeal. Brown grass. Dead plants. An eyesore for the ages—anything but a showplace. "It was in pretty bad shape, if that's what you're referring to."

"Exactly. It's never been one of our priorities, and the Condo Covenant Committee has been on our butts to do something about it for a while now. They've been threatening a heavy fine because some of the neighbors have been complaining. The busybodies that put on airs, you understand. So we went to talk to Arden Wilson about sprucing us up. Everybody knows Miz Liddie's gardens are the most spectacular in Rosalie, and Arden is the reason. We paid him a good little chunk of change to get our yard up to code so the committee would get off our case."

"You paid him in advance?"

"Yes. Why not?"

"So when is he going to do the work?" Ross said. "He hasn't done it yet, according to what I saw recently."

"Soon," Beau said. "Arden says certain things have to be planted at just the right time. He must know what he's talking about judging by his work. Everyone in Rosalie knows that he's the man."

"So this is all about Arden Wilson having a green thumb, then. All very aboveboard, I take it?"

"You got it." Beau lifted his chin and flashed his most predatory smile. "If I didn't know better, Mr. Rierson, I'd say you looked downright disappointed. Did I just bust your pet theory? That Charley and I had paid Arden to poison my mother, saddling Miz Liddie's cook with the blame? Is that how you wanted it to go down? Maybe you just better think again."

"We have to consider all angles, Mr. Lewis. Meanwhile, you've just presented me with a story that explains everything neatly, but that doesn't mean it might not have some holes."

"Easy enough to verify it with the committee and Arden Wilson. That's our ace in the hole."

"Believe me, that's next on my agenda," Ross said. "And by the way, you seemed a little too happy that my theory was busted. Maybe even relieved?"

"Now, Mr. Rierson. Be a good sport. Keep it up, and I'll have to get my lawyer on the case. Don't quote me, but I'm pretty sure he'll tell me that you won't hear a peep outta me and Charley from now on."

So here Ross was, back with Arden Wilson and his hipster, deadpan, dead butterfly persona, and he didn't like the man any more the second time around than he had the first. It was Arden's conspicuous lack of respect for authority that annoyed him more than anything else. There was a part of Ross that eagerly relished the prospect of Arden being the culprit, for whatever reason, on behalf of whatever other party or even himself. Yet it had been his experience as a detective that it often didn't work that way. The most obnoxious suspect was not always the guilty one. Sometimes the most attractive persons of interest—female or male—were the ones who had done the deed. So it remained important not to jump to conclusions or lose objectivity throughout the investigation.

"I was intrigued as to why you would have me come in again," Arden was saying to Ross in the interrogation room, fidgeting with his man-bun as if he had much better things to do than suffer the police. "But I never thought it would be because of the Lewis Brothers."

"And why is that?"

"They're such deadbeats."

"So their check bounced?"

"What check? They paid me in cash for services rendered."

Ross looked supremely smug. "So you admit they paid you for something. And no paper trail. Smart."

"Come again?"

"What services were rendered?"

Arden remained unflappable, even sounding bored. "They hired me to green up their front yard not too long ago. I haven't gotten around to it yet because I've had trouble getting some good St. Augustine sod in. I have to order the stuff from a nursery over in Alexandria, Louisiana. Of course they came to the right person to do it. It was either pay me or pay a fine to their Covenant Committee. They were between the old rock and the hard place."

Ross leaned forward, putting both hands on the table and then backing off in one smooth motion. "A convenient explanation. Both you and the Lewis Brothers definitely got your stories straight. But let me propose something else to you. Let's say they came to you and asked you to find a way to off their mother because she was frittering away their inheritance. They paid you handsomely to do it. You stirred the potassium cyanide into the sugar bowl whenever you found a moment, knowing Merleece would take the blame. You made sure you were there to witness her actually fixing up the coffee to make the case against her even more open-and-shut. So, how did it feel to take out four people at once with that move? Did that make you feel all-powerful? It makes you a monster in my book."

Nothing seemed to faze Arden, however. "Make up all the fantasies you want, but I took out no one. And I'm quite sure that it was Merleece who saw me and the Lewis Brothers from the kitchen window. Who else could have? Seems like she's trying to divert attention from herself. But we were there for a legit purpose, conducting legit business, and you're dreaming if you think you can pin this on me. Or them. We're all three of us telling you the truth, and you can write it down in your book."

"That remains to be seen."

"Face it," Arden said. "This has been Merleece's doing all along. You cops amuse me. There the solution is right under your nose. All the evidence and motive and opportunity you need, and you keep beating around the bush instead of issuing a warrant for her arrest."

"That's our job, not yours, sir," Ross said. "But it's quite clear that accusing Merleece has been a priority of yours from the beginning."

This time there was indignation in Arden's tone. "Hey, I was there watching it all happen. I didn't make anything up. And by the way, where do you cops get off thinking I would be willing to murder the most lucrative employer I've ever had? I worked very hard to make Miz Liddie's gardens the showplace of Rosalie, and I achieved that. Everyone admits it. When I rushed into her dining room that afternoon and saw her and her friends in the throes of death, I was in shock. I could barely call 9-1-1. You're barking up the wrong tree thinking I was behind this in any way. Yes, it's true, Merleece and I didn't get along at all, but I did not frame her for murder. So you're just gonna have to look elsewhere for your solution, Mr. Rierson. You might not like the fact that I take out butterflies, but I don't take out human beings, and that's my final word on the subject."

"Nice little speech," Ross said with slow-motion, mock applause. "So, now that Miz Liddie is no longer around, whose gardens will you be tending?"

"That's already set," Arden said, as if anticipating the question. "Miz Crystal Forrest has employed me to make her gardens the equal of Miz Liddie's and even more spectacular than that. She wants to take a back seat to no one in Rosalie in that regard. She says she'll stop at nothing to be the envy of the town."

"Stop at nothing. That's an interesting way to put it, don't you think? That was also a pretty quick hire Miz Crystal made. Any chance the two of you had a deal in the works beforehand? Maybe Miz Crystal paid you to take out Miz Liddie."

"Man, you cops never stop, do you? That's a ridiculous accusation if I ever heard one," Arden said with a sneer. "The truth is, there was no provision made for me to continue upon Miz Liddie's death. Stella Markham told me my services would no longer be needed, so Miz Crystal and I met halfway. I told her my situation, and she readily offered me the position. It was all completely aboveboard. So the deal is I'm moving down Minor Street a few houses. Anyone who wants to compare my work doesn't have far to walk."

"Word on the street is that you've been wining and dining Miz Crystal. For instance, you were spotted having lunch at the Toast of Rosalie," Ross told him.

"So? You guys tailing me or something? Miz Crystal just wanted to take me to lunch to celebrate my coming on board as her gardener."

Ross moved on. "Why weren't your services required any longer at Don Jose's Retreat? Your reputation is impeccable."

Arden took his time and then stuttered anyway. "It . . . it beats me. You'd have to ask Stella Markham for the particulars on that one. All I know is Miz Stella said she will be moving into her mother's house to take care of it after the estate is finally settled, and she evidently has other plans for the gardens. She flat out told me that they did not include me. Maybe she wants to do it all herself. You figure it out. You're supposed to be the pro."

"Since you asked, I have a theory about that," Ross began, careful to keep the humor in his voice. "You and Miz Crystal sure did get chummy real fast. Try this on for size: if Miz Crystal couldn't pay her way into The Rosalie Bridge Club, perhaps she could steal Miz Liddie's gardener and have the best-looking gardens in town. There's still the real possibility that someone paid you to do the dirty work for them, since none of them left any DNA or fingerprints in the kitchen; let's see, we have an entire list that might have required your services: the Lewis Brothers, Miz Crystal, maybe even Miz Selena. All of them wanted Miz Liddie out of the way or to get revenge for one reason or another, and you had the means to do it for them stored away in that gardening shed."

Arden got right up in his face with his answer, appearing not the least bit anxious. "You turn up a paper trail for a transaction like that, and you've got me dead to rights, sir. But I know that if you had one, you'd have already arrested me, or Miz Crystal or the Lewis Brothers or whoever. Instead, the finger keeps pointin' to Merleece doin' it on her own without any help."

"Just keep doing me a favor and stick around," Ross told him. "We may yet turn out somethin' that nails you. Or somebody else who's been workin' with you."

After Arden had been dismissed, Ross tried his best to

make some sense of what he had just been told about the gardening scenarios. One wealthy lady dismissing him and another picking him up, both after four heinous murders had been committed. More importantly, what did either of those facts have to do with the poisonings, if anything? Was there to be no clear-cut answer to the crimes other than to arrest Merleece? After all, Judge Lahey's warrant at Harry Keller's behest would be issued anytime now.

CHAPTER 16

Wendy had made what some might have considered a curious decision. She would go back to the basics of bridge to help her with The Grand Slam Murders. Maybe it was because she was frustrated with the way the investigation was unfolding, clearing everyone except Merleece, the one person she was certain had not done the deed. Or maybe she just needed a mental vacation from the pressure of the questioning and the speculation and all that came with trying to figure out what had happened on that fateful day in Miz Liddie's house. And why it had happened. Besides, she had not been trained in the disciplines of law enforcement; hers had been no matriculation in the Rosalie Police Academy. She was strictly on her own in using whatever she thought would help her get the job done.

Then there was this. She had never lost sight of the notion that Miz Liddie had to be the starting point of both the investigation and the first feature story the *Citizen* was going to publish soon. That meant returning to the woman's love of the game of bridge, even if her love was somewhat of a manipulation of social standards. Impossibly high social standards.

So she turned on her computer in her cubicle at the *Citizen* for the first time that morning and started reading an online article on the rules of bridge. True, it was old hat. But what could it possibly hurt?

> The basics: four players, two teams . . . the team that won the auction called declarers, the team trying to defeat the contract called the defenders . . . thirteen, fourteen points needed to open in most cases . . . an ace counted four points, a king three, a queen two, and a jack one, length in a suit made it more valuable . . . a discussion of the minimum number of points needed to raise your partner's opening bid . . . sometimes six, sometimes seven . . . another about how many points were needed for game . . . less in minor suits, more in major suits . . . instructions on making sure all four suits were covered in a no-trump auction . . . a daunting introduction to the various conventions used to determine the feasibility of a slam, Little or Grand . . . asking for aces, asking for kings . . . what did it mean to be vulnerable . . . when to double a contract and when not to . . .

She ran through these many explanatory paragraphs in a perfunctory manner. She had all these technicalities down pat. That much her fledgling membership in The Rosalie Bridge Club had done for her. So what was she accomplishing, and what would Dalton Hemmings say if he knew she had abandoned that boring list of engagement announcements piled up in her in-box to amuse herself with the rules of a card game? Or even putting aside working on the first of the Gin Girls' features. The man had nearly had a cerebral hemorrhage when he discovered that a recently hired sportswriter in the newsroom had been watching porn on his monitor. Mighty damn short stay at the *Citizen* that was. He was fired on the spot.

After a while, Wendy realized it wasn't the rules of bridge she was after exactly. That was not the path of enlightenment she needed. She knew all the rules pretty well, even if she had not played long enough to call herself halfway competent and certainly not worthy of competition.

No, it suddenly came to her that there was something half-remembered she was trying to dig out of her brain. Something someone had said to her over the past few days when she had been interviewing and questioning and starting this sleuthing business up in earnest. But reading over the rules of bridge wasn't doing it for her. It wasn't making her remember that something she felt had a crucial bearing on the case. Something no one else had thought of. So what would draw it out of her?

Perhaps remembering who had said those words, that phrase, that sentence to her. Very well, then. Time to be methodical and make a list: Mini-profiles of all those whom either she or Ross had interviewed, including tidibts here and there her father, Bax, had contributed in various conversations.

Merleece Maxique—loyal servant who fixed up coffee with poisoned sugar
Stella Markham—well-organized, devoted daughter of Liddie Rose
Sherry Herrold—childlike, devoted daughter of Sicily Groves
Hyram Maxique—runaway son of Merleece with a bad reputation
Arden Wilson—bizarre butterfly collector and gardener with deadly chemicals
Selena Chalk—disgruntled restaurant owner, called out by the Gin Girls

Crystal Forrest—nouveau riche, wealthy resident, hell-bent on acceptance
Beau and Charley Lewis—immature, wealthy divorced men on the prowl
Peter Markham—Stella's ex, presumably an addict, though a pharmacist
Hermes Caliban—exercise guru and more to Hanna Lewis, one of the Gin Girls

Perhaps she was being naïve, but she was also certain one of those people, either directly or indirectly, had handed her the key to the crimes in some offhand remark. And once again, she was also convinced that whatever it was that had been said had something to do with bridge. For some reason, she decided to search her memory where the first four were concerned: Merleece, Stella, Sherry, and Hyram.

She went about it logically. Who had she spent the most time with, spoken with most often? Merleece, of course. Did the odds therefore favor revisiting conversations she had had with her first? She decided that they did. The next step was to connect conversations with Merleece about and to the game of bridge. The two of them had had more than a few in a casual way, mostly behind the scenes in the kitchen while the Gin Girls were trying to make their contracts or defeat those of their opponents. While they were busy playing out their hands and drinking their gin and gossiping and not having a care in the world. *Playing out their hands.* But they weren't playing out their hands the day they were murdered.

Something was shimmering tantalizingly on the surface of Wendy's brain. She almost had it at her disposal. Another second of concentration and it would be there in the palm of her hand to use. That phrase, those words, the person who had said it. It was all she needed to plow ahead.

A deep, phlegmy voice suddenly startled her, shattering her focus completely. "Miz Winchester?"

Whatever it was that was about to reveal itself to Wendy went *poof.* She could almost hear it sounding just like that in her head, and she quickly shut down the screen as Dalton Hemmings entered her cubicle. "Yes, Mr. Hemmings?"

"I've decided we'll be running the article on Miz Liddie this Friday. Have you done enough research to put it together for me so I can give it a read?"

Thinking on her feet, Wendy told him she had, but the truth was she had been neglecting her feature work for the investigation. She had not even written the first paragraph, so obsessed had she become with solving the murders herself.

"Good. Then I'll expect it on my desk tomorrow morning and we'll take it from there."

"Yes, sir. I'll have it for you."

As Hemmings walked away, she had to restrain herself from sticking her tongue out at him. The only thing that remained of the epiphany she was so desperate to achieve was the realization that it had been Merleece who had said something vital to her. She was certain of that much now. But she was going to have to find another level of concentration to return to that "aha" moment. And now she had this deadline looming. It was going to be difficult for her to play detective for a while. Damn Dalton Hemmings and his ill-timed entrances and exits!

It was around midmorning that L'il Jack Horner—fresh from his constant monitoring of the police scanner—popped up out of his cubicle and pulled another of his rare "I'm a real person with real emotions after all" stunts, playing to the entire newsroom. "Merleece Maxique has been arrested for the murders of the Gin Girls. And her son, Hyram Maxique, has been shot."

Wendy felt a mixture of adrenaline and fear surging through her as Jack continued all full of himself. "When they went to arrest her, it appears her son pulled a gun on the police, and they put a bullet in him."

Wendy hurried over to Jack's cubicle as her pulse continued to quicken. "Is he . . . is he dead?"

"What we know is that they have him on the way to the ER right now, according to this report."

The anxiety and guilt Wendy felt were palpable. If Hyram died, would she bear some of the responsibility? The information she'd just been given was sketchy. There was no guarantee he would survive. She had warned Hyram about his gun. Perhaps she had not emphasized enough the danger of waving a gun around when the police appeared. She was certain that was what had happened. And then there was the inescapable fact that she had withheld her knowledge of Hyram's presence in Rosalie from Ross and the police department, itself. Should she have told them? Was this truly on her? But Rosalie was not a police state. This was America. Ordinary people like Hyram had a right to show up and leave as they pleased without being reported to the authorities. Unless there was a warrant for their arrest.

Standing in his office doorframe, Dalton Hemmings was the first to say out loud what most everyone in the newsroom was thinking. "Well, I guess they've finally got their man—or woman, in this case. Jack, you and Oscar run down to the station, get an official statement from Captain Winchester if there's a press conference in the works, and interview the arresting officers."

"Will do," Manning said, doing an unconscious parody of a salute for the benefit of his boss.

Wendy was struggling mightily to hold her tongue. In a perfect world she ought to be the one handling the story, but she hadn't earned her wings yet. She had never felt such frustration in her life. But at least she did have the advantage of being Captain Winchester's daughter. A quick phone call from her cubicle would put her in the thick of things, even if Jack Manning would be the one getting the byline.

She would have been better off not getting through to her father at that particular time, however. His was an unexpectedly blunt, harried demeanor.

"I'm up to my eyeballs in work right now," he told her. "But, yes, Merleece is in jail, and her son is at the ER, and I won't pull any punches with you. Ross was the arresting officer."

The last sentence exploded like a bomb in her brain, and for a while she seemed to have lost the ability to form words.

"I've got to get busy, sweetie," Bax said next. "Got a big presser to organize pronto."

"Wait. Why was Ross the arresting officer?" Wendy said, recovering her faculties. "Why couldn't someone else have done it?"

"Because he was the lead detective. Judge Lahey issued the warrant on behalf of Harry Keller, and that was that. It was out of our hands. Listen, sweetie, I've really got to run."

"But please tell me Ross didn't shoot Hyram Maxique," Wendy said, continuing to fight back the panic that was overwhelming her.

"No, Ross didn't do the shooting. It was Ronald Pike, his partner. They haven't told us anything more about Hyram yet. Talk to you later. Gotta go."

And with that, Wendy was disconnected.

A half hour later, Wendy used her lunch hour to make a date with Ross at the Bluff City Bistro, even though she wasn't the least bit hungry. With Bax's hastily called press conference to announce the arrest out of the way, he had agreed, as he was looking forward to ordering his usual at their favorite table by one of the windows overlooking the river.

"Hyram's doing fine," he had told Wendy right after sitting down. "He just got winged."

"That's a relief."

"Bax should have told you everything over the phone about Merleece," he said, right after the waitress had walked away with the menus and their orders. "I asked to be the one to arrest her and read her rights to her once the arrest warrant was issued."

"Daddy said it was because you're the lead detective. I thought you didn't have a choice."

He unfolded his napkin and laid it in his lap. "Partly. But I wanted to be the one to tell her what was happening. I didn't want it to come from a stranger on the force. I've spent more than a little time with her these past few days, and I wanted to make it as easy on her as possible. I know that might not sound like much, but I wanted to do what I could."

"And how *did* she take it? Was she hysterical?"

Ross cringed. "No, she closed her eyes and swallowed hard, but she told me she understood. She knew it wasn't personal with me. She even said she'd been expecting it to happen and that she knew it was just a matter of time. At that point I thought it was going about as well as it could. But then her son came rushing into the room out of nowhere and pulled a gun out of his pocket, screaming, 'Nobody's takin' my Mama to jail,' and that's when Ronald took him down with a bullet to the arm. He's always had the quickest trigger finger on the force. It all happened so fast, it was like a reflex action on Ronald's part. He didn't know whether the guy was going to fire or not. You don't have time to lose in situations like that. If you hesitate, you're dead. But I can tell you this. Ronald knows how to shoot not to kill better than anybody else I know. He wasn't aiming to take the guy out—just to take out the threat."

Being a police officer's daughter, Wendy knew what came next. "Thank God, Hyram's okay, though. Was Merleece able to post bail?"

"No."

"What about a lawyer?"

"Howard Usry has been appointed."

"And the arraignment?"

"In two days."

Wendy caught a glimpse of a long barge tow struggling against the current in the distance and let it distract her for a moment or two. It was confession time. "I've come to realize that I'm really not cut out to be in law enforcement."

"Well, the fact is, you aren't in it, of course. But I didn't realize you ever wanted to be."

"No, I didn't. But I've been trying my hand at this amateur sleuthing thing, and it looks like it involves some of the same things."

"You don't have to have a gun to solve crimes, if that's what you're getting at," Ross said.

"I was referring more to my judgment calls," she told him. Then she explained the sequence of events starting at the gas station that had brought about her last visit with Merleece and how she had tried to convince Hyram to keep a low profile and keep his head no matter what happened.

"So you knew he was in town and didn't mention it to me. You're right. That wasn't the best decision you could've made. That was valuable information we needed to have."

"That's what I meant by my judgment calls," she said. "Would it have made a difference if I had mentioned it?"

Ross pressed his lips together for a brief second and took a deep breath for good measure. "It might have. We would have known he was there and that he was armed. We might have been better prepared to handle the situation, and Hyram might not be in the ER right now having a bullet removed from his bicep. Or, God forbid, even dead."

Wendy was obviously avoiding his gaze. "Are you angry with me? Please say you're not angry."

Ross's familiar smile slowly returned. "Only if you're not angry with me for arresting Merleece and reading her rights to her. It seems to me we've both been put in awkward positions, but it doesn't mean we're bad people."

Wendy felt an enormous sense of relief. "Thanks for saying that." She took a moment to squeeze the lemon floating atop her water glass and then stir it in. "This all still leaves a terrible taste in my mouth, Ross. I know deep down that Merleece is innocent, but it looks like she's going to take the fall for this. Harry Keller and his ilk must be on cloud nine."

"Bax and I and some of the other detectives have been over and over this, though. We have no proof anyone else did it themselves or had someone else do it for them. Plenty of theories, plenty of suspects, but Merleece is the only one who lines up according to the evidence and the DNA. Follow the evidence is pretty much the mantra of law enforcement, and that's what Harry Keller is doing. It's almost gotten to where our hands are tied."

Wendy took a sip of her water and made a sour lemon face. "Then we're all looking at the evidence wrong. Somehow, one of us has got to go beyond the circumstantial and get at the right angle. This morning, I almost had it."

"Almost?"

The frustration clearly showed in the lines across Wendy's forehead. "I was doing some mental gymnastics at my cubicle at the paper, and I had finally hooked up Merleece with something she had said to me about the ladies playing bridge. A second or two more and I would have made the actual connection, but then Hemmings comes along with his nasty, throat-clearing ways and throws me off completely. He has a gift for doing that."

"Do you think you can get it back?"

"I can try," she said.

Ross's burger with fries and Wendy's Caesar salad arrived a moment later, and for a while they ate in silence. Then Selena Chalk lumbered over to their table with a worried look on her face.

"Is it true they've arrested Miz Liddie's housekeeper for the murders?" she said. "Everyone who's come in for lunch has been buzzing about it. You can't keep anything quiet for long in this town."

Ross downed a couple of ketchup-covered fries with his fingers and said, "No, *they* didn't arrest Merleece Maxique. *I* did, Miz Chalk."

"Then you think she's guilty?"

Ross shook his head. "It doesn't matter what I think. Judge Lahey issued the warrant, there's enough evidence for probable cause, and I wanted to be the one to break the news to Merleece."

Selena leaned down, lowering her voice and adding another chin to her wide, fleshy face. "Well, just so you know, I don't think she did it, even though I'm sure Miz Liddie and her friends probably gave her cause. They gave lots of people cause. I know what I'm talking about. I'm still fighting hard to keep my head above water with the restaurant after that snarky review they got published in the paper. The worst of it is, they exaggerated something awful about the food and the service. Nothing like they described ever happened to them here."

Wendy decided to chime in. "I'm just curious, Miz Selena. Tell me. Who do *you* think did it?"

"I couldn't say for sure," Selena said. "But I'm a great fan of mysteries. I read them all the time. It's always the person you least suspect. So that would automatically leave out Miz Liddie's loyal housekeeper to my way of thinking. You just mull that over for a while and see where it leads you." Then Selena changed the subject. "How's your food, folks? You know I always have to ask."

"Hits the spot, as usual, Miz Selena," Ross told her, giving her a ketchup-smeared thumbs-up.

"Couldn't be more delicious," Wendy said, as Selena nodded and then turned to head back to the kitchen with a satisfied smile.

When she was out of earshot, Ross said, "I suppose you know you can't go by what Miz Selena just said. I mean, that line about the person you least suspect. That's like saying the butler did it. It's a cliché. It's the evidence that leads you where you want to go."

As Wendy was finishing up her salad, she began seriously contemplating what Ross had just said. Perhaps he was right. After all, the *least likely* person to have committed the murders had to be Sherry Groves Herrold. Why would she want to kill her mother, Miz Sicily? Or the other ladies? Even after Ross had described her as "an emotional mess." Had she somehow fallen off the edge of the earth and done the utterly unthinkable?

And then the next *least likely* was surely Stella Markham. Obviously devoted to her mother and the other Gin Girls, as well as a loyal alternate in The Rosalie Bridge Club whose company she, herself, had enjoyed and appreciated, it made no sense that she would want to take all of them out. She had them all up on pedestals. What could possibly have been her motive? It made no sense.

What did make sense to Wendy, however, was to take a break from all the murder speculation and get cracking on the pressing assignment Dalton Hemmings had delivered to her in person a couple of hours ago. Time to write glowingly about Liddie Langston Rose and her family—with more than a few references to the Gin Girls and The Rosalie Bridge Club. Time for that tribute the entire town of Rosalie had been anticipating while the murders were still fresh in their minds.

After hurrying through the annoying pile of engagement announcements she had been ignoring for too long, Wendy devoted the rest of the afternoon at her cubicle to putting together a rough draft of the feature on Liddie Langston Rose. It was turning out to be not nearly as difficult as she thought it would be. The family biographies that Stella Markham had helpfully provided her were coming in handy in creating a skeleton of an article. Even putting flesh on the bones was turning out to be enjoyable. But she had one caveat to consider. Should she or should she not include that little episode Sherry Herrold had described about Miz Sicily and Miz Bethany climbing on top of the sorority house roof at Ole Miss and drinking themselves into a school spirit stupor? An episode that had led to their dismissal from college. Or the one about Miz Liddie ordering up spiking the punch at the Baptist Student Union party?

Well, why not? It definitely reflected who all of them were as the hell-raising Gin Girls of Rosalie, Mississippi, whose citizens were hardly shy and silent about their love affair with liquor. It was said that if you hadn't had a drink shoved into your hands at some social gathering by the time you were fifteen in the town of Rosalie, your parents or grandparents or aunts and uncles were all greatly remiss in their child-rearing practices. In fact, Wendy fully expected that excluding such amusing anecdotes throughout the series would have most Rosalieans up in arms, coming after her with torches and pitchforks. Some dry, stuffy summary of the lives of the Gin Girls was certainly not in order.

Shortly before four o'clock, Wendy walked into Dalton Hemmings's office and handed over what she considered to be a remarkably polished effort considering the short time she had devoted to it.

"Here's the piece on Miz Liddie as requested," Wendy said, obviously quite pleased with herself.

Instead of picking it up from his desk and tearing into it, however, Hemmings said, "There's been a slight change of priorities. Stella Markham called about an hour ago and wanted to know how you were coming along with the feature on her mother. I told her it just so happened you were winding it up right about now and that we had it scheduled for publication tomorrow."

Wendy saw no reason to do anything but shrug with a smile on her face. "Great. She should be pleased, then."

"There's a little more to it, though. She asked me if it would be okay if you brought it out for her to look over before it went to press. I told her you'd be more than happy to do just that."

Then Wendy remembered how Hemmings had admitting to buckling under to Miz Liddie and her social coverage demands over the years. This was obviously an extension of that very generous policy. "Okay, I'll take it out there. You want me to do it right now?"

"Please. Let's get this ready to roll."

"What if she decides she wants changes? Are you going to give her editorial carte blanche?"

Wendy wasn't quite sure she was okay with that part. She didn't think her article needed a thing in the way of revision. It might even qualify for her first minor masterpiece. After all, this would be her first assignment of any substance since being hired. Hemmings had never even considered editing any of her puff-piece, social tidbits. Really, there was nothing to edit. Engagements and weddings and showers were straightforward facts with a few "baby's breath and bouquet" garnishes for those precious touches that never failed to please the people who cut them out and put them in their scrapbooks.

"I'll be the final judge of what goes in the paper, as I don't have to remind you," he told her. She felt like she was being scolded once again. What else was new with being a female under his authority?

Wendy was sitting across from Stella Markham in her cozy breakfast nook surrounded by cheerful sunflower wallpaper, studying her face closely as she was reading the feature article on Miz Liddie, the Langstons, and the Roses. It was a roller-coaster ride of interpretation with Stella moving her lips while frowning here and grinning there. It was quite evident that an in-depth and perhaps controversial discussion would soon follow, and Stella did not disappoint.

"I admit you got all the facts straight," Stella said. "I certainly can't criticize you for that."

Wendy steeled herself for the *but.*

"But," Stella continued on cue, tapping her index finger on the table for emphasis, "I wonder if you needed to go into quite so much detail about Sherry Herrold's anecdote on her mother and Miz Bethany climbing up on the sorority roof and getting drunk. Not to mention getting expelled from Ole Miss. And are you really going to include that story about spiking the punch at the Baptist Student Union to-do? I mean, really. Considering the unthinkable way my mother and her friends left this world at the hands of Merleece Maxique, it's my opinion that a more respectful approach is needed here. I told you Merleece was up to something, and that she was the one who did it all along, if I recall. Her arrest doesn't surprise me one bit. I also told you that Mother suspected she and Arden might be up to something all along."

Well, there it was—the controversy Wendy had anticipated. Something ached in the pit of her stomach as the words sunk in.

"Yes, you've suggested that to me more than once," Wendy said. "And your mother's finger-pointing proved she suspected something to the end, right?"

"Exactly," Stella said. "It just looks like Merleece was the one who got caught. But back to your story about Miz Sicily and Miz Bethany drinking and singing like drunken sailors on the sorority roof and the business about the Baptist Student Union. I told Sherry to restrain herself when she talked to you about our mothers' wild and woolly Ole Miss days, but she never listens to me. She's like a naughty, spoiled child, really. She's always seeking the spotlight in her pathetic little way. I don't know how she ever grew up into a responsible adult. As long as she can do her incessant shopping and playing like a little child at recess, I suppose she's as happy as she can be."

"I don't think the anecdotes are disrespectful at all," Wendy said, ignoring the comments on Sherry. "They're definitely humorous—or at least typical of collegiate foolishness. Which one of us hasn't been guilty of that? I remember a few stupid moves I made at Mizzou. And most Rosalieans already know why Miz Sicily and Miz Bethany were expelled. I think this just puts it in perspective and makes them more lovable. And, anyway, wasn't the motto of the Gin Girls to 'raise hell' just about everywhere? Including Heaven? I think these stories fit that motto perfectly."

"Of course, but it's a matter of emphasis," Stella said. "So why not spend more time on the charitable activities that benefited all of Rosalie? I firmly believe we should showcase the noble side of the Gin Girls."

"I mentioned their charities."

"In passing. It seems to me you were much more interested in devoting many more paragraphs to the roof incident and the spiking the punch episode. As you say, we all did our foolish, regrettable things in college. It comes with the territory. But why call excessive attention to these foolish choices years later? You don't seem to realize what all Mother was going through—"

Stella came to an abrupt pause, and something came over her suddenly. It was there in her eyes. Was it confusion? Or more like fear? After a rush of breath, she appeared to recover. "I'm sorry. I got a bit overdramatic there. This has been . . . a very difficult time for me as you can imagine. I have to see that things are done right."

For the first time since they had met over six months ago at one of Miz Liddie's bridge luncheons, Wendy realized how much alike Stella Markham and Liddie Rose really were. Not physically, of course, but both liked to control things, telling people what to do and when to do them. Stella's playful side had emerged during her turns as a bridge alternate, but it had been completely overridden now by a domineering streak that showed no signs of retreating anytime soon.

"I'm also willing to bet that Dalton Hemmings will want to cut out all that risqué business you went on so long about in the article. His has always been a conservative newspaper," Stella continued. "Mother always swore by him, and he never let her down."

"I would certainly agree with that. Sometimes I think he was around when Gutenberg invented the printing press," Wendy said, not caring whether Stella found the remark humorous or not.

In fact, she did not, giving Wendy a hurried glance that was both superior and skeptical. "Don't you think it's a bit reckless to go around making fun of your boss? He might take a dim view of it."

"I have nothing to lose, actually. I think I've offended His Hemmings-ness about a thousand times since I started working there. If he really minded, he would have fired me a long time ago. You see, he and Daddy are great friends, so I do have that as a safety net."

Rising from the table to signal that their conversation had ended, Stella handed back the article Wendy had printed out for her and offered her hand once again. The gesture was polite but on the cold side. "That's fortunate for you. At any rate, I do hope you'll express my concerns to Mr. Hemmings. You should put your best foot forward when you do these pieces on the Gin Girls. I'm sure their many admirers around Rosalie will thank you."

"I promise you I will do my very best writing," Wendy told her, enjoying the cryptic nature of her comment. Then at the last second she remembered something that had emerged in one of her discussions with Ross. "I was just wondering, Stella—has your mother's will been read yet? I was thinking about it now that Merleece has been arrested."

Stella did not hesitate, now fully in control of herself once again. "It has not. These things take a little time, you know. But I can assure you that all the plotting Merleece did will be for naught, no matter how much my mother left her. I think it's quite clear that justice will be served in the end, as it should be. I have no idea why you want to defend Merleece the way you appear to be doing."

"Merleece is still innocent until proven guilty. She'll have her day in court like everyone else."

"I'm sure she won't prevail," Stella said. "I assure you my mother knew what was going on."

CHAPTER 17

Wendy and Dalton Hemmings were going round and round in his office about the content of the feature on Miz Liddie. She was determined to stand her ground, particularly after she learned that Stella Markham had called up Hemmings right after she had left and complained about certain passages to him. Apparently, she intended to leave nothing to chance, making a huge fuss.

"But why go out of our way to offend Miz Stella and some of the others out there?" Hemmings was saying as they faced off across his desk. They had now been at it for a good half hour, well past her shift, which had ended at six, and neither of them appeared to be giving an inch.

"You said yourself right after reading the article that you thought it was the best I'd ever written," Wendy said.

"I did say that. But there's nothing wrong with balance, Miz Winchester. I've always been an advocate of that."

Though already weary of arguing with him, Wendy drew herself up and tried again to prevail. "The balance is already there, Mr. Hemmings. I spent several paragraphs on the charity work of the Gin Girls, even though Stella Markham described it as merely passing it all over when I talked to her today. It is no such thing. It's just that there's not much interest in stating such things, however noble they are. They're just dry facts. Why not include a few humorous anecdotes to bring the ladies to life a little more? Why would that be such a bad thing?"

He leaned back in his chair and made a teepee of his fingers, the impatience clearly showing on his face. "I clearly recall telling you right after I approved this assignment that you would have to tread carefully. We simply have to err on the side of the families who are going through this awful trauma. We can't publish everything over their objections. If you can't understand that, then you're no journalist, but I firmly believe you are."

Wendy conceded his point with a reluctant sigh. "I do understand it. I'm just wondering if you think the piece is a bit too obituary-like without the humorous asides."

"Obits can have their lighter side, but we'll take our chances with the way things are, Miz Winchester. Especially since Miz Stella has made such a big deal out of it. She called both before and after you visited with her. This clearly means a great deal to her, and we do want to get this right."

Wendy knew then that she had lost the battle. There would be nothing colorful or amusing about her work—at least not this time around. Dalton Hemmings would edit out anything he considered remotely inappropriate, and the article would go to press as a straightforward summary of Miz Liddie's life with no asides to distract from the pristine image Stella Markham was bound and determined to protect. In effect, someone else would end up writing the guts of the article, taking away any charm it might have possessed.

"What about the other articles?" Wendy said. "Will there be nothing lighthearted about them, either?"

Hemmings leaned forward again, his tone not quite as resolute. "That will depend on what the other families want.

They may not hold us to such stringent standards. But let's worry about that when we get there. Let's get this one out there and see how the public reacts."

Wendy retreated to her cubicle feeling as if some force were pushing down hard upon her, trying to nail her in place to the ground. A couple of engagements had appeared late in her in-box, and for some reason, she decided to stay even later and get them done. She did not want such uninspiring busy work to be waiting for her when she returned the next day. Everything that had been buoying her up lately seemed to have abandoned her—keeping Merleece out of jail and creating a phenomenally entertaining piece on Miz Liddie—and she had the sense of sinking to the bottom of her career. It was all falling apart.

By the time Wendy reached her car after leaving the building, it was nearly dusk. It had also started to rain, causing her to frown at the low, gray sky above her. Where had that come from? There was no precipitation in the forecast. It wasn't particularly hard rain, more like a late-spring shower, but it made her slide into her front seat hurriedly, somewhat oblivious to her surroundings. She was completely preoccupied with the defeat she had just suffered at the hands of Dalton Hemmings as she made her way through town onto Lower Kingston Road toward her bungalow. It began to rain harder, but she was so distracted that she did not slow down. The threat of hydroplaning had not entered her mind.

Instead, as it grew darker by the minute, she returned to that elusive piece of the puzzle in her head that had been within her grasp before Dalton Hemmings had interrupted her train of thought with his annoying, phlegmy noises. What was it Merleece had said that had tantalized her so? That had made her think that the solution was near at hand if only she concentrated hard enough.

She felt it bubbling up again. She was all around it. Something about the ladies playing out their hands. Why did that resonate with her so much? A vicious crack of thunder made her heart nearly skip a beat, and she almost lost control of the steering wheel for a second. But she steadied herself, and then—as if the thunder and the spurt of adrenaline it had produced behind her sternum had been the catalysts—what she had been searching for so determinedly came to her at last.

Merleece had summed it up precisely when she had said something to the effect that *the ladies had not gotten to play out their hands this time.*

They had died before they had gotten the chance to do so. That practice hand that was going to help them win the duplicate title in Jackson had never happened.

What was the significance of that? What difference could that possibly make in the scheme of things? Wendy started to play *what-if*? If Merleece were truly innocent, then there was another remote, nearly insane explanation that might make sense, that might make all the pieces of the puzzle fit. How had she stumbled upon such an outrageous idea? Was her detective muse working overtime? Did she truly have a gift that was now being put to the test? Or was she just out of her mind?

No, what she had suddenly envisioned could not possibly be. It was a solution that made Wendy catch her breath as it began to take form in hideous fashion. More than ever, she thought that she, Ross, Bax, and the rest of the police department had all been looking at everything and everyone—Merleece, Arden Wilson, the Lewis Brothers, Selena Chalk, Crystal Forrest, Stella and Peter Markham, and Hermes Caliban—as if they were all reflections in a mirror. On what side lay the reality? And there was that word again: *mirror.* Another soon followed: *makeup.*

But that had all been resolved. Or had it? There was also

the phrase *missing bridge games* to consider. Stella Markham had attributed it all to her mother's rosacea and then had substituted for her in the club from time to time. Attributed it to her mother's vanity. That seemed to make sense on the surface. But more than one person Wendy had interviewed had described Miz Liddie as "almost being another person in the same body" or some such conceit. Stella had mentioned that Wendy *didn't realize everything that her mother had been going through*—. Could this possibly be about more than rosacea?

Wendy returned to her off-the-wall scenario that was giving her chill bumps. She felt just like the seven-year-old who had pointed to the right pieces of her parents' jigsaw puzzle without an explanation in sight. That island of knowledge, that remarkable gift for problem solving beyond the ordinary had kicked in. But the wanton, bizarre scheme she was considering needed proof. And even with the proof secured, what was the reason behind it?

Perhaps she should start with the basics, overlooking nothing. Where were the hands the ladies were supposed to have played? That Grand Slam contract they were supposed to tackle. They had been classified as evidence from the start and were neatly and individually wrapped and bagged at the police station, Ross had told her. That had been a very smart move, but then there had been no follow-through as far as she knew. She must ask Ross to examine the hands closely on her behalf—on behalf of the investigation—as quickly as possible. Not for fingerprints. Not for DNA. That had been done. The only fingerprints found were those of Miz Liddie, which made sense considering that she had dealt out the four hands. Wendy was willing to bet now that this was the key; this was the tidbit they had all been ignoring or glossing over without thinking it through. The examination of the hands must happen before the arraignment. There was precious little time to lose, and she must get Ross on this right away.

Then, two other phrases popped up to excite her further: *attention to detail* and *brand-new decks*. Together, they were two more pieces of the puzzle.

Suddenly, Wendy was aware of an unbearable brightness—a spotlight on her brain—that rudely brought her out of her speculations. Out of nowhere, a car had begun tailgating her with its high beams blinding her. Worse—they were halogen lights, uncomfortably annoying, sometimes even blinding—to all drivers even on low beam.

Had the car been there all along, not tailing her quite so closely, then gradually creeping up until it was practically on her bumper? Had her mental detective work blotted out everything else passing by or behind her so that only now she was noticing what was upon her? She tried to adjust the rearview mirror to lessen the glare, but it scarcely helped. Whoever was behind her surely knew how uncomfortable they were making her, how dangerous it all was with the rain coming down harder and harder. Then whoever was threatening her began to lean on the horn. The effect was maddening at first, then ear-piercing, and finally frightening to the marrow of her bone.

It came to Wendy with a chilling clarity that whoever was behind her was trying to kill her, to drive her off the road to her death down the embankment or out among the impenetrable stands of hardwoods lining the road, where she could only collide with huge, immobile tree trunks. They would not give an inch, but the metal of the car would crumple and buckle until it no longer resembled what it was supposed to be. There was no shoulder to speak of, only a severe drop-off with no room for error for the most skilled driver. Even a Hollywood stuntman would have had problems negotiating the terrain under the circumstances and might not emerge alive and intact.

In her panic, Wendy's brain switched into high, adrenaline-soaked gear, and the only words it was allowing her to think were: *this is it . . . this is how and where I'm going to die.*

It was raining so hard now that the windshield wipers could barely reveal to her what was in front of her. The fireball of light behind her felt like death closing in on her, and the misophonic accompaniment of the car horn only heightened her sense of doom. In its volume and pitch it had taken on the character of a freight train barreling down the tracks. Could she possibly retrieve her cell phone and summon 9-1-1? But it was inside her purse, which was on the far side of the front passenger's seat, leaning against the door due to all the swerving she had done. She would have to remove her seat belt to reach it. Could she take one hand off the steering wheel long enough to do so safely? And then she would have to pull it toward her and then mix around in it until she located the cell. This was one of those occasions in which she devoutly wished she hadn't kept everything but the kitchen sink in that purse. Furthermore, she was asking so much of her brain, of all her senses, to keep her from going off the road—and indeed, from going off the deep end before that even happened. This was what was meant by falling to pieces, and she was well on her way.

Lower Kingston Road's sharpest curve lay just ahead. It was one she had often had trouble negotiating in broad daylight when the road was dry and there was not so much as a bird in the sky flying around to distract and disturb her. It never should have been designed that way. There was no line of sight whatsoever—it was the essence of blind. She and her father had often joked about it, blaming a drunken monkey for engineering it in such a dangerous fashion. But nothing had ever been done about it over the years, despite the fact that at least four people had lost their lives in wrecks that had occurred right at that spot. The county supervisors had merely shrugged at the horrifying statistics, examined the costs of straightening the road, and finally settled for the cheapest out—putting up a sign that said: SLOW DANGEROUS CURVE. Little good that had done. There had been at least one more fatality at that location since the erection of the sign—making the last of the fourth to date. Now, Wendy found herself thinking that the curve might just claim a fifth victim any second now.

Somehow, she managed to unbuckle her seat belt and stretched as far as she could while steering with one hand. Then, just as she was able to reach her purse, the car behind her rammed her bumper, almost causing her to lose control of the wheel then and there. It rammed her a second time, causing her to lurch forward since she had not yet managed to buckle her seat belt again.

The last jolt finally did the trick. Wendy careened down the steep embankment halfway through the curve and headed toward a stand of hardwoods that had no notion of the laws of physics. Their mission was just to stand there and grow—rigid and tall—taking no heed of creatures that had the gift of motion and moved at various speeds, often making sounds they did not have the capacity to understand. Unknowingly, unfeelingly, the trees had taken lives before, and their leaves, branches, and trunks had paid no mind. Would they do so again?

The last thing Wendy remembered was the explosion of the air bag against her face. The rough texture, the gasping for air, her blood turning to a stream of fear throughout her body. Then, there was nothing.

CHAPTER 18

The first thing that came into focus for Wendy was a blur in blue scrubs. Then a musical female voice entered her hazy, surreal world. It was nearly as high-pitched as a flute.

"Miss Winchester?" it said.

Although she did not feel in control of her vocal cords, Wendy somehow managed to say, "Yes?"

"Miss Winchester," the voice continued, "you're in the ER of Rosalie General Hospital. Now don't worry about a thing. You're gonna be just fine. All your vitals are nearly perfect now."

Wendy's vision began to clear, and she noticed that she was tied to telemetry in a triage room hemmed in by curtains. She made no effort to free herself from all the equipment, however. Hers was an inertia unchallenged.

The voice, which came with a ponytail of blond hair and a sweet, valentine-shaped face, introduced itself. "I'm your nurse, Mandy. You had a terrible accident out on Lower Kingston Road, and you took a little bit of a blow to the head. We're not sure how that happened since the paramed-ics said your air bag was fully inflated when they pulled you out of your car. My opinion is sometimes these air bags get a little too rough with the passengers. They can do damage themselves. I think the car companies should do something about that."

Wendy strained to remember what Nurse Mandy was referring to but could conjure up nothing at the moment. "How did I get here?"

"A motorist passing by after the accident called 9-1-1 for you, and we just came and got you with our sirens going full blast," Nurse Mandy said with a smile in her voice. "That's what we do, you know."

"That was nice of whoever that was." Wendy reached up tentatively and touched the bandage atop her head. "How serious is this?"

"X-rays and a CAT scan will tell us the whole story, but at this point you seem to have had a miraculous escape." Nurse Mandy paused for a moment. "I do have some difficult news for you, though. The paramedics said your car was a total mess. Emphasis on the total."

Wendy actually managed a wry smile. "Better it than me. Besides, I have good insurance."

"You also have a couple of visitors," Nurse Mandy said next. "They've been waiting on the other side of the curtain for you to come around."

"Show them in by all means," Wendy said, suddenly finding her sense of humor. "I'm ready to receive my fans."

Nurse Mandy pulled back the curtain to reveal Ross and Bax together, their expressions quickly changing from concern to relief. Then she stepped aside to allow them to have a private conversation.

"How ya doin', daughter a' mine?" Bax said, moving to her quickly and leaning down to give her a big kiss on the cheek. "You gave us both quite a scare for a while there, you know."

"I'm not in any pain, if that's what you mean," she said. "I think I'm all in one piece, too."

Ross followed suit, gently taking her hand and kissing it. "It all sounded much worse than it was when the hospital called your father. Man, when are the supervisors gonna do something about that curve? Bax, you and I oughta start a campaign tomorrow. This foolishness has gone on long enough."

"Damn straight," Bax said, his voice full of anger. He even made a fist of his left hand as he spoke the words.

Wendy's faculties were returning with each second that went by; then finally she gasped as everything that had happened earlier rushed in on her all at once.

"What's the matter, sweetie? Do you need me to call the doctor or the nurse back?" Bax said.

"No, Daddy, I don't." She firmly caught his gaze and then switched to Ross with equal intensity. "You both need to know something. I did *not* have an accident out there this evening."

It was Ross who took the bait first. "What do you mean?"

"I mean that I was forced off the road. Someone was trying to kill me. They tailgated me for at least a mile with their high beams on and their horn blaring, and then they rammed me twice. That's when I went off the highway and off into the woods. That was no accident."

It was difficult to say which man looked angrier and more shocked, but it was Bax who spoke up. "Did you get a look at the car by any chance? Could you tell us anything about it?"

Wendy was reluctant to tell them that she had been totally distracted while trying to solve the murders in her head, but this was no time for holding anything back. "Just that it seemed like it was a larger and heavier car than mine, judging from the ramming. And it had those halogen headlights that are so bright they blind you even when they aren't on high beam. Other than that, everything was a blur."

"That's still something to go on," Ross said. "We're looking for a big car with halogen headlights—maybe an SUV or a truck—that might have sustained damage to the bumper when it rammed you."

The triage curtain pulled back, and a pleasant older woman with a graying bun atop her head moved in with some highly technical equipment. "Excuse me, gentleman, but I'm Lorraine, your friendly neighborhood X-ray technician. I'll need you both to move out while we do this. It'll only take a minute."

While the technician readied her by placing a plate behind her back, Wendy continued to speculate about the murders and her own near miss. A couple more bits of behavior floated up to the forefront of her brain: *the finger-pointing* Miz Liddie had done at the dinner table and then the "*You!*" as Merleece and Arden had rushed into the room. She, Ross, and her father had discussed before what it all could possibly have meant besides the obvious accusatory implication. Bax had even brought up the idea that perhaps Miz Liddie hadn't gotten to finish her sentence and that she was implicating neither Merleece nor Arden Wilson, rather than either one. But Wendy had tackled it all long enough now that there was one further possibility that none of them had considered—her bizarre island of knowledge solution—and it made nearly all the pieces of the puzzle fit together to Wendy's utter horror.

When Ross and Bax reentered the room after the technician had left, Wendy took up where she had left off. "Don't you see what this means? There's Merleece tucked safely away in jail and her son is in the hospital, and someone's out there trying to drive me off the road and kill me. The case can't possibly be closed. I'm convinced we've all been looking at this the wrong way around."

But before she could say anything further, the curtain was pulled back again. "Hi," a lean, young male nurse with a scruffy beard said. "Time for us to go get a CAT scan, folks. We're gonna cover all the bases tonight. Doctor's orders."

As Wendy was detached from telemetry and then rolled down a series of tin-type hallways in her bed, she latched upon yet another intriguing idea to reinforce her burgeoning solution. *The motto of the Gin Girls.* Could she remember it? Yes, of course she could. It was catchy.

Raising hell in high school,
Raising hell in college,
Raising hell in marriage,
Raising hell in Heaven.

All through the tedious CAT scan procedure, she continued to turn it over and over in her head. She scarcely cared or noticed what the technician was doing or saying as her brain cells lit up. It was the last line of the motto that stayed with her. Then certain words from that line. *Hell. Heaven.* She felt as if her thought processes were truly on fire now. Soon she would be there.

The bridge game—that Grand Slam contract—the one that was never played and with a new deck. The one that Miz Liddie had been so excited about according to Merleece. The one that was finally going to win them that championship in Jackson after so many unsuccessful tries. Those four hands that were bagged at the police station as evidence. To her way of thinking, they were unexamined evidence—except for fingerprints. The conceit of Miz Liddie posing at mirrors with too much makeup and then missing those bridge games while searching for a cure for rosacea. It was an explanation that needed to be extensively revisited.

It was on the way back from her CAT scan to her triage

room that Wendy settled once again on what had to be done immediately. Not later. Not tomorrow at someone's convenience. But right now.

"Ross, you need to go to the station right this minute and examine those bridge hands," Wendy told him even before the nurse had positioned her bed and hooked her up to telemetry once again.

His expression was a curious mixture of smile and frown. "What?"

"I'm deadly serious. You have to leave and go look at those hands. Call me back on my cell and tell me exactly what cards are in every one of those hands. Daddy will stay here with me, won't you?"

"Of course I will. But what do you expect him to find?" Bax said, gently taking his daughter's hand.

"The truth about what happened that day at Miz Liddie's," she told them both. "I want to be proven wrong, but I don't think I will be."

"If you have some theory, share it with us," Bax continued. "It looks like we need all the help we can get, considering what just happened to you."

Wendy gave her father her most affectionate glance. "Maybe you can cut me a little slack, Daddy. I don't want to look the complete fool if I'm wrong. I don't want to be pointing to the wrong pieces of the jigsaw puzzle all of a sudden. After all, I'm just an amateur."

"I won't tell anyone, daughter a' mine. But if you end up solving this thing, I'll proudly shout it to the rooftops of Rosalie."

She managed a bright little hiccup of a chuckle. "Thanks. We have some time to spare waiting for the results of the X-rays and the CAT scan. Just humor me, please. I nearly bought the farm today."

Bax glanced at Ross, and they both shrugged. "Okay,

please humor her, then," Bax told him. "Get going. Do what she says, and get back to us as soon as you can. I have the feeling my daughter may be on to something."

Dr. Garvin Fore of the Rosalie General Hospital ER sauntered into Wendy's triage room about forty-minutes later with the widest smile he could manage. It complemented his healthy tan, mop of thick dark hair, and even features; in fact, he hardly looked like he was out of college, much less medical school.

"I'm happy to report that there's nothing broken, nothing bleeding, and you're all clear, Miss Winchester," he said. "Looks like you walked away from that wreck with just that contusion on your forehead. I think you've been here long enough for me to authorize your discharge."

Bax leaned down again and gave his daughter another big kiss on the cheek. "Well, thank God for that."

"Guess it just wasn't my time," Wendy said, trying to sound nonchalant about it all when she actually didn't feel that way. Despite everything, there was the inescapable fact that someone out there had tried to kill her, and she had never felt so vulnerable. "How long will it take to discharge me, Doctor?"

"You should be out of here in about fifteen or twenty minutes," he told her. "It's just a matter of the paperwork, you know."

Wendy should have been smiling but wasn't. "Well, I was expecting an important call, Doctor."

"Ross will be able to reach you no matter where you are," Bax said. "You've got your cell over in your purse, remember?"

"Oh, that's right," she said. Then she finally smiled. "Must be my contusion acting up."

After Dr. Fore left, Bax tried quizzing his daughter again using his paternal wiles. "So you're absolutely not gonna share this solution to the murders with me? With your dear old dad?"

"We'll see what Ross has to report. And even then, I still don't think I have all the answers. I just think I'm on the right track."

As if on cue, Wendy's bouncy ringtone sounded, and Bax moved quickly to retrieve her cell. "Ross?" he said. After nodding, he handed over the phone.

"Hi. What did you find out?" she said.

"Well, I'm sure you know the only thing we did with the cards was to dust them for fingerprints, and the only ones we found on them were Miz Liddie's. That makes sense since she was the one who was supposed to have shuffled and dealt them. We're no bridge players here at the station, of course," he told her.

"I already know that." Her tone was decidedly impatient. "We already know she dealt the hands and had them ready and waiting for the ladies at the bridge table. Stop stalling. Tell me what all four hands look like."

"Where do you want me to start? The bags are labeled NORTH, SOUTH, EAST, and WEST. It was Merleece who pointed that out to us."

There was more impatience in her sigh. "North. That was where Miz Liddie always sat according to both Merleece and Stella Markham."

"Okay," Ross said. "I wrote it all down. The North hand consists of the entire spade suit—ace through two."

"All thirteen cards?"

"All thirteen."

"Continue with the South hand, then."

"It's got all thirteen hearts."

Wendy's gasp contained elements of both regret and satisfaction, if such a thing were possible. "I already know what

East and West look like. The complete diamond and club suits, right?"

"Right."

"Do the cards look new? I mean, does it look like a new deck?"

There was a pause. "I guess they're new. I don't see what difference that makes. If you mean do they look worn, the answer is no. They smell new. So what does all this mean in bridge terms? I've never played the game before, you know."

"It means that the deal cannot possibly be the Grand Slam contract that Miz Liddie told the ladies they were going to play in order to practice for the championship in Jackson. It also means that you are looking at a new, unshuffled deck. Miz Liddie just separated the suits and left it at that. She didn't even try to disguise things. She lacked attention to detail."

"What do you mean—disguise? What was she trying to accomplish by doing something like that?"

Wendy was becoming slightly impatient. She couldn't believe Ross didn't see it yet, and he was supposed to be the pro. But then, neither had anyone else at the police department, including her father. "I'm pretty sure she knew they were never going to play bridge that day. It was just a ruse—a ploy to get all the ladies into the house, presumably to practice. She didn't bother with the minute details, though. If she had, it would have been a foolproof scheme. She just picked up a deck, fanned out the suits, and stacked them up four ways. She took the path of least resistance. I suspect she got lazy about it and didn't think it would matter."

"Lazy? Help me out here. I'm not a card shark."

"I mean she didn't think it through."

"You make her sound like some sort of criminal."

"Yes, I'm implying that. I would dearly love to be proven wrong, but the cards tell a different story."

Ross took a deep, noisy breath at the other end. "Okay. Let's have the full story as you see it."

"I don't have it all figured out yet," Wendy told him. "But I believe Miz Liddie committed suicide and murdered her three best friends. We've been looking at this backward all along. We assumed that she was the likely target in all of this—or maybe one of the other ladies was. This was the ultimate inside job, and it was Miz Liddie who did all the killing."

There was silence at the other end of the phone for a good while.

"Ross, have you gone to sleep down there? Do you understand what I'm saying to you?"

"Yes, I understand. But I'm not sure I believe any of it. It may be the most outrageous thing I've ever heard in all my years of detective work. Why on earth would Miz Liddie do something like that? Is that the part you haven't figured out yet, assuming you're right about the other part?"

"Yes, I don't know why she did it yet. But I think there's someone who can confirm what I've told you and perhaps can give us the rest of the answers," she told him, sounding supremely confident.

"Who's that?"

"The person who was closest to her in the world—her daughter, Stella Markham. I think you should pay her a visit immediately. You should also check out her car, particularly the bumper and the headlights. I've never been so sure of a hunch in my life. I guess you could make a case that I'm a sleuth on a roll, and I'm also the little girl pointing to the pieces of the Mississippi River jigsaw puzzle all over again. But it gives me no pleasure to say that."

Ross made a sharp, whistling sound. "Good Lord, Wendy. When did you come up with all this?"

"I've been working on it since I got the assignment from

Hemmings, of course. And you and Daddy have helped me a lot by leaking things here and there. I don't know why you're surprised that I paid attention the way any good detective would. But I promise I'm not after either of your jobs." Then she managed a conspiratorial little chuckle. "They say sometimes a bump on the head can rewire your brain in positive ways. Maybe that little accident I had was my crowning achievement." She caught herself and giggled. "Oh, and no pun intended. You know—crown, head." She giggled again.

"All right, then. But make sure they don't release you until you've taken all your meds," he told her, sounding more serious than he needed to. "You sound a bit out of it. But I'll get going on interrogating Stella Markham right away. You'll tell your father about what I found and what you think it all means, I assume?"

"Of course I will. He's been making the craziest faces at me all this time we've been talking." She paused and took a deep breath that seemed to exhaust her. Was this the price of doing brainwork overtime? "And for the record once again, I hate being right about all of this. I don't think I'll ever get the horrible taste out of my mouth no matter how long I live."

Ross felt like he was playing a role in some bizarre film noir. The set piece of choice was Stella Markham's ornate living room, where she sat on the sofa looking wild-eyed and jumpy. His partner, Ronald Pike, had already discovered and inspected the dent on the front bumper of Stella's SUV parked in front of her house, and she had eagerly confirmed that she had halogen headlights. Her cooperation with both of them seemed almost gleeful. But she hadn't stopped there.

"And yes, I tried to kill Wendy Winchester this evening, as a matter of record. Why should I hide it?" she said next as if she were telling them both that she had just fixed herself a salad for her supper.

Despite the shock he was feeling, Ross exchanged frustrated glances with Pike, who was standing next to him, and then continued. "Why did you do such a thing, Miz Stella?"

"I know you police types like for people to cut to the chase. So, here goes. I liked her well enough when we first met at the bridge club as alternates, but it turns out that she's an aspiring busybody," Stella said, the contempt shooting out from her eyes. "I could tell from her attitude that she wasn't going to let up on my mother and the rest of the Gin Girls with those features she was writing. I had to stay on it with Dalton Hemmings to make sure she didn't embarrass Mother and her legacy. That's all that's really important, you know. The reputation of the Langstons and the Roses had to be protected at all costs, and I could tell that Wendy didn't respect that. She was out to make a name for herself at my family's expense. All these cutesy, humiliating anecdotes she wanted to include, you know. So I figured if I could get her out of the way, those articles would never be written, and she wouldn't be able to dig up any more dirt on my mother and the ladies. You know they knew everything about each other, don't you?" Stella lowered her voice to a whisper. "The sort of things you'd rather keep locked up in a closet, don't you know?"

"What I do know is that you don't seem upset at all that you tried to commit premeditated vehicular homicide," Ross said, noting particularly the facial tics that kept showing up here and there across Stella's face.

"I'm not the least bit upset, and I can't believe she actually survived," Stella said, pounding the sofa with her fist. "I rammed her as hard as I could twice, and I was certain that steep embankment or the trees would take care of her. Pardon my language, but I was royally pissed when you rang my doorbell and told me otherwise. I would've much preferred the Avon Lady. I'm running out of a few things to keep myself looking as pretty as I can." Stella pointed to her cheeks and laughed. "Rouge, rouge. Running out of rouge."

"Well, if you don't mind me saying so, you are really quite the piece of work, Miz Stella."

"Thank you," she said, giving him a disdainful, crooked smile. "I've always tried to live up to my mother's superior standards."

"So superior that she would have approved of what you tried to do this evening?" Ross said, frowning.

"I believe she would, yes. Considering . . ."

"Considering what?"

Now Stella turned coy, averting her eyes after batting her lashes. "I'm not ready to tell all yet."

"Whatever the case, Miz Stella Markham, you are under arrest for attempted vehicular homicide," Ross said. Then he began reading her rights to her, after which he told his partner to cuff her.

Stella calmly offered up her wrists with a flippant attitude and said, "I have absolutely no regrets about anything I've done. There are those of us who don't have to adhere to the rules that were made for the common folk, or the little people, if you will. Some people are superior, others are inferior. Then there's the whole Darwinian thing. Sometimes you have to help it along. That's the way my mother saw it, and I see it the same way. But I would like to go ahead and make that one phone call I'm entitled to once we get down to the station."

"To your lawyer?" Ross said.

"Oh, that. He'll know what to do when the time comes. Probably plead insanity for me or something along those lines. Maybe I am. Who knows? No, I'd like for Wendy Winchester to visit me in jail. I figure she's entitled to the rest of the story since she's such a survivor. I have to give her credit for that. I thought it would be all over by now—that Merleece would end up in prison or on death row, and that Wendy would be dead and buried to a big chorus of boo-hoos, and that would be the end of it all. I would move into Mother's house and make it a shrine to her and the other ladies. I intended to take it off tour, by the way. It was just going to be my private little place to worship them all as the best thing that ever happened to Rosalie. At least that's the way it was supposed to go."

"So you want to talk to Wendy about the murders, then?" Ross added. "You realize we'll be recording everything you say down at the station, don't you? We'll know everything."

"Of course I know all that. And what else would I be talking to Wendy about? My favorite recipes? Tips on bridge? You don't happen to have her number, do you?" she said in a tone that was cavalier rather than concerned.

In fact, it was Ross's opinion from years of experience and observation in the down and dirty business of law enforcement that Stella Markham had to be seriously "hopped up on something"; not to mention that the conversation he had had with her ex came to mind immediately—the one in which Peter Markham had adamantly declared that it was *she* who was the controlled-substance addict and not himself. It was now abundantly clear which one of them had been telling the truth.

"You can talk to Wendy later," Ross told Stella, almost as if she were a naughty child. "Meanwhile, I want you to take my advice and call your lawyer when we get down to the station."

Stella shrugged with half-lidded eyes. "You realize you're taking the fun out of all of this, don't you?"

"There's nothing remotely funny about attempted murder," Ross said, while Pike slowly but surely pushed her toward the front door.

"Suit yourself," Stella said, not appearing to have a care in the world. "But I've decided I will only speak to Wendy now that I'm under arrest. Why, we're the only two members of The Rosalie Bridge Club left, you know. That counts for everything in this world."

CHAPTER 19

Protected by a wall of sturdy plastic, Wendy sat down across from Stella the next morning at the detention center and picked up the receiver of the intercom phone in front of her. She noted with some degree of annoyance that Stella was laughing in her orange jumpsuit while emphatically pointing at Wendy's bandage over and over again with her index finger.

"You mean to tell me that that's all the damage I did?" Stella said for an opener on the other side of the plastic.

Wendy steeled herself, remaining as calm as she could. "I'm afraid so. Sorry to disappoint you."

"I'm not a very good reckless driver, then, am I?"

Wendy resented Stella's attempt at humor and took her time answering, "No, you're not."

"So we're going to be monosyllabic today, are we?"

"I'm told you wanted to tell all to me, so I'm here to listen to what you have to say, Stella," Wendy told her. "I may have a comment or two at some point, but this is your moment to shine, if you can call it that."

Stella grew a bit more somber. "It is, isn't it? My dark moment to shine. I like the sound of that."

"I'm sure you do, and no one knows the truth the way you know it, I suspect. So go ahead and explain this from start to finish."

Stella smiled again and rubbed her hands together like a fly, making Wendy cringe slightly. How could she not have detected the unhinged nature of this woman before now when everyone could clearly see that she had snapped? Still, perhaps she shouldn't be so hard on herself since this was her first case, and Stella, as it turned out, was a two-faced devil.

"Where do you want me to start?" Stella said.

"At the beginning would be nice. There are some things I don't understand about all of this. Maybe you'll clear them up for me—for all of us. It's my belief that your mother killed herself and murdered her three best friends in the world. It's the why I don't quite get yet."

Stella backed away from the plastic, her mood shifting drastically from sassy to sullen. "None of you got it. Well, you came the closest, Wendy. You should pat yourself on the back."

"I don't want compliments, Stella. I want the truth. Am I right that your mother was behind this from the beginning?"

Stella gave her what could only be described as the stare of a horror film monster. Her eyes could not have been more wide open, her nostrils more flared, and her teeth more bared in nothing short of a grimace. "You make it sound like Mother actually did something wrong."

"Oh my God. You think she didn't?"

"She did what she had to do . . . because . . ."

Stella could not seem to finish her sentence, and Wendy waited as long as she could. "Go on . . . because?"

Stella's monstrous pose disappeared, and she lowered her voice. "Because she was dying."

"Of what?"

"Of liver cancer. Late stage when she first discovered it."

Wendy was trying her best to process what she had just been told, but all she could say for the moment was, "How awful. Why didn't she tell someone?"

"She told *me*. I'm someone."

"Go on, then."

Stella took a little time to gather her thoughts and then continued. "Mother started losing weight about five months ago, and she had some other peculiar symptoms. She didn't think anything of it at first, but she finally gave in to her worst fears. So she went down to MD Anderson in Houston for a battery of tests. She had her suspicions, you understand, but only the best for my mother, of course. No local doctors who might spread the word, embarrass her, or give her less than the finest treatment available. That was the first time I subbed for her at the bridge club. That was about the time she decided to let you join."

"Are you saying that that was the reason she let me in?"

Stella nodded and gave her a sarcastic smile. "Yes, in the beginning she was looking ahead. She told me that if anything happened to her, I would move up from alternate to regular, and you would become the new alternate. That was before she found out she was definitely terminal and there was no protocol or clinical trial that could help her and before she . . . well, I'm jumping the gun a bit."

"To be honest with you, I did wonder why I made the cut when no one else in Rosalie could," Wendy said.

"Now you know. Anyway, when MD Anderson didn't even have a clinical trial that would help Mother, she went up to Sloan Kettering in New York, and I subbed for her on that trip, too. She was looking for second opinions, even thirds, but they all told her the same thing no matter where she went, and no matter how many times I subbed. She had a couple of months to live maybe, and they all recommended she consider going into hospice. They told her that chemo or radiation or any of the rest of the protocols would produce worse effects than the disease was producing at that point. Her world came crashing in around her, and she had no answer for it. Except for choosing how she would leave."

"I'm sorry it came down to that," Wendy said. "That must have been a nightmare for your mother to face."

"You have no idea what Mother went through during that period. She kept going back and forth about it, but in the end, she decided to do what she did."

"Which was?"

"Not to go into hospice despite the advice of all the clinics she visited," Stella began. "She didn't want to die in a hospital-type setting or have lots of people fuss over her while she was trapped in a bed. She was claustrophobic about that. She didn't want to relinquish the control she'd enjoyed all her life. So she got enough painkiller scrips and other meds from oncologists she visited to help her navigate the last part of her life. It changed her personality completely. She was often in pain despite the meds, and she was often very drowsy as well. Of course, she also snapped at everyone, including me, because she was never really comfortable. She really did become a different person. Who wouldn't, being as sick as she was? Finally, she called me up and told me to come over one evening. She'd had enough of indecision about which way she should leave, and she was seriously worried about *what came next,* she told me."

"You mean what comes after death?" Wendy said, now genuinely mesmerized by the story Stella was telling her.

"Yes, she told me that she knew she'd done some terrible things in her lifetime, including to her best friends, the Gin Girls. I already knew she had slept with Miz Hanna's husband, but she revealed to me that she'd also slept with Miz Sicily and Miz Bethany's husbands, too. *Because she could,* she told me. She wanted to prove to herself that there was no man in Rosalie she couldn't have if she set her mind to it. There were other things that bothered her. For instance, things about my father that a couple of the ladies knew but kept quiet about—namely that my father had cheated their husbands out of investments he'd made for them. She said she wasn't sure whether she'd meet my father in Heaven or Hell, and she was concerned about her own destination. That was really why she did it."

The last statement pulled Wendy out of the incredible tale Stella had been weaving. "*What* was why she really did it?"

"The fear that if she left the others behind, they would reveal what they knew about her morals and my father's financial tactics. The family reputation would be completely ruined. Not only that, she said that she wanted her Gin Girls with her when she faced whatever judgment was coming her way. And she did believe something was coming. It was part of their motto, she said. *They would raise hell in Heaven together.* So that's why Mother put on gloves, went out to the gardening shed, put the poison in the sugar bowl the night before, and then deliberately pointed to both Merleece and Arden Wilson when they entered the room that day. Her intention was to implicate them in the murders with the last word she would ever speak on this earth—the word *You!*"

Wendy thought for a second and frowned. "Wasn't she taking a chance that she would die before getting it out?"

Stella shook her head. "Maybe. But she knew Merleece or Arden would take the blame no matter what. She didn't care which one. She believed they were far beneath her in the scheme of things. What did they really matter?"

The last sentence caused Wendy to shiver slightly, but she found the appropriate reply. "The superior standards of Liddie Langston Rose."

"Yes, and they're mine, too." Stella's tone had not an ounce of remorse to it. "Matter of fact, I'll tell you something else that'll probably shock you. All those charities Mother got the other ladies to contribute to and support—she didn't really believe in any of them. In fact, she was downright cynical about who really got the money. She said she thought the executives who ran those places got most of the money. But she told me she looked upon supporting them as an insurance policy. 'Maybe all those donations will make up for the not-so-charitable things I've done in my life,' she'd said. For her, they weren't even so much a tax deduction as they were a hope that she might be forgiven for her mistakes there at the very end."

"I don't know what on earth to do with all that," Wendy said. "So many mixed messages there."

"You and your easy judgments."

"So neither of you had any compunction about cutting short the lives of people who trusted you, despite the ups and downs of lifelong friendship? Did it occur to you that she might have developed a psychosis by then?"

"Again, that's easy for you to say. You weren't in my shoes. Or my mother's. You'd have to be there to understand. At any rate, I have no compunction whatsoever about the whole affair."

Wendy continued to work things out in her head. "So the rosacea thing really was a lie, wasn't it?"

"Yes, I thought it was rather clever, myself. But in between her desperate trips to various clinics, Mother started using makeup to cover up her sallow complexion due to the cancer. She also bought some padding so she could fill out her dresses better as she lost her appetite and lost more weight as a result, and the others couldn't really tell the difference as easily, including Merleece. She was always checking herself out in all the mirrors around the house. She also thought changing her hairstyle would distract the others from what was really going on with her physically. They could just interpret it as a whim or something. The Gin Girls liked to do things like that all the time. The thing is . . ."

Wendy could tell something at last seemed to be troubling her. "Yes?"

"There were moments—more than once—when Mother did balk and almost backed out of taking the ladies with her. When she was in that mood, she told me she had decided it would be better to just take her own life and hope the others would only speak well of her in her absence. I told her I'd go along with her on it and even suggested it might be a lot simpler that way. At that point I actively lobbied to let the other ladies live. I pulled every argument out of the hat I could think of. I did honestly try. But then she would reject my pleas. She just couldn't take a chance leaving them behind. As she had in life, she wanted to have them around her once her life was over."

"Leaving them behind would have been an improvement over what she actually did. She seems to have gone back and forth several times. What finally decided things for her?"

For the first time, Stella sounded more exasperated than flippant. "That last week both Miz Selena Chalk and Miz Crystal Forrest barged into the house and attacked her viciously about various things. With Miz Crystal it was just words. But Miz Selena actually tried to push her around, Mother said. She told me it really upset her so much that her pain meds had almost no effect. She thought that was just a sample of what people who didn't like her would say once she was gone. It turned her back toward getting it all over with sooner rather than later and letting the chips fall where they may. That day they were supposed to be playing out that Grand Slam contract, she loaded up with as many pills as she could and still stay awake. She said she was determined to get it over with. She couldn't go on like that anymore. She even said that maybe she'd made a mistake by not going into hospice, even though it meant putting herself in the hands of other people she didn't know. So she returned to the conviction that she wanted to face whatever she had to face with her Gin Girls at her side. She was certain they wouldn't mind in the end. They would all be in it together."

Wendy closed her eyes, hoping that that would somehow clear her brain of the monstrous plot that had just been revealed to her. But no such luck. The raw reality of it would not be going away anytime soon. She envisioned many nightmares ahead of her.

"I understand completely that cancer is no picnic and that she wanted out," Wendy said, "but she had no right to take three other people with her like that. Who knows? They could have ended up falling back on their better nature and defending her from all the gossip and hearsay. How could she have betrayed them like that by taking their lives?"

Stella waved her off with her free hand. "Say what you want, but there would have been people like you to dig it all up for the sensationalism. You didn't listen to me either time you came to visit, did you? But I have to say that I did enjoy immensely feeding you and your boyfriend all that foolishness about Merleece and Arden Wilson having some sort of conspiracy going on behind Mother's back. That was her idea, actually. She said she would stage everything and do the finger-pointing at the last moment, and I could throw even more suspicion upon them by claiming they were huddling and plotting against her. You bought it all hook, line, and sinker."

"I wouldn't say that was the case at all. We kept on probing until we got at the truth, one way or another."

Stella winced briefly, but her unhinged, smug look soon returned. "Mother had it all planned down to the last detail. She told me that she was going to pick a fight with Merleece that morning about making the drinks for the bridge game.

Mother lied and told her that the ladies had been complaining about how weak the drinks were lately, so she told Merleece to put an extra jigger or two of gin in those Bloody Marys. It was all very considerate of Mother, I thought."

"Considerate?"

"That's what I said."

"In what alternate universe?"

"You don't understand. Mother wanted them all good and lubricated so they wouldn't feel the effects of the cyanide so much. Same for herself. You know—feeling no pain as they had so many times over the years when they'd gotten a few drinks under their belts. She knew it wasn't going to be pleasant—she'd done the research, believe me—even if the effects of the potassium cyanide would be relatively brief in the scheme of things. I think it took a lot of courage to do what she did. There was a method to her madness, you see."

Wendy sat horrified, unable to find the words immediately. "Courage? Hardly. I think madness is the operative word here, though."

"Another judgment from you? You're very good at that, you know. People who don't have the proper background usually do. I'm speaking of genes here. It takes generations to produce superior people who know what's best."

This time, Wendy had no response. She could think of none that belonged in the real world.

"Why, I believe I've finally shut you up, dear," Stella said with a smirk. "And by the way, I had such wicked good fun trying to implicate Peter in this by telling the cops he was the one with the drug problem. It wouldn't have hurt my feelings at all if he'd ended up being nailed for the murders. Mother couldn't stand him, either, you know. Of course, I did what I could."

"I don't understand why you're telling me all of this now?

You could've kept all these details to yourself. You could have lied. It seems you're almost delighted for you and your mother to be found out. They say there's a certain type of criminal who won't rest until everyone knows exactly what they've done. You certainly fit the mold, and you've played to the camera beautifully."

The look that came over Stella's face was nothing short of demonic again, and Wendy sensed another verbal attack on the way. "My, my. Aren't you suddenly the expert? The social columnist thinks she's got everyone pegged. Well, there's a quandary I'm going to leave with you, my dear. You probably have no idea what's coming down the pike for you, I'm sure."

"What do you mean?"

Stella leaned forward, her face nearly touching the plastic. "Which article are you going to write about the murders? Are you going to tell the whole truth, or are you going to leave out a few things and let the public wonder? Plus, you'll have Dalton Hemmings to deal with. No matter what you write, he'll second-guess you and make the final decision on what actually gets published. I can just picture it, can't you?"

"No," Wendy said, "I can't."

Stella outlined the square shape of a newspaper with her hands. "Oh, but I can. Hemmings will let you reveal that Mother committed suicide because of her cancer. That's sympathetic enough. Everyone will be so sorry to hear that. But I'll bet you anything he makes you write that the others were a horrendous accident of some sort. I assure you I know how he thinks. I've talked to him enough. So did Mother. He and your father are pretty close, and I'll bet they'll both do what's best for Rosalie in the end. The truth is too ugly to reveal."

"Don't you dare speak for my father like that. He's an honorable man," Wendy said, raising the tone of her voice. "He would never consider a cover-up. Besides, what makes you think Hemmings will even let me write the murder story? That's L'il Jack Horner—uh, Jack Manning's beat."

"Even better," Stella said. "Hemmings will practically dictate what that dork writes. Mother and I pretty much had the *Citizen* in the palm of our hands, and we knew what everyone who was anyone did there. Meanwhile, all I've confessed to is trying to run you off the road. My lawyer will see to it that I'm sent off for rehab or a stay in an institution somewhere for a while, and that will be the end of it. Mother's dead, and I guarantee you Hemmings won't want to sully her good name."

Wendy was becoming angrier by the second. "You're still an accessory to the murders before and after the fact."

"A mentally unstable, Lortab-addicted accessory for starters, dear. Try this on for size: I simply lost my mind when my mother told me what she wanted to do. Could anyone out there blame me? What would you have done? And I actually did try and stop her. I'll be sure and emphasize that. Need I say more? You can record what all I've said until the cows come home, but my defense will be the same. I need to go to rehab for drug addiction. Maybe even a mental hospital for a short stay. I know I can talk my way out of that by charming my shrink. Who knows? Kyle Welton has been on retainer for the Rose Family for decades now. Let's just say that he's friends with just oodles of judges on the bench. In the end I'm sure they'll see it my way."

Wendy rose from her chair. "I think I've heard more than enough. I need a breath of fresh air."

"I don't wonder. Perhaps you should go back to writing about weddings and baby showers. There's nothing threatening about that to anyone. And here's something that might amuse you—you're not likely to get run off the road for anything you whip up on those saccharine subjects."

"I feel very sorry for you, Stella. It seems as if you've chosen to bypass your humanity and your moral compass, just as your mother did," Wendy told her. "Heaven versus Hell, indeed."

"Pontificate all you like," Stella said. "But see if you don't end up right back on the society page after all is said and done."

"I assure you I'd quit if that happens. The *Citizen* isn't the only newspaper in the country, you know."

"Playing around with words for a living," Stella added, her eyes half-lidded. "What an inferior occupation. But if it amuses you, by all means, continue to pursue it for whatever paltry salary you're offered."

"Your mother didn't seem to think journalism was such a waste of time, the way she wanted everything she did socially to appear in print. I ought to know. Dalton Hemmings put all her announcements and events on my desk with ***RUSH*** written across the top in big red all caps. I always had to drop whatever I was doing to take care of them."

Stella did not sound the least bit impressed. "At least you knew your role—to take orders from your superiors."

"I'm afraid your 'giving orders to inferiors' days are over for good," Wendy said, getting in the last word.

CHAPTER 20

Bax gave Dalton Hemmings his most determined look, leaned across his desk, and then repeated what he'd just said: "Well . . . isn't that a shocker?"

He'd just shown his old friend the tape of Wendy's jail visit with Stella Markham from start to finish, and Hemmings was indeed speechless.

Finally, Hemmings managed a curious response. "So, what are we gonna do about it?"

"What do you mean?"

Hemmings settled back in his chair and squinted, while taking a deep breath. "I mean, do you have any idea what this'll do to Rosalie?"

"I'm sure they'll be just as shocked as we are," Bax told him. "I know I didn't see this one coming."

Hemmings shrugged, but there was a hint of hostility in the gesture. "Who would? But the point is that I've been running the *Citizen* for decades now. I've been deciding what Rosalieans should and should not know for their own good. It seems to have worked out well enough."

"That's a lot of power for one man to have, Dalton. When you wield it, you need to have a little humility."

Hemmings sniffed the air contemptuously. "You should be the one to talk, Bax. I believe you've bent the rules here and there down at the police station. You've consulted with this lawyer and that to make things happen for certain people. Don't you think controlling things for the common good comes with the territory in a small town like Rosalie?"

"Technicalities, Dalton, technicalities," Bax said. "You're talking about things like my recommending that a teenager not be tried as an adult. Or giving someone a second chance to prove themselves on probation before actually sending them off to jail. I've always done that sort of thing based on the knowledge of the person's character. I don't regret any of the decisions I've ever made in that regard."

Hemmings plopped his hands down on the desk and offered up a wry grin. "Yeah, you've made friends with more than a few judges. So what is it you hope to accomplish by telling everybody the whole ugly truth that Stella Markham revealed? In a way, I think it gives the whole town of Rosalie a black eye that it'll never recover from in our lifetime."

"How so?"

"Let's face it," Hemmings said. "Rosalie has always been a law unto itself. We've all encouraged and even applauded the quirkiest, most bizarre behaviors among the elite families. We let them get away with anything and everything because of their pedigrees. People in other towns would've been arrested for doing the same things. The rest of Mississippi looks at Rosalie as a medieval kingdom of sorts answerable to no one. We laugh at our citizens here as if they were actors in Broadway plays."

Hemmings paused and adopted a dramatic pose. " 'Oh, it's just the Such-and-Such Family,' we say. 'They're always doing things like that, you know,' we say. The fact is, Rosalieans are the ultimate example of the truth being stranger than fiction. If any writer ever came in here and tried to string some of these anecdotes together into a plot, I'll betcha anything their editor would tell 'em they can't use any of it—it's just too unbelievable."

Bax was looking off in the distance and shaking his head solemnly. "That may be true, but to my knowledge, we've never encouraged and applauded murder. That's the real issue here, and it's not very pretty to look at. You know, my daughter was the one who figured out what really happened that day at Miz Liddie's, don't you? If you ask me, she's gonna make some newspaper one helluva investigative reporter. Might as well be yours."

"Ah, yes, Miz Wendy," Hemmings said. "I know she's your beloved daughter and all that, Bax, but she's been a very difficult employee to work with. She's not very happy with her job, I'm afraid."

"Are you thinking of firing her?"

"No, of course not. But she wants more responsibility than she's been given here. I think you've been aware of that for some time now."

Bax gave him a quizzical look. "And it hasn't occurred to you to do something about it?"

Hemmings straightened up in his chair a bit. "It has. I gave her the features on the Gin Girls as a trial. You already know that. But I warned her from the beginning that we were gonna have to tread carefully so as not to offend people. That's true now more than ever because of what actually happened to them. They're no longer with us, so we have to be respectful of the dead."

Bax made a fist and slammed it on the desk. "Who in hell are you afraid of offending, Dalton? Miz Liddie is dead. She killed herself. She killed the others. Her daughter is a basket case who wrong-headedly thinks she's gonna get off scot-free for trying to kill my Wendy. This is the story of the century for this crazy little town, and you're giving me the impression that you want to bury it in the classifieds or somewhere."

Hemmings pushed his right hand forward and shook his head emphatically. "Not true. It just occurred to me right this second what to do with the story."

"Which is?" Bax said with a skeptical glance.

Hemmings began pointing his index finger emphatically as he spoke, as if chastising a naughty student in school. "We admit that Miz Liddie committed suicide because that's the truth of the matter. People will be very sympathetic because of the terminal cancer. Everyone can relate to the despair and depression of that. But we could save the town of Rosalie a lot of head-shaking and chest-beating by saying that the other three deaths were a mistake, a horrible accident. We could say that the tainted sugar bowl was carelessly left out and the others helped themselves to it. I mean, what harm could it do? Miz Liddie is gone and can't stand trial for the murders she committed, and Miz Stella is obviously headed toward some mental institution unless my eyes and ears deceive me. She's absolutely bonkers. And that housekeeper, Merleece What's-Her-Name, will be exonerated. What's wrong with that?"

"Look, Dalton," Bax said, rising from his chair and gesturing wildly with his hands in response to all the finger-pointing, "You and I, we go back a long way. We watched each other get to the top of the heap in this town. We've done about a zillion favors for each other, and we've even paid the price a coupla times for doing that. But we have to tell the truth here, and there's the matter of the survivors possibly suing Miz Liddie's estate for wrongful death. Just because she's dead doesn't mean they can't go that route in court."

"They wouldn't if they didn't know what actually happened."

Bax's impatience was verging on outrage. "Castrating the

story won't necessarily get rid of that possibility. A case could be made that the other ladies wouldn't have died had it not been for Miz Liddie's gross carelessness. That is, if that particular lie were passed off as the truth. Don't slide down that slippery slope."

"You really think this town can survive knowing that one of its social divas committed premeditated murder due to her own vainglory? Doesn't it put the whole town on trial in a way?"

"Here's a bulletin for you. Miz Liddie had her detractors, believe it or not. Just because you bowed down to her every time she knocked on your door doesn't mean everybody did, you know," Bax said.

The two of them sat with the sarcasm for a minute or two; then Hemmings said, "I don't care. I think it would be a huge mistake not to doctor this up a bit. I'm sure it wouldn't surprise you to hear I've altered the facts on a story now and then. Editorial discretion, so to speak."

"And I think you should let my daughter write the version that doesn't hold back anything. It'll pull no punches. It'll contain everything that was recorded at the jail and whatever else Wendy and Ross, the crime lab, and myself have all discovered during the investigation. Opt for integrity, Dalton. Opt for the truth. This isn't the old Soviet Union."

Hemmings did not answer right away. He nervously drummed his fingers on the desk for a while and finally exhaled noisily. "I don't think it'll ever be put to bed in this town if we call it murder instead of a mistake. Rosalieans will be talking about it for generations to come. But I'll do as you ask and tell Wendy to write it up for me, and I'll take a good look, I promise." He paused as if suddenly uncomfortable. "I . . . uh . . . I'm also gonna have an important announcement to make shortly that has nothing to do with the murders. I've been thinking about it for some time now."

"That sounds mysterious and very much unlike you. Not gonna give me any sort of hint?"

Hemmings looked perplexed. "Let me fully convince myself, Bax. I'm almost there, but not quite. I just gotta be sure what I want to do is the absolutely right decision for me."

Wendy had never had so much trouble transferring her thoughts from her brain to the computer screen. "Write the truth. The unadulterated truth," her father had told her a couple of hours ago after his meeting with Hemmings. Then he had explained the ultimate implications of her work. But once she had settled down to compose in her cubicle, she realized that she was going to have to overcome the powerful urge to editorialize in her writing. In fact, it was all she could do to stop herself from marching into Hemmings's office and asking him if she could be the one to write an actual editorial on the murders, something she was sure he was preparing to do in his usual self-serving manner.

How would it be possible to put a reasonable face on premeditated murder? It was distasteful beyond belief. Miz Liddie had taken four lives, including her own. The part about having terminal cancer would resonate with everyone, of course. What a wretched, unforgiving disease it was—turning on babies and children, young adults, the middle-aged, and seniors indiscriminately. It respected no one and cast a wide net of sorrow. Some people might even understand, if not excuse, the decision to commit suicide. But to "take her friends with her" made her an arch-villainess of the highest order in Wendy's mind.

Finally, she began to put her sentences together, blending facts from the bios of all the women with what Stella Markham had revealed in her mentally unhinged, taped interview. She read through it all after the first draft. It was brutal, but it was the truth. She thought the writing was strong, straightforward, and even impeccable. And she had made a decision: if Hemmings failed to publish her article and instead went with some sort of cover-up—even the slightest hint of one—that Jack Manning would surely be assigned to write, she was going to offer him her resignation right then and there. There was no good reason to work for an editor who was that committed to manipulating the truth.

She reviewed the last paragraph with great satisfaction.

> And so it was that four women who had been lifelong friends drank a toast to winning the bridge championship that had eluded them for so long. In good faith and trust did three of them do so, with only the sociable task of successful bidding and playing out a contract before them. They believed there was nothing more at stake than that. Little did those three realize that their lives hung in the balance and that the only contract that would be bid and made on that fateful day was one for heinous and sudden death, making it a grand slam of horrors that will never be forgotten.

Despite the pride she felt for her article, however, Wendy decided to give it a polish for good measure, and by four-thirty in the afternoon she had her work ready to present. It was time for the showdown. Wendy printed out what she had written and approached Hemmings's office door with great trepidation. She could almost hear his words after he had read through it: "I'm very sorry to have to tell you, Miz Winchester. But I've decided to go another way on this."

Then L'il Jack Horner would get the byline and the bogus narrative, and she would start looking around for another job in another town.

Patiently, Wendy waited for Hemmings's verdict as she sat across from him. There were a multitude of expressions on his face as he continued to scan it quickly, few of which impressed her as favorable. Then he looked up from his task and noisily cleared his throat. That usually meant something bombastic was on the way.

Instead, he said, "It's very nice work. Well-researched and actually very riveting to read."

She managed a surprised, "Thank you."

"You've gone ahead and editorialized a bit, particularly there at the end. That's not your job as a journalist."

Wendy knew he had a point but decided to engage him, anyway. She hadn't come this far to wimp out. "I thought my job as a journalist was to tell the truth. Miz Liddie committed suicide and wantonly cut short the lives of three of her friends. What I stated there at the end was just a summary of what actually happened."

"I have no quarrel with your style, of course. Bax and I talked about this at some length. The two people who are guilty in all of this—Miz Liddie and Stella Markham—won't be around to prosecute. Unless you want to bring charges against Miz Stella for what she tried to do to you. Do you? She'll still be up for charges as an accessory to the murders."

Wendy shook her head, having thought it over, and decided that she did not want to pursue the matter further. Stella Markham was desperately in need of medical and psychiatric help, and the buzz already was that her lawyer was going to ask the court to consider a plea of diminished capacity. Wendy was okay with that—as long as Stella wouldn't be able to run around loose and drive a car in Rosalie or anywhere else for that matter. Perhaps a padded cell or a straitjacket would suffice quite nicely for the foreseeable future.

"I kinda thought you wouldn't," he said. "Miz Liddie's not around to punish for her misdeeds, of course. So what do you say about it all, Miz Winchester? Do we publish this or not?"

The last thing Wendy had expected was to have the ball thrown back into her court. "You're asking me to make the decision?"

Hemmings's expression looked particularly inscrutable. "Well, why not? You be the editor for a moment. I'd like to see what you're made of. It'll tell me a lot more about you, even though I know a lot already."

Feeling suddenly emboldened, Wendy forged ahead. "All right, then. As editor, I would publish it as is. Tell everything. All the shocking details. Anything less would be an insult to what good journalism is all about."

"Have a care, my girl," Hemmings said, his tone at its most patronizing. "It's very easy to slip into tabloid sensationalism these days. It's best you don't go there."

"I'd be mindful of that. You have a point."

"That's pretty much what I thought you'd say. On the other hand, I think I would alter parts of it because of the messiness," Hemmings told her, still pressing his narrative.

"I'm sure I know which parts, but I vehemently disagree with you."

Hemmings did not seem upset by her remark. Instead, he exhaled slowly as if it were his last breath. "I understand, but I have something else to say here. You have no way of knowing this, but I'll be seventy years old in December. Seventy. I've been at this bid'ness a very long time. Too long, I think sometimes. You're from a different generation. Your standards are higher than mine. I'll admit it, but I'm not particularly ashamed to admit it. I've lived through so much change down here in the South. So much violence, so much restlessness, so many grievances aired openly. I've done the best I could to make that change palatable to my readers by manipulating a few things. But perhaps that attitude has outlived its usefulness. Perhaps it's time for me to move on."

"I'm glad to hear you say that."

Hemmings remained stoic. "The bottom line is I've been thinking about retirement for a coupla years now, and I'll shortly be announcing that I'll be stepping down after the Christmas holidays. Tell me frankly, does it please you to hear that? Is that good news for you?"

Again, Wendy was caught by surprise. "I . . . well . . . I'd rather not answer that. But if it's really what you want to do, then fine."

"I think it's the right decision. I told your father a few hours ago that I had a big decision to make soon, and this Grand Slam Murders case has brought it to a head for sure. I've had things my way for a long time now. Maybe it's time for some fresh thinking in Rosalie. And to be honest with you, I'm tired. Bone-tired. The quirkiness of this town takes its toll, believe me."

Now Hemmings was making a deep connection with her. The layers of Rosalie were often impenetrable, impossible to peel back and survey with any sort of certainty. But everyone knew that they were there—solid as the growth rings inside an old, gnarled tree. Rings that never saw the light of day while they were part of a complicated living organism.

"I can understand that," Wendy told him. "There have been moments when I've thought I needed to move somewhere else to achieve my long-term goals. Should I try to be the proverbial big fish in the small pond or swim with the sharks in the ocean? Forgive the clichés. I know it's not good journalism."

Hemmings cracked an odd little smile that looked somewhat paternal. "Well, there's more I have to tell you. This piece you did *is* very good journalism. What it tells me is that you're being wasted as the society columnist, and I'm sure you'll be pleased to hear that I'm creating a new position for you. You'll be the *Citizen*'s full-time investigative reporter starting next week. And I promise not to interfere with your assignments. You'll have carte blanche to do things your way all the time. There'll be no second-guessing."

Wendy sat with her jaw dropped for a full fifteen seconds, but that was soon replaced by her awkward, stuttering attempt at gratitude. "I . . . I . . . can't believe it, Mr. Hemmings. Please . . . please say . . . you're not kidding."

"I'm not."

She popped up impulsively, offering her hand, and the two shook on his offer. "I can't thank you enough. This is what I've been dreaming of . . . for years."

"I gathered as much. Oh, and you'll get a substantial raise, of course. Five thousand more a year. Does that suit you for starters?"

Wendy felt overwhelmed and wondered for a moment if she should pinch herself to determine whether what was going on was really happening; but then she couldn't help but smile as she realized she had dredged up yet another cliché with the pinching thing. She must stop relying on them in her head so as not to find them strewn haphazardly throughout her work by default. Finally, she answered him.

"Five thousand more sounds like a dream come true." She sat back down and added, "For now."

Hemmings appeared to be amused. "You're no pushover. You're a tough nut. But you might prepare yourself for some blowback on this, though. You'll have gone from the—let's face it—innocuous to the scandalous in one fell swoop. There are people out there who will always want to shoot the messenger, and some of 'em have very good aim. I'm pretty sure you've never gotten hate mail. I have, of course. Nowadays, that translates into hate e-mails."

"I've thought of that before, believe me," she said, trying to sound nonchalant about it all. "But I think I'm a big girl."

"Yes, you are. You'll be putting your big-girl journalism pants on permanently now. I'm sure your father will be very proud of you, too."

As somewhat of an afterthought, Wendy said, "Do you have any idea who'll be taking your place? Have you been training anyone on the staff? What about promoting Mr. Brady?"

Hemmings looked at her as if she were insane. "Logan? He's just a few years younger than I am. Besides, just between the two of us, I've already approached him about the job. He says he doesn't want that kind of responsibility at his ripe old age. He's happy with being assistant editor, doing his design and layout thing, and leaving it at that."

"Ah," was all Wendy could manage.

Meanwhile, she had to fight off the disturbing idea that L'il Jack Horner was even remotely a candidate for the position. Being the editor's good, little lap dog for years was hardly a qualification in her estimation. Surely, Hemmings wouldn't go in that direction. But if he did, she couldn't imagine herself taking orders from the person she respected least on the staff. She would just have to find employment elsewhere—which she was more than confident she could do.

"Would you advertise for the job and bring someone in from the outside?" Wendy continued.

Hemmings did not answer her but produced a sudden, boisterous laugh, which ended in another of his coughing and throat-clearing extravaganzas that caused Wendy to lean back in astonishment. It flashed into her head the kind of damage he could do if he were ever contagious with anything.

"What's so funny, Mr. Hemmings?"

"You mentioning the issue of my successor at all. It's just that I thought for the longest time I would drop dead at my desk at some ungodly age. Retire? Not this old dog. They'd find me stiff at my computer with my cursor blinking impatiently for the next letter. But as you can see, I've changed my mind. There's no guarantee that you'll get along with whoever comes in here and sits at this desk, of course. You may have to fight different kinds of battles at that point. But to answer your last question, we'll probably advertise for the position, and there's no telling who'll get the job. Might even be someone crankier and more opinionated than I am, if that's possible. On the other hand, it could be someone who thinks just like you do. You could be a match made in heaven, to use another cliché."

"I think I'll be up to the challenge no matter who it is."

"Yes, I think you will be, too. You have your father's determination and integrity. I knew that from the moment I hired you. Of course, I didn't show you that I knew. I'm pretty tough on everyone who works for me. Just part of the persona I've deliberately cultivated all these years; plus, I think it keeps everybody on their toes. You always want your employees to try a little harder to please the boss. It's a psychology that really works, and it's enabled me to squeeze every ounce of ability out of people who didn't know they had it in 'em."

Overcome with the feeling that they were at last on equal footing, Wendy said, "I never looked at it from that angle—I mean, from your point of view." The realization brought a smile to her face, and she pressed on. "What do you think you'll do with your spare time once you step down? Have you given it a thought at all?"

"I think maybe I'll travel a bit," he said, making a sweeping gesture as if the whole world were in the room. "Don't know quite where yet. But I think I need to get out of Rosalie for a while. I need a breath of fresh air most of all. Even with all its many architectural treasures and rich history, this town can put people out to pasture before their time. They don't even realize it's happening to them. They lose the common touch. They get caught up in things that don't mean as much anymore in modern life. Maybe that's what made Miz Liddie believe she was above the law in doing what she did. Seems to me like no one had ever said no to her because of who her family was and her social position. I know I never did—and maybe I should have once in a while. Maybe she'd have been far less inclined to think that poisoning her closest friends was something she should even consider pulling off."

"Surely you're not taking any of the blame for this, are you? That's just not your style."

Hemmings hung his head. Wendy had never seen him so drained of energy and so lacking in confidence. The face that had been so intimidating to so many for so long now seemed like a pale imitation of itself. "No, I would never go that far. I don't play any of those 'society is to blame' games, even if I've played around with the truth now and then. I'm just saying that worshiping the past and what your ancestors did while not taking responsibility for the things you do in the present can get you in serious trouble. We have only to look as far as The Grand Slam Murders to demonstrate the damage."

Wendy nodded, saying nothing further. But she was completely astonished by what she was hearing from the man who had been bossing her around for years without impunity. Where had this version of Dalton Hemmings been hiding all this time? Perhaps the prospect of finally stepping down from a position where he had stayed far too long and had played far too loosely with the truth was restoring a bit of his humanity and humility. Then she thought about the bridge game that was never meant to be played but had fatal consequences anyway, and it caused her to shudder involuntarily.

Death, as it turned out, was sometimes a cruel surprise—lingering in the most unlikely places.

CHAPTER 21

Wendy could tell that Merleece was having a great deal of trouble processing what Miz Liddie had done to herself and her best friends. The two of them were sitting side by side on Merleece's cozy living room sofa, and Wendy had asked her father and Ross if she could be the one to go over and explain everything after Merleece was released from jail. His arm in a sling, Hyram was sprawled out in a nearby armchair, joining his mother in frowning at everything that had just been thrown at them.

"I cain't believe she did all that, Strawberry," Merleece said in an anguished tone. "What kinda awful pain she musta been in to think up somethin' wicked like that. I never would believe it in a million years. You think she up and lost her mind there at the end? Sound like it to me."

Wendy saw no reason to downplay the situation. Miz Liddie's treachery had nearly cost Merleece a prison sentence or even worse. "Unfortunately, she was lucid enough to plan everything so you or Arden—or even both of you—got the blame for her vanity. If she had taken her life and left it at that, it would have been more understandable, even though still very tragic. I do think her daughter had definitely gone off the deep end since she tried to kill me, though."

Merleece shuddered and then squeezed Wendy's hand. "I'm so glad Miz Stella, she didd'n take you out. I woudda cried and cried. You never know about some folks, do you?"

"No, you don't. But considering how I lost control of the car and tumbled down that embankment the way I did, I'd have to say it just wasn't meant to be. Or if you'd like, you can just call it a miracle."

Hyram shifted his weight and groaned audibly, and Merleece said, "Your arm actin' up again, son?"

"A little bit, Mama. It itches more than anything else. Wish I could scratch it, but I'll live." Then he caught Wendy's gaze and managed a smile. "I guess here's where I should thank you for savin' Mama. When you talked her into not goin' back with me to Chicago and then the police showed up to arrest her not too long after that, I thought it was just gonna be another example of the white man's justice. I was pretty mad at you. I guess I'm lucky not to be dead, too, the way I rushed out into the room and pulled my gun on those cops. I admit I'm kind of a hothead, as Mama can tell you."

"Hyram, please. Stop carryin' on so much. The cops, they not gone press charges 'cause you pull that gun on 'em like you did. You could be in serious trouble, so we both need to be thankful for that," Merleece said, looking his way.

Wendy felt pangs of guilt, recalling Ross's statement that she should have told him about Hyram being in town immediately after she had found out. "No, he has every right to be angry, Merleece. There were some mean-spirited people in Rosalie who wanted to railroad you, and there's no way that should be happening in this day and age."

Hyram made a contemptuous snorting noise and lifted his chin defiantly. "You think things have changed all that much down here in the South? Or around the whole country for that matter? Lemme tell you—Chicago's no shining example of racial harmony, either." He turned toward his mother. "I haven't told you a lotta things that've happened to me up in there, Mama."

Merleece's eyes widened noticeably. "Like what?"

He started to say something, but then shook his head. "Never mind. Sorry I mentioned it."

"Guess I'm better off not knowin', then," Merleece told him.

"Prob'ly."

"I'm sure you know what you're talking about, Hyram," Wendy said. "But I'm just happy I was able to prevent a grave injustice from happening here in Rosalie right where I live. You do what you can, and that way, you change things bit by bit."

"I know that's right," Merleece said, blowing Wendy a kiss. "Strawberry, I owe you my freedom, girl."

Wendy leaned against her affectionately and said, "Somebody had to dig out the truth, and you actually helped me get there because I remembered something you said to me that I just couldn't get out of my head."

Then Wendy carefully explained to Merleece how her comment about the ladies not getting to play their hands out had somehow triggered her curiosity about what the cards had actually looked like that day. She had asked the question that apparently had not occurred to anyone else. Was it or was it not the Grand Slam deal that Miz Liddie had raved about to Merleece and the other ladies? That creative conjecture had ended up solving what had presented itself as a genuine enigma to the Rosalie Police Department, causing them to arrest the wrong person. As a result, she had become a genuine hero to everyone in the department from her father on down to the greenest rookie fresh out of the academy.

Bax had even put it to her in a half-joking manner just

before she had left to explain everything to Merleece. "You sure you don't wanna consider joining the force, daughter a' mine?"

"I've got what I've really always wanted now," she had told him, and they had both smiled proudly.

In the present moment, Merleece was brimming with pride herself about the daughter she never had. "You the smart one, Strawberry. I always knew that 'boutchoo." But Merleece's smile quickly vanished. "Now, it all make sense to me. The way Miz Liddie, she disappear into her room to say she want a nap all the time. I figure she gettin' older, so why not? And then, she only have her coffee for breakfast, she don't have lunch, and I fix her dinner and leave it in the fridge for her to warm up after I leave, so I cain't see if she eatin' or not. How I'm s'pose to know she that sick? And then the makeup and the mirrors and the trips and all the rest she use to hide everything. I still say she musta been in some kinda pain the way she snap at me and everybody else for nothin'. Knowin' she shoudda been in a hospital all that time make my heart ache, even if she try to make it look like I'm the one who was guilty."

"She actually should've been in a hospice, but even so, she had plenty of meds according to Stella Markham," Wendy said. "But they probably weren't helping her very much there at the end. She could have left this world with grace and dignity. But she chose not to do that. Instead, she went to a very dark place, and I'm sure she suffered unnecessarily and did something no one has the right to do—deliberately take another human life, much less three of them. And for the most specious of reasons."

"You suppose I should say somethin' like 'rest her soul,' even though she did what she did, Strawberry?"

"You should say whatever you feel, Merleece. You're the one who's still alive with a future. No thanks to Miz Liddie, of course. So I think you should take that into consideration before you go out of your way to bless her. I'd leave that to the universe to handle."

Merleece mulled that over for a while and then gently pointed in Hyram's direction. "Time to talk 'bout somethin' positive, then. Tell Strawberry what you decide to do, son."

Hyram seemed reluctant at first, wriggling around a bit, but finally said, "I'm gonna stay down here with Mama for the time being. I made some mistakes here in Rosalie a while back, but that's in the past. I'm gonna try to make things right."

"I think that's wonderful," Wendy said. "So there's no one waiting for you up in Chicago?"

"Please, girl," Merleece said with a hint of disgust. "That's somethin' that Arden Wilson make up to confuse things. My son, he'll start over fresh down here where I bring him up. I got my baby back now."

"I'm gonna try to do right, Mama, I'm gonna try. Need to find me a job first, but I got a little saved up in the meantime."

"Are you going to continue to work, Merleece? Do you have any prospects?" Wendy said.

"Funny you bringin' that up now, Strawberry. Miz Crystal Forrest, she call me up as soon as she read the article in the paper this mornin' and axe if I'd come to work for her, since she say her maid quit on her. So maybe somethin' good did come of her bargin' in on Miz Liddie that day and screamin' and hollerin' the way she did. Miz Crystal say she never did see such a clean house as Miz Liddie have. I'm startin' over there at Concord Manor next week. I never did mind workin' hard—long as I was paid well for it. The only bad thing I gotta deal with at Miz Crystal place is Arden Wilson, 'cause he workin' for her, too. I almost told Miz Crystal I wouldd'n take the job at first. But I think I know how to handle that butterfly-killin' so-and-so now—I mean, I got enough practice at it."

Wendy laughed gently. "Yes, I'm sure you have. I think I saw you put him in his place a couple of times. By the way, I don't want to seem nosy or anything, but is Miz Crystal paying you more money than Miz Liddie did?"

Merleece grinned and gently rubbed Wendy's arm. "Now, you know I don't go round talkin' 'bout exactly how much money I make. But lemme say this much to you right now—I got no complaint."

"I'm thrilled for you. You deserve it. And who knows? Maybe Miz Liddie did leave you a little something in her will after all, that is, when they finally get around to reading it."

Merleece waved her off energetically. "Now, lissen to me, Strawberry. I'm not holdin' my breath on that one. Miz Liddie say she gone do that when we have too much to drink together every now and then after Mr. Murray finally die. That threw her in a tizzy, you know. It was fun doin' that kinda socializin' with the boss, but I think it was the liquor talkin,' if you want my opinion. She wudd'n the leader of the Gin Girls for nothin'."

Ross had just proposed a champagne toast at the Bluff City Bistro to Wendy's new promotion at the newspaper, but for some reason, Wendy remained a bit leery of what lay ahead. He had seemed incredibly euphoric ever since he had picked her up right after work at the *Citizen.*

"I've got a very big evening planned for us," he had told her, adding a sly wink to his words.

She had read between the lines and speculated that there might be something more afoot than a quiet dinner overlooking the Mississippi River, and she was trying her best to anticipate and formulate a plan of action. But Ross wouldn't shut up long enough to let her think straight.

"So, here's to this milestone in your career," he said as they clinked rims and each took a swallow. "And who knew you'd achieve it so soon? I gotta feeling you're gonna be the best reporter this town or any other ever had. You're gonna get to the bottom of a million stories. I gotta be honest with you, though, and tell you that I didn't think it would happen until Dalton Hemmings keeled over. That doesn't sound too ugly, does it?"

"Nope, I probably thought it myself more than once while sitting in my cubicle describing bridesmaids' bouquets and grooms' cakes. 'He can't last forever,' I would tell myself over and over whenever I got too depressed about the suffocating nature of my job."

Ross had more of his champagne, seamlessly fought back the customary carbonated belch that always accompanies a healthy sip, and cracked a smile. "Maybe I shouldn't have said anything to you about it. He and your father are pretty tight friends, aren't they?"

"They've had their buddy-buddy moments over the years, that's for sure. I happen to know they've had their clashes, too. They've probably seen it all," Wendy told him. "Daddy's a bit younger, though, and I'd be the first one he'd tell if he were thinking about retirement like Hemmings is."

"Yeah, you gotta make choices in life," Ross said, downing the last of his champagne. "You hope you make the right ones, of course. So, I was thinking that maybe you and I should . . ." He paused and wagged his brows a couple of times, as if expecting Wendy to read his mind.

The intriguing fact that she *could* did not mean that she was about to let him know that. She could play oblivious better than anyone else she knew—male or female. "Should what?"

"You know. Settle down together as a couple. Get married. Or at the very least, get engaged."

And there it was.

She had guessed rightly that it was coming down the pike

on this particular evening, and she had even rehearsed how she would respond if Ross actually ended up saying those words to her.

"Don't you think we're rushing things just a bit?" had occurred to her first during her practice rounds.

Or its first clichéd cousin: "I think we should really get to know each other a little better, don't you?"

But now that he had actually brought it up, she knew she had to be completely honest with him and not settle for some trite expression that did nothing but cause bad feelings between them. They had been too intimate for too long for that. So she took his hand and looked straight into his eyes. "Ross, you're the only man in my life right now. You have to know that. Other than my daddy, that is. But of course that's a completely different kind of relationship."

"I hope so," he said, managing an awkward chuckle.

"Ross, I'm serious. What you've got to understand is that I'm really at the beginning of a new career—the one I've always wanted. I have a lot more responsibility than I ever had trying to make baby showers sound colorful and interesting to anyone other than the baby's mother and her doting friends. I do think we've got something good going, but you're already a pro in law enforcement. You know the ropes. Right now, I've got to concentrate on becoming a pro at my career. Hemmings has promised not to interfere with my assignments. You have no idea what that means to me, even though I know I'm going to be on my own for the most part. I really think I'd shortchange you trying to be a wife at this point when my passion is to learn how to become a great investigative journalist. And you've got to admit, I didn't do a half-bad job as an amateur sleuth, either. I basically solved an extremely complicated murder case—with a little help, of course."

"Glad you added that last part. I really wasn't supposed to share as much as I did with you," Ross said, gently withdrawing his hand and then pouring himself another glass of champagne from the nearby magnum on ice. Then he refreshed her half-full glass without asking, as any ardent suitor would do.

"Now you know good and well I'm not after your job," Wendy said as she focused with a kind of girlish delight on the brand-new bubbles rising spiritedly toward the surface of her dainty little glass. "You've just got to give me some room to spread my wings for a while. We can still go out and do things together, or stay home if we feel like it. I don't want any of that to stop. But I don't honestly think I'm ready for the kind of commitment you want—at least not yet."

Ross reached into his pants pocket and pulled out a small black box, displaying it in the palm of his hand, unopened. "Then I guess I don't need to show you this engagement ring I've got in here, sweetheart."

Wendy gave him a gracious smile and took her time. She did not want to come close to hurting his feelings. "I'm tremendously flattered, of course, and I'm sure it's beyond beautiful, Ross. But don't tempt me just yet. Let's keep things the way they are for a while longer. I think we'll both know when it's time for you to open that box and put that ring on my finger."

Ross quickly put the ring back in his pocket and pointed toward the menus they had largely been ignoring so far. "Fair enough. Let's go ahead and order, then. The waitress has come over twice and we've put her off. I even think she had a bit of an attitude last time."

"Did she? I didn't notice." Wendy suddenly laughed out loud. "I wonder if she was the cause of the Gin Girls' letter to the *Citizen*?"

Ross looked taken aback. "Don't think so. I know I've never seen her in here before. I bet she's new."

"Then by all means, let's look everything over before we

starve to death. Except I have no idea what I'm in the mood for. You'll have your usual burger with blue cheese, I guess?"

"Nah, I think I'll go for something different this time. I'm kinda stuck in a rut, I do believe. Maybe I'll try something a little fancier."

"Fancier than blue cheese?" Wendy said, both amused and surprised. "I've never thought of blue cheese as exactly blue collar, you know."

"Yeah, I know exactly what you mean," he said, holding his hand up. "People say it's an acquired taste because it really does stink to high heaven. Some even say people's feet smell better. You either love it or hate it."

Wendy had to agree. She was in the hate it camp. The stuff made her gag. But she loved the way Ross appeared to be handling what amounted to a rejection right there in public. She made a mental note to give him credit for being a grown man about her request that they wait a while longer before making any life-changing decision about their relationship. When the time came—if it indeed came—she didn't want to hook up with a peevish little boy who had to get his way right then and there, or else. Her interaction with the Rosalie Police Department on The Grand Slam Murders case had shown her what a dangerous and difficult job Ross had every day he showed up for work. She had no intention of backing down from slightly putting on the brakes with him, but it had been like that from the start for them—an affair that ran hot and then tapered off to lukewarm after a while. Then without warning, it would zoom back to hot. But she had never been the sort of conventional woman who worried about biological clocks or role-playing—not at this stage of her exciting young life. Or possibly, she conjectured, at any stage for that matter.

Ross sensed she was lost in thought and said, "We don't have to order anything, you know."

"No, I want to. I'm really hungry. I do feel like celebrating and having a good time. Just don't pay any attention to me. I'll make up my mind eventually. I mean about everything, too." The wink she gave him was full of affection, and he returned it with his signature smile.

Wendy continued scanning the menu, still unable to decide on what she wanted to eat. Then, out of the corner of her eye, she caught sight of a long barge tow heading downstream toward the twin Rosalie bridges. Virtually every time before, when she had eaten with Ross at the Bluff City Bistro—or even by herself—the tows were headed upstream, going against the current and struggling mightily against the principles of physics and the laws of nature. She had often wondered when she was going to witness the opposite and why it was she hadn't done so before now.

No matter. She continued to watch the tow glide effortlessly atop the high muddy waters of late May, transfixed by it until it had disappeared from even her peripheral vision. It was at that moment that she felt life was flowing in the right direction for her at last.

Connect with